Sawdust and Sixguns

**Center Point
Large Print**

SAWDUST AND SIXGUNS

MAX BRAND®

CENTER POINT PUBLISHING
THORNDIKE, MAINE

This Center Point Large Print edition
is published in the year 2005 by arrangement with
Golden West Literary Agency.

The text of this Large Print edition is unabridged. In other
aspects, this book may vary from the original edition. Printed in
Thailand. Set in 16-point Times New Roman type.

ISBN 1-58547-664-1

Library of Congress Cataloging-in-Publication Data

Brand, Max, 1892-1944.
    Sawdust and six guns / Max Brand.--Center Point large print ed.
    p. cm.
    ISBN 1-58547-664-1 (lib. bdg. : alk. paper)
    1. Large type books. I. Title.

PS3511.A87S28 2005
813'.52--dc22

2005012867

29.95

CHAPTER I

THE FATES, WHEN THEY DECIDED TO COMPOSE Anthony Castracane, began operations in widely separated parts of the world.

In the first place, they took Filipo Castracane, a youngster of good birth in Lucca, and made him drive a knife through the heart of another youngster of even better birth than himself. So much better that though the fight was perfectly fair, Filipo was forced to flee for the border, dodge his way to Nice, and thence over the seas to the United States, which in that part of the nineteenth century was still a country with regions of fable in it.

Then Susie Murphy, lady's maid in Dublin, proved to be so pretty and with such an enchanting smile that one day her mistress found it worth while to say: "Susie, take fifty pounds and go to the States and forget for a few years that there is such a country as Ireland in the world!" Now, Susie knew all that was in her lady's mind, and the good ground that her ladyship had for her fears, but it happened that Susie preferred fifty pounds and a chance for adventure above an opportunity for a rich marriage. So she took the money and said good-by to green Ireland.

When she got to the new land, Susie felt that some higher destiny than a maid's life awaited her. She cast about her for an opening, and presently, because she had spent most of her life with horses, she blossomed forth in short skirts and a "property" smile as a bareback rider in the Green and Wagnall Circus.

Susie's blue eyes and red hair upset the hearts of everybody under the big tent, from the roustabouts and the strong man to the chief aerial star and Mr. Wagnall himself. But of all who admired the blue eyes and the red hair of Susie, there was none so acceptable, she thought, as a tall, athletic, dark, and beautiful young man who performed with the lions every evening, clad in shining white tights, with a spangled girdle about his middle. He wore the odd name of Philip Castracane. And a week after their first meeting, Susie and the young Lucchese were married.

Still another week, and a fretful lion made a pass with his paw at the tamer. And the next day they buried Castracane.

Poor Susie grieved until her heart almost broke, but at least she had her ponies to console her, and she worked on earnestly. In the course of time she became the mother of a fine, red-headed, blue-eyed, dark-skinned baby. And she called him Anthony.

Those were the antecedents of him who was called by so many, in the later days of his life, Anthony the Great, and by others, borrowing from that wild man of the revolution, Mad Anthony.

For the first few years of his life, little Anthony hardly knew which was bigger or more important—the blue of the sky or the great arch of the circus tent. And as he grew older, he naturally stepped into the life which he found around him. He was hardly more than a baby when his mother included him in her act; he was still an infant when he stood up on the back of a cantering pony and galloped it around the arena while the mothers in the audience held their breath and the children shrieked with joy.

So early in life as this, Anthony learned that applause is sweet, and that it is usually to be purchased with hard falls!

He learned to ride, without knowing how, until he was as much at home on a horse's back as any wild Tartar or Indian. Or even more so, because they learn their tricks casually; but Anthony from the very first had to acquire the professional touch which makes the hardest thing look easy.

So that, when he reached his tenth year and his mother died, Anthony was already too valuable to be turned adrift. He was a rare and high-priced solo performer with his horses, who could keep his balance on a cantering horse while standing on his head, and turn a somersault from the withers to the haunch of his broadest and safest pony.

But horseback riding was not his only work. He turned his hand to many things. Not that Anthony was ambitious, but because he "liked whatever he looked on, and his eyes went everywhere."

Sometimes he was up in the air for an hour at a time with Signor Piraneschi, the great trapeze artist, who taught him how to think only of the swinging bar and forget the distance which lay beneath to the ground.

And again, for long, long hours, he was working with Jumbo the strong man, who had loved Susie, and now loved her son. Jumbo was growing a little gray, but his muscles were more massive than ever. And after drinking in the admiration of the boy for a time, he drew him apart one day and imparted the greatest secret in his heart, which was that he had not been *born* strong, but that he had made himself what he was by patient exercise! If Anthony cared to take lessons and try . . .

If Anthony cared! His heart swelled almost to bursting, when he thought that one day *he* might be able to hold up with one hand a platform upon which three men performed gymnastics! Of course he cared, and of course he took lessons, and practiced at them with the infinite patience which he had learned with almost his first year.

Those were dreadfully difficult tricks which Jumbo taught him. To stand upon his hands, for instance, and slowly lower himself until his chin touched the ground, and then, more slowly still, to raise himself to arms' length again—and to continue this.

They used to send a stinging, blinding rush of blood to Tony's head, these dreadful efforts, but he would have been ashamed to stop trying.

Then there was that wonderful couple, Barney and Kilpatrick, who performed in a side show, Barney a wrestler and Kilpatrick a boxer, contesting furiously to show which was the superior art of combat. They drew in the admiring Tony. Each decided to make him a disciple, and so poor Tony was in for dreadful hours of mauling, learning the punishing wrestling holds, and learning, also, the uncanny craft and lightning speed of Kilpatrick.

"Only," Barney would say to him, "of course these fights that me and Kil put on, they're faked up to look exciting. But if it come to a *real* fight, you could put your money on me. I'd *kill* that skinny Irishman!"

Other influences, too, came into Anthony's life and stayed there. But the greatest of all was Abdullah Khan, the mighty magician and sleight of hand artist!

Abdullah performed in a flowing gown from which he could produce almost more things than other men's minds could conceive. He had a great, curling, black, flowing beard, and a turban, and dark, overhanging brows through which his keen eyes glittered mystically, and while he worked, from a censer on either side of him, streams of sweet incense climbed weirdly into the air toward the heaven of Mahomet. But with Tony all men unbent, and even Abdullah was no exception.

When he had finished his performance, pulling oddities out of his sleeves or sticking knives around the outline of a pretty girl who stood with arms held crosswise against a great slab of wood—when he had finished these things and dexterous card tricks and all the rest—Abdullah Khan was fond of sitting down with Tony and taking off gown, turban, beard, and eyebrows, and smoking a pipe, and talking about the good old days in Brooklyn, when he used to fight with the other ragamuffins of the empty lots until he made the mystical discovery that the hand is faster than the eye.

To keep fifteen balls in the air! That needed space, a steady hand, an eye of lightning. Or to palm a deck of cards and make them act as though every card had a listening, obedient mind! But greatest of all, said Abdullah Kahn—alias Isaac Levy—was to hit with a heavy knife, at a distance of twenty steps, a single thin pencil line on a board! Too hard a trick for a circus, but beautiful when it happened.

"Y'understand me, kid," said Abdullah Khan, "nothing is worth while trying that ain't really too hard to do, except once in a long while!"

The Khan, too, spent his long hours with Tony, and taught him how to make of his hand an illusive fairy wand that disappeared from human ken, dipped here and there at leisure, and appeared again, having performed a miracle. And he taught him how to keep the fifteen balls in the air and how to hit the line with a heavy knife.

"Why couldn't *I* be a magician someday?" said Tony after he had gone through almost the whole list of Abdullah's tricks without a flaw.

"I'll tell you why, kid," said Abdullah Khan. "You ain't got the face for it. You can't be serious. You're always laughing and smiling; and that's what comes from working with those nags of yours all the time. Always laughing, when you're on the backs of your ponies, doing somersaults and other stuff, and climbing under their bellies, and riding three at a time!"

"I don't see what's wrong with that," said Tony a little sadly.

"I'll tell you what's wrong," said Abdullah. "It's cheapening, that's what it is. A young guy has got to take care what influences comes into his life. Look at the way you pal around with that big slumgullion Jumbo, trying to lift a ton at a time. And why? And look at the way you spend hours wrestling with that scum Barney, and that roughneck Kilpatrick—is it true that you knocked Kil down yesterday?"

"It was a mistake," said Tony. "You see, he left himself a bit open when he was rushing in—"

"Aw, I wish you'd knocked his block off!" said Abdullah Khan. "But the fact is, kid, that you ain't gonna make a success of nothing until you find something that you're gonna be serious about, and something that you like not so much that it makes you laugh but so much that it half scares you. You hear me talk?"

And he automatically picked up his turban, settled it on his head, and frowned impressively upon Tony, forgetful of the clay pipe which was still between his teeth and which spoiled the effect of the picture somewhat.

Tony could not help smiling, and the Khan looked darker than ever.

"There's another thing wrong with you, kid," said he. "How old are you now?"

"Sixteen," said Tony.

"Sixteen! It's too young. You've learned too much for your own good. I tell you what, Tony, you'll never make no mark for yourself until you get hold of something that you can't learn right offhand!"

CHAPTER II

PERHAPS THERE WAS A GOOD DEAL IN THE ADVICE which Abdullah Khan gave to Anthony Castracane, but there was one important thing which kept Anthony from taking that advice too seriously. At sixteen he was tall and rather slight, except that his wide shoulders were heavily furnished with muscle due to the laborious exercises through which Jumbo put him. But big as he was, his body was still developing and flowering at an amazing rate. The big bones were still solidifying and extending and growing thicker, and tendons were becoming daily more mighty. Thus, his physical existence was a wide empire to be watched over and supervised, and its care absorbed all Castracane's energies. And year after year he remained with the circus, though it was gradually dawning on Anthony that a circus life was not all that he cared to undertake.

He had had to give over the ponies, before this. They were too small and they looked too childishly fragile, compared with Anthony's bulk. He had long ago passed the two-hundred-pound mark. So Mr. Wagnall introduced a troupe of huge Cleveland Bays, lofty creatures, with the beauty of blood horses and such a bulk that they looked formidable even when compared with their rider. And on their backs Anthony careered around the arena, night after night and day after day, with his blue eyes shining and his long red hair blowing behind him. He was a headline performer now, and he never failed to bring wild applause. But the horses were not all. When Jumbo fell sick for a whole month, his part was taken by Anthony, who performed all those monstrous feats of weight lifting with a consummate ease, even though his arms were not half so massively made as the older man's. With such ease, indeed, that Mr. Wagnall, sweating with anxiety, had said: "Can't you stagger a little, Tony? Damn it, don't make things look so simple!"

Or, again, when Kilpatrick was forced into a vacation owing to a wrenched leg received from Barney's mighty hands, young Tony took his place in that exhibition, but made it all too short. For at the very first rush he planted a gloved fist on Barney's head, and the wrestler fell limp and heavy to the mat, while the spectators howled for their money back. And again, they tried Anthony in the role of Abdullah Khan himself. But even the long beard could not keep Anthony's happy smile from flashing forth, and the audience shrugged their shoulders and yawned. They wanted mystery—and here was only sleight of hand! They wanted to be overawed, and here was only a made-up boy who glided happily from parlor trick to parlor trick. Even when the pretty girl stood against the slab of wood, there was no thrill because she could not help laughing as she looked into Anthony's dancing eyes. It was plain that she had no dread at all of the knives! And in Anthony's gleaming hands they flew forth to their marks so rapidly that it seemed they were drawn down a glancing wire to their appointed lodging in the wooden slab.

"You got to make the easy things look hard!" said Wagnall. "Even the horses are falling down on you. You got to make them act like they was wanting to tear you to bits, Tony! You got to make them wilder!"

They brought in two truly wild horses, savage and fierce. And for a fortnight crowds of spectators screamed and cheered with delight while Anthony struggled with the team. But at the end of the two weeks it was the same old story over again, and one would have said that the horses were cantering about the arena because they loved Anthony, not because he was *making* them perform.

Wagnall went to his most profound performer, Abdullah, and talked it over.

"The kid is too good," said Wagnall. "He's got to be given a fall!"

"It won't work," said Abdullah. "He's had his falls aplenty before he was ten years old. Failure don't scare him, it just makes him patient. I tried him out last year. I gave him a set of bum knives with lopsided weights in the handles—why, in two weeks he had them going like the good ones again!"

"He's *too* good!" said Wagnall. "He ain't a headliner for me any more. He never gets a cheer from the crowd. And yet he's the best man under my tent—except you, Abdullah, of course! What *can* we do with him?"

"Get him rattled," said Abdullah. "Get him nervous. Find out something to do that, will you? Get him *scared* for once in his life! And then his circus stuff will come to him hard enough, if that's what you want. But he's got to find something that ain't a joke!"

Mr. Wagnall bowed his head, and finally a thought came to him. Once, in his youth, he had been set upon by a stalwart and beaten most dreadfully with hard fists. If such a thing happened to his young star . . .

Mr. Wagnall went straight to that formidable ruffian of the ring, Canada Charlie. "This is what I want you to do, Charlie, for fifty dollars!"

"Sure," said Canada Charlie. "Big, but the bigger they are, the harder they fall. I'll trim him good!"

"Not too good," said Wagnall, "but just enough!"

"Leave that to me," said Canada.

The next day a note came from a hospital to Mr. Wagnall.

"I tried, but something slipped and the sky fell on me. Please send that fifty by bearer!"

Mr. Wagnall sent the fifty and along with it the curt note: "Get a couple of your pals to try the same job for a hundred."

Two men, certainly, would make short work of Tony!

So, in the dark of an alley, two men converged suddenly upon Anthony and assaulted him with the weight of trained fists. He took the first man by hip and neck, whirled with him, and dashed him at his companion.

Then Anthony picked up one human wreck under either arm and stepped into the doorway of the next house.

"Have you some hot water and some spare rags for bandages?" said Anthony. "These two men just ran into each other."

The householder came to see.

"Humph!" said he. "Ran into a dray, and under it, you mean!"

But Anthony went smiling on his way.

Mr. Wagnall was in despair and he told Abdullah about his troubles.

"Hell, chief," said Abdullah, "why d'you ask me? Ain't I been trying for years to fix him? Go ask your wife. She's got a head."

Mrs. Wagnall indeed had a head. By means of it she had risen and raised her husband from juggling in a side show to their present eminence. She listened to the story from beginning to end, her knitting needles clicking with a constant rhythm. For that matter, she had known about Anthony's case for a long time, but she never believed in speaking until the right moment came. In ring parlance, she held back her punch until the other man was played out.

"You go get a pretty girl and turn her loose on big

Red," said Mrs. Wagnall.

"Pretty girl? Pretty girl?" sneered Mr. Wagnall. "Why, Maggie, you talk like a fool. Ain't all the girls in the circus been breaking their hearts over his handsome face? And ain't the circus girls as pretty as most?"

Said Mrs. Wagnall, slowly and evenly, while her needles still clicked:

"What are they to him? He was raised with 'em. Short skirts and spangles and tights and make-up— why they're as natural to Red as the sawdust. Try another kind."

"He's got no eye for girls," said Wagnall. "He spends his time with that fat fool, Jumbo, or with Abdullah or Kilpatrick. He ain't like other boys."

"Hank," said Mrs. Wagnall, "there ain't any man in this world but what some woman can make a fool of him. There's Queenie, that has got a pretty cousin living right here in Nashville, by name of Muriel Lester, that's going West, pretty soon, to marry somebody. Now, let her try her hand with Red. I've seen her. She's got a smile that makes men dizzy!"

"It won't do," said Wagnall. "She's a good girl. Money wouldn't tempt her."

"Bah," said Mrs. Wagnall. "The game of it would, though."

"But I say," said Wagnall, "that we got only two more days in Nashville."

"Two days," said his spouse, "is as good as two years, if a girl knows her business, and this Muriel

17

Lester is too pretty not to know what she can do with men."

"It'll never work," said Wagnall.

"Leave it to me," said Mrs. Wagnall. "I'll guarantee that when the circus leaves Nashville, Red will have forgot how to smile. And if he ain't absent-minded enough to get his neck broke is all you'll have to worry about. Now clear out, and I'll start."

Mr. Wagnall, with many misgivings, "cleared out," and Mrs. Wagnall "started."

Not an hour later she sat with Queenie in the Lesters' house, a quaint little white house behind a deep rose garden, and as they talked on that warm spring day the fragrance from the garden blew in softly about them, and all was so sleepily quiet that no one, surely, could have guessed the mighty troubles which Mrs. Wagnall's active brain was hatching apace, and she least of all!

"You run along, Queenie," said Mrs. Wagnall, "I want to talk business to your cousin."

"Business?" said Queenie. "Are you going to try to ring her into the circus? You can't do it, because she starts West in two days to get married. Don't you, Muriel?"

"The sooner she leaves, the better," said Mrs. Wagnall. "Now, you run along."

So Queenie walked in the garden while the other girl's great eyes were fixed on Mrs. Wagnall's broad, wise, good-natured face.

"I could never do it!" she said at first.

18

"Tush!" said Mrs. Wagnall. "You see, child, that it's for his own good. And will it hurt you to smile at him half a dozen times in two days? Besides, you'll never see him again, because you're going West, and the Circus leaves town. But I want you to take the heart of our Tony West with you!"

"But it seems wicked," said Muriel, growing very pink.

"Come," said Mrs. Wagnall. "Men's hearts don't break. They don't even crack. I know!"

CHAPTER III

IT IS BEST TO HURRY THROUGH THIS PART OF ANTHONY'S history, because, of course, what is important is what happened after he became that fellow whom we all knew as "Mad Anthony." But all of this is important, in its own way, because if it had not been for Muriel Lester's quiet, lovely face, and Mrs. Wagnall's wits, that cyclone would never have been turned loose in the West. It cost me a great deal of pains to get at the history of Mad Anthony before he reached Dodge City, because it was generally taken for granted that men *had* no history before arriving there. And no one in the world could have been more surprised than I was when I learned of Anthony's strange beginnings, and the sort of explosion that tore him up from the old rootage of his life and flung him West.

What always most astonished me was that such a

girl as Muriel Lester could ever have taken such a part on herself. But she was only a youngster, hardly nineteen years old; and since she was about to rush out West and be married, she took it for granted that one small, small flirtation, guaranteed harmless, and undertaken for the good of the man in question, couldn't possibly be wrong.

At any rate, that same evening they met. Mrs. Wagnall arranged that. And Red Anthony was to talk with Mr. Lester about taming an intractable horse which Lester owned—that was excuse for the meeting. So he and the father talked horses to their hearts' content, and Muriel appeared in the conversation only with a smile, now and then. But somehow, those smiles seemed to convey a vast admiration for the wisdom of all that Anthony was saying, and a vast sympathy for all that he was.

Now this is to be understood in the very first place, that of all the girls in the world there was none purer in heart and thought than Muriel Lester, none franker and gentler, and none, perhaps, with a heart more set on her husband to be. And yet, even so, she was a little angry because her smiles had seemed to have so little effect while Red Anthony chatted on about horses with a sort of foolishly boyish enthusiasm. So, when the time came to say good night, she looked straight into his eyes, gravely, and let her hand linger in his just a fraction of a second longer than was necessary.

It had a most remarkable effect.

It does not take much to start a snowslide. Perhaps

for half a century the snows have been piling up high and higher. And finally the mere displacement of a pebble's weight starts a tiny mass in motion which gathers headway from moment to moment until finally it is a raging torrent, cutting away whole forests in its sweep downward.

And here was poor Anthony, who had spent his life among pretty girls and taken them as much for granted, as Mrs. Wagnall had observed, as if they had been so many wooden images. But now, as he left Muriel, his eyes were opened to the fact that she seemed a little different, and as he walked home through the night, the difference between her and others seemed to grow and grow in importance until, when he reached his bed, it was a vast thing. And he wakened in the middle of the night, convinced that she stood apart in the whole human race—like a separate species.

Help Mr. Lester tame his wild horse?

He was down at the Lester place at an absurdly early hour, and yet, to his vast delight, not too early for Muriel. There she was with her father at the pasture gate, to watch Anthony saddle the gelding and mount with a leap lighter than any with which he had ever graced the circus tent.

It was a glorious battle, while it lasted, but it did not last overlong. This was a tried and true-bucking horse perfectly accustomed to flicking riders off its back with as much unconcern as a boy snaps melon seeds away between his fingers. But it found upon the saddle a heavy weight, and its body was crushed by two mighty legs, and a terrible hand of iron controlled its mouth. It could not buck wholeheartedly with its chin drawn back against its chest, but that was where that chin had to be while Anthony rode.

And suddenly the gelding forgot to pitch and stood still, worrying fretfully at the bit and the reins.

In another hour, he was going docilely back and forth, and then nothing was to be done except to take Red Anthony into the house and sit down with him, and praise him for his good work, and offer him a handsome little sum of money for this bit of artistic horse taming. But Anthony's face grew more red than a berry when money was offered, and his eyes turned rather wildly toward the girl as if he would have said: "You understand. Therefore, tell him that I can't take money!"

Anthony, in short, was desperately and deeply in love. And though, as Mrs. Wagnall had said, every pretty girl knows fairly well just what power is in her smiling, yet Muriel Lester was too astonished to be entirely happy. She was accustomed to making men admire her. She was not accustomed to overwhelming and annihilating them.

And this young madman knew no sensible stopping point. In fact, he was completely possessed, floating in air, giddy, and half sick. And the first instant that he found himself alone with Muriel, that day, he was telling her with a stammering earnestness that he worshiped her, that she transformed the ground upon

22

which she walked, that her breathing filled the air with fragrance, that her beauty rushed through his blood like music, and that at the sight of her, his heart pounded like the stamping of wild horses.

Up to the tip of her tongue came the truth, that she was hugely flattered, that she admired and liked him very well, but that she was leaving, the very next day, for the wild West, to marry.

But something held her back. I hardly know what. It could not have been merely that she wished to play out more of the game, as Mrs. Wagnall had desired her to do. For she could see, now, that she had played it all too well. I think it must have been a plain reluctance to surrender entirely her control over such a great force. If one has a thunderbolt placed in one's hand, one is sadly tempted to hurl it—only once!

So she told him only the first half of her thoughts, and left the bitter part of the truth unsaid. Only, when the end came, she wished to have a little more time to think of what he had said to her. And if he would come to the house at noon the next day . . .

He went back half mad with joy. He felt already that she was his. And that night, for the first time in years, he fell in the middle of his act while making a somersault. Mrs. Wagnall saw and touched her husband's arm, and Mr. Wagnall swore softly with joy and surprise while the audience shouted appreciation as the red-headed giant bounded up and returned to his work. He was no longer a bland young trickster, but like a giant half dazed and trying to work by force, not skill.

So he received an ovation that night, and Mr. Wagnall embraced his wife and called her the light of his life.

Never did hours drag so wearily on as they passed for Red Anthony before noon of the next day when he stood at the door of the Lester house and rapped, and received no answer, and waited in amazement, and then thundered with his fist until a neighbor ran out to see what caused this odd disturbance.

"The Lesters? Why, they've gone down to the station to see Muriel off for Dodge City on the train—"

The universe was wrenched from its hinges and crashed about Anthony's ears.

All the way to the station he sprinted. And he arrived in time to see the Lesters waving farewell, and Muriel leaning from a window of the departing train.

She saw him, she could not help but see him. And yet she would not give him a glance.

A bulldog fury rose in Anthony. He rushed for the last platform as the train whirled out from the station, but it was traveling too fast for even his grip of iron, his hands were torn loose, and he rolled in the cinders.

He stood up, dusty, heavily bruised, but unconscious of his hurts. And he went back to the circus tent.

If there had been anyone to explain the little affair to Anthony, even then I don't think that he would have believed or understood. Nothing but a word from the girl who had dealt the blow could have made him see the truth.

He sat in his dressing room with his head between

his hands. Then he went out and found Barney, who knew the world.

"Barney," he said, "where is Dodge City?"

"In hell, son," said Barney without hesitation.

"I mean," said Anthony, "seriously!"

"Serious is what I am," said Barney. "Why d'you ask?"

"Because I'm curious. I'm bound for Dodge City today."

"Hey, Tony, are you wild? Ain't you got a contract?"

"Confound the contract!" said Anthony.

"Dodge City!" gasped Barney. "Why, lad, Dodge City is in hell and Dodge City *is* hell. It's where old Nick has his private lodgings. You keep away from that town and you keep away from trouble!"

To Wagnall the news was a thunderclap. But Mrs. Wagnall was more calm.

"He'll be back," she said. "He's going to see that girl once more, and when he does, she'll bring him down to earth with a bump. There ain't anything more cruel than a good woman, Hank!"

There was never a swifter series of good-bys said than those which separated Anthony from the circus where he had been born and bred. But he was like a man who walks in a dream. He saw nothing that was around him. Faces passed in a haze. And there was no clear vision to him until, the next day at noon, he was on board a train bound West, with his luggage at his feet.

But how the train crawled for Anthony! How it

dragged wearily over the tracks!

For his thoughts were already far before him, at the side of the girl, touching her arm, making her turn around with her mild eyes to confront him, and to answer the question which he would put to her.

One thing, at least, was certain. She could not have lied to him! Then what was the explanation? What mysterious thing had happened to tear her away from her home and start her West toward that city which, as Barney said, was in hell?

CHAPTER IV

SOME PEOPLE HAVE SAID, WHEN THEY LEARNED THE truth about the origin of Red Anthony, Mad Anthony, Anthony the Great, that the wildness which was in him was predestined to find some sort of expression, sooner or later, but I have always felt that if his old life had never been torn up by the roots, he would have gone on quietly, living the circus life, thinking few but circus thoughts, with perhaps only vague desires for other things wakened in him from time to time. Certainly he had proved that he was susceptible to the influence of a lovely woman, but in the ordinary course he would never have been fascinated by any girl more completely than he fascinated her. He would simply have drawn her into his own life; and it was only the craft of Mrs. Wagnall which devised matters so that Anthony was swept away from himself and his old life. She had succeeded far better than she dreamed. She had started the pebble rolling, and the pebble in turn became a landslide, and it is the devious and terrible course of that landslide which we are now trying to follow.

First, I should like to have you look at Anthony Castracane as he sits by the window in the train; ordinarily, it would be difficult to watch him without meeting his blue eyes which are now filled with the beginning of that wildfire which was never after quite to die out of them, but now he sees nothing except the plains and the mountains which unroll in the distant horizon. His heart is flying out there toward the edge of the sky where Muriel Lester has gone before him. So we have a moment to study him as he is, leisurely, stroke by stroke, printing the lines forever in our memories, since he is worth much study!

We see, first of all, that mass of dark-red hair. It is like red-gold flame in the sunshine; it is almost the dark blue-red of blood in the shadow. The forehead is craggy and uneven. Then the eyes are set deep beneath the brow, keeping a shadow around them, after that godlike type which the Athenians were forever putting into stone. They are blue eyes which have been half dreamy or wholly smiling all Castracane's years, but now the new fire is in them, barely visible, now that he is silent and quiet, but smoldering like a spark which, on the instant, can be blown into flame. And there is a bold nose, slightly arched, such as befits a conqueror, with sensitive, almost translucent nostrils.

There is a mouth beautifully made, but, taken in conjunction with the bold, rounded, swelling curves of the chin, rather a cruel expression lingers about it. And when one stands off and sketches in the face from a distance, straight in front, it is a freely made oval except for the somewhat bulging squareness of the brow and the slight and significant output at the base of the jaws.

When you see this head, you feel at first that it is too roughly cast to be anything but ugly, and the flowing hairline gives it a further startling effect of wild motion. You feel, too, that the head is too large, quite out of proportion to the possibilities of any body.

But that is before you have accurately measured the thickness of the throat or the ample width of the shoulders. As a matter of fact, it is an arresting face, young, ardent, sincere—almost overearnest.

But when you see Castracane in action, you will have quite another impression of him. We will come to that in good time.

They speed west and west. Other men mount the train at little towns. They wear hair as long or longer than Red Anthony's, they are dressed in buckskin suits, Indian style, or else they at least have boots with tops wonderfully ornate, and they are fond of wearing gay sashes about the waist. They are going to the frontier. But what is the frontier and what are these frontiersmen?

We have no frontier, now. Fast-driven passenger expresses snake across the country from end to end, blotting out time and distance. Or if a man's thoughts must be sent and not his person, he flashes them instantly and cheaply across the wires. And ten thousand newspapers pour forth floods and floods of news so that nothing can happen in one corner of the country that is not known in every other part of it, so long as it is beautiful, strange, terrible, or in the least degree important. From East to West, from North to South, we read the same papers and books, hear the same music, and live according to the same standards. Our food is the same, our clothes are the same, and our thoughts are the same. And every moment of existence welds this gigantic empire into a closer-knit, stronger unit, furnishes it with a stronger and more universal ideal, links every particle of it into an entity called the United States which in physical power is to the Roman Empire what the Roman Empire was, let us say, to a single sprawling province like Africa. So we have no frontier.

And because we have no frontier, we are forced to digest the poison which is generated in the social body, and take it back into the blood, so that who can say to what ignominious end our muscular greatness will come?

But in these days when Anthony Castracane started for Dodge City, there was a frontier indeed! The frontier was a meeting place. On the one side civilization pressed against the wilderness. On the other side the wilderness pressed back against civilization. And where there is pressure heat must be generated, and where there is heat there must be destruction, great or little. The wilderness furnished itself along the frontier with its hardest wall of spirits, men of steel, half-breeds, Indians, whites gone wild; and civilization combed its ranks and selected the atavists who were capable of meeting force with force. Numbers were always on the side of civilization, and so the frontier went west and west, but very slowly.

We are apt to feel that the wildness of those old days has been exaggerated, but exaggeration is hardly possible. Let us remember that a single judge in a single court which had a jurisdiction over a part of that no man's land in a few years condemned four hundred criminals to death. And it is safe to say that the law paid at least a life for a life in apprehending these capital criminals.

So no man went to the frontier unless he loved adventure and excitement and money more than he loved mere life. Therefore life became almost the cheapest commodity in which men could deal. It was an age when criminals never repented or confessed, and when marshals gave one warning and then shot to kill.

It was the age, too, of the great cattle trails. The stockowners in the southwest had discovered that the cattle which they raised cheaply and in myriads through the winter were apt to grow starvation thin in the summer, too thin to stand shipment to the eastern markets. So they would drive their lean herds north, and north, and drifting them softly along, let them fatten on the way until they converged at a shipping point, like Dodge City, where tens of thousands were often waiting for the trains. And the men who followed the cattle trails out of the heart of the wilderness were as reckless as any legion of devils—a gay legion, hunting for amusement, willing to die almost for the sake of a jest. In Dodge City and other towns they met the men from civilization, the atavists. And so the frontier was fringed with blood, and men died by the half dozen at a stroke, with their boots on, forgotten almost before they fell.

Into Dodge City came the train, and down from the train stepped Anthony Castracane, with his ponderous valise light in his hand, striding into a new life and totally unconscious of his destiny.

It seemed a strange place to which Muriel Lester had come. And he was more sure than ever that there was something mysteriously wrong, which he must discover by craft and set right by force.

On the whole, Dodge City was like a great village which had been rushed up over night. It had been built so rapidly that it seemed the builders expected it to decay all as suddenly. They had made no preparations for it to endure through the next winter's storms. The shacks were simply set down with little or no foundation. And the men who moved up and down the streets—for there were almost no women—seemed to Anthony to be questing just as he was. They were in a great hurry. They were like men hastening to an appointment. And what men!

He had hardly a chance to begin his survey of them when with a great bellowing and lowing a herd of cattle came down the street. The crowd pressed back on either side, laughing, good-natured, and then came the cows, a bristling phalanx of horns, red-eyed creatures tossing their heads and tails. Behind them rode *vaqueros* in five-gallon hats, on little, rough-coated horses. Before the dust cloud was half settled, the pedestrians had swarmed back into the center of the narrow street once more, and the babel of voices began again. Ragged beggars, gaudy cowpunchers, hunters from the plains in deerskin suits, tall men in black frock coats with black hats, and dark-eyed Mexicans and half-breeds and Negroes—the eye of Anthony Castracane, trained in the lightning arts of jugglery, flicked from face to face, and from form to form, and saw everything. And nothing did he see that seemed to him a fitting background for such a girl as Muriel Lester. The sense of mystery grew in him. The sense of determination grew also.

Then, just in front of him, "Bear back, boys! Here's guns!" shouted a voice, and the crowd surged back and left Anthony on its rim looking into an open space where he saw a man on either side of the street, each damning the other with a profusion of oaths, each a little crouched, each with a right hand at the butt of a revolver. It dawned suddenly upon Anthony's mind that this meant business of the most serious order, and not the sort of a fight that mere fisticuffs could settle.

Two guns flashed at the same instant, two arms were

32

thrust up, hip-high, and at the same instant a double explosion split the air. The man on Anthony's right hand tossed up his hands, whirled, and fell upon his face. He rolled over and strove to crawl into the nearest doorway. A second bullet struck his body with a heavy spat, like two hands struck together, and he went down again.

Anthony stared in bewilderment, in horror, and disgust. Here were a hundred armed men looking on and yet no one interfered!

A third bullet appeared to miss the target as the wounded man struggled forward again. Then Anthony followed his instinct with a movement a little faster than thought. He snatched the heavy bowie knife from the belt of his right-hand neighbor in the crowd and threw it with the same motion. It glanced in the sun and drove straight through the gun arm of the victor!

CHAPTER V

IN THIS MANNER ANTHONY STEPPED UPON THE STAGE where he was to appear so often. Two men in the crowd have told me that the instant Cherokee Dan dropped his gun and gripped his wounded arm and they saw Anthony stepping forward, they guessed that someone of importance had appeared in Dodge City.

The defeated contestant in the gunfight had gained the safety beyond the doorway by this time, and

Cherokee Dan, scooping up his fallen gun with his left hand, turned with a yell of agony and rage to confront the crowd and exact retribution. He whirled straight into Anthony as the latter advanced. Somehow—Cherokee Dan could never explain it—a crushing grip caught his left wrist, turned his hand numb, and made the gun fall a second time, and he heard a musical bass voice saying:

"I'm sorry that I had to hurt you—but I couldn't see any other way of keeping you from killing that other fellow."

The crowd had packed closely in around them. Curious eyes were lifted to the face of the big man, and none more curious than those of Cherokee Dan.

"Damn me and burn me!" said Cherokee. "*You* couldn't think of any other way? You throwed that knife, you—"

"Hush," said Anthony. "You're losing blood fast. Is there a doctor here?"

"Damn you and your doctors! You'll need a doctor for this here bit of work. Pete, gimme a hand, will you? Tommy, I need you too—Joe!"

Various friends of Cherokee pressed suddenly around him, and Anthony Castracane stepped back. And men gave him room readily enough, gaping at him as he moved to the door through which the first victim of the fight had passed. A man with a rifle dropped into the hollow of his left arm blocked the way.

"And who the devil are you?" he asked of Anthony.

"I've come to see if that wounded man was badly hurt," said the latter.

"One through the shoulder and one through the leg. But he'll live, and worse luck for some of you gents that have been—"

"Now, pipe down, Bill. This is the gent that knifed Cherokee!"

"Ah! You're him? And you're a friend of Loftus, then? I didn't know that he *had* any outside friends in this town. Come inside. You can tell where Loftus is by the swearing."

Profanity, indeed, spouted in a steady stream from the rear room of the shack, and stepping to the doorway, Anthony looked down on a bearded man who was stretched on the floor with two others busily bandaging and cleaning his wounds.

"Who are you?" he snarled at Anthony. "Did Cherokee send you to finish his dirty work? Go back and tell Cherokee that the next time I'll have a gun that *won't* hang in the draw!"

"Shut up, Loftus. This is him that stuck the knife through Cherokee's arm. Lay back! Wait till I get this bandage on you."

"*You* knifed Cherokee!" said Loftus, staring wildly at Anthony. "Why, I never seen you before! Did you have a grudge agin him?"

"This is the first day I've spent in Dodge City," said Anthony in his mild, deep voice. "But I thought you seemed in trouble. It looked like murder to me."

"You didn't have nothing to gain?" yelled Loftus.

35

"I'm glad that you're not fatally hurt," said Anthony, and he backed from the door.

"Bring him back!" cried Loftus. "Lemme find out a tenderfoot that knows how to handle a knife like that. Hey, Doc, stop him——"

But Anthony was already in the street.

To his amazement, all signs of the fight had passed over. Men were once more pouring up and down through the dust. And Cherokee Dan and his friends had disappeared. For a moment, Anthony surveyed the scene up and down, and he was about to continue down the street when a voice said beside him: "I think you owe me something, stranger."

He looked down at a thick-set man of middle age, with a square jaw and a gray-sprinkled mustache.

"I owe you a knife which I took a moment ago," said Anthony. "I'll be glad to pay you, if you'll tell me what it was worth."

"You'll pay me, eh?"

"Yes, of course."

"Put up your money," said the other, "because money don't pay me for that knife."

Anthony stared, bewildered again.

"I'll tell you about the knife," said the stranger, "and you can pay me for it by telling me about yourself."

"Why," said Anthony, "that seems more than fair."

"But in the first place, it don't look like none too good a spot for talking, where you've got to look at me and can't guard your back."

"Guard my back?"

"I mean, from Cherokee and his set."

"Guard my back?" echoed Anthony. "From a shot from behind?"

"Why," said the other, looking more sharply at his companion, "do you think that Cherokee and his lot care whether you face up the wind or down when they want to get you? Tell me, stranger, how long you've lived west of the Mississippi?"

"One day," said Anthony, "lacking a few hours."

"By God," said his new friend, "I almost guessed it! Now, you come in with me."

They passed into a saloon.

It consisted of a long, narrow room, with just enough height to permit Anthony to stand upright. On one side a long clutter of chairs and benches extended. On the other side heavy planks, laid upon upturned barrels, served as a bar, and behind this bar, in turn, were the bottles and the kegs which made up the trade. It was a slack moment in the room. There were not more than a dozen men drinking at the bar, encouraged by a great sign painted across the wall: IF DRINKING HURTS YOUR BUSINESS, QUIT YOUR BUSINESS.

"My name is Parker," said Anthony's new acquaintance.

"My name is Anthony Castracane."

"That's half a yard too long for this part of the world. They'll probably call you Red. What are you drinking?"

"I'm not drinking," said Anthony.

"Keeping steady for today, eh?"

37

"I never tried whisky," said Anthony. "It makes one's hand shake, I've heard."

Parker regarded him with a genial eye.

"Makes your hand shake so you can't do what?"

"Why," said Anthony, looking vaguely around him, "this for instance."

And, for lack of anything better to do, he picked a heavy tumbler from the bar, set it upon the tip of his finger, and put another on top of it.

They stood as stiffly straight as though they had been glued together. So Anthony caught away the lower one, and the top glass dropped down and stood firmly, solidly, upon the extended tip of his finger.

"It is very simple," said Anthony, "but you have to have steady nerves for it, really."

"Humph!" said Parker, "I guess that you really do. Come over here and sit down in the corner. This is better. Now you've got a wall at your back and you can keep your eyes on everybody in the room, ready to flash your guns out if Cherokee or any of his lot come in—"

"Guns?" said Anthony. "I have no guns."

"No guns? Good God!" exclaimed Parker. "Raising ructions in Dodge City with your bare hands?"

And he fairly gaped at Anthony.

"Ah, well," said Anthony, "I shall not be here long. I hope to leave in a day or two, and so I won't need—"

"Wait!" said Parker. "It begins to drift in on me that you *are* a tenderfoot, and one of the tenderest. You understand me when I tell you: Time in Dodge City ain't like time in other places. Half an hour here is as much as a day in other towns. A month here is pretty near a year, and a year is the bigger part of a lifetime."

Anthony nodded, but his eye was rather vague.

"About this gun business," said Parker in continuation. "I don't have to ask you whether or not you know how to handle a Colt, because I've seen you flash a knife. And even allowing for luck in hitting the mark, it was a very neat pull and cast!"

"Luck?" echoed Anthony.

"Well?" said Parker, frowning a little. "I suppose you *knew* you'd hit his arm?"

"Of course," said Anthony, "as long as it was stationary."

A sarcastic rejoinder curled upon the lips of Parker, but before he could speak, Anthony went on blithely: "But, as a matter of fact, I've never fired a gun in my life."

Now, Parker had heard and seen some very odd things from this young man in the short interval of their acquaintance, but he had heard or seen nothing that caused him half as much amazement as this announcement.

He could only grip the sides of his chair, for a moment, and then he said slowly: "Then, young fellow, what are you doing in Dodge City? Trying to commit suicide?"

"No," said Anthony, "I am only hunting for a girl, and as soon as I find her, I'll be going back home."

"A girl!" echoed Parker. "Here?"

"Yes."

Mr. Parker fell silent, and drummed upon the table with the tips of his squared fingers.

Then he said gently: "A girl, and in Dodge City? Might I ask you how long you knowed her before you came here to find her?"

"Let me see," said Anthony. "Two days, altogether. Though it really seems a good deal longer."

Mr. Parker looked deeply into his young companion's face.

"I got an idea that it *does* seem longer," said he.

"And, to tell you the truth," said Anthony, who had not yet mastered the art of hiding emotions: "I expected to see her the very day that she left. I had an appointment, in fact. But she had to go West."

"Humph!" said Parker. "West, eh?"

"Yes," said Anthony, with a sigh. "I was to meet her at noon. But it happened oddly that that was the very moment when the train pulled out for Dodge City."

"Ah-h!" drawled Parker. "And you had knowed her two days—why, it sort of seems to me that I see through this here thing!"

CHAPTER VI

PERHAPS IT DOES NOT NEED TO BE EXPLAINED THAT there was one serious lack in Anthony's nature at this time in his life. He had no sense of humor. And when he heard Mr. Parker speak in this manner he quite failed to understand a little glimmer of sarcastic light which was in the eyes of his companion. He laid a lightning hand upon the arm of Parker and stammered with eagerness:

"You see through it! Do you see through it? Then tell me, quickly!"

"Take your hand off!" said Parker. "You're smashing the bone of my arm."

"I beg your pardon!" said Anthony, confused, and he caught back his hand and held it in his other with such a grip that his finger tips turned blue.

There would have been something girlish in that attitude and gesture had it not been for the quivering force that was in it. And Mr. Parker regarded those long, rather bony hands with a most considerate eye while he rubbed his bruised arm. He had read of a hand of iron. Now he felt that he knew it by experience.

"I beg your pardon," said Anthony, "but you seemed to understand—and this has worried me a great deal, you know!"

"Why, Castracane," said the other, "what I understand is what any other man should understand at once. The girl put you on a wrong trail. She just doubled past you and got away."

But Anthony leaned back in his chair with a sigh and shook his head.

"It can't be that!" said he.

"And why not, then?"

41

"Because," said Anthony, "she is not that sort of a girl."

"You knew her two days?" said Parker.

"Yes."

"Son," said the other, "listen to me! The wisest man that ever lived in the world never could get to know the simplest girl in only two days. Not if she cared to cover her cards! Did you find out who could have *made* her go West?"

"I didn't stop to ask questions," said Anthony. "I just came on at once."

"Humph!" said Parker. "And how long do you plan to stay?"

"Until I find her, of course. That should be in a day or two."

"And if you don't find her in a day or two?"

"I shall stay longer."

"A month, then?"

"Or a year, or ten years," said Anthony calmly. "Because I shall never stop hunting."

Mr. Parker began to smile, but his smile presently went out. There was such a mixture of childish impulse and manly resolution in his new acquaintance that he hardly knew what to think or to say.

But at length he said gently:

"Suppose that you met this girl, partner, and that she had along with her a fellow who didn't *want* her to go back?"

"In that case," said Anthony, "of course I should find out what Miss Lester wished."

"And?"

"And then, if she really wished to go back, I should try to find some way of taking her—"

"In spite of the other gent?"

"Yes, in spite of him."

"And if it meant fighting?"

"I should not like that," said Anthony, "but I should have to do my best!"

"Hum!" grunted Parker. "Don't you see no snag in front of you?"

"I don't know what you mean," said Anthony.

"It's like this, son," said the other. "Here you sit, the only man of your age west of the Mississippi that ain't able to use a Colt or a rifle."

"Ah!" murmured Anthony. "You mean that the other man might use a gun on me?"

"Might? Might?" chuckled Parker. "Why, lad, fifteen years ago I came into this part of the world and *I* didn't know how to use a rifle or a revolver. And do you know what happened to me?"

"I m very interested," said Anthony devoutly.

"This!" said Parker.

He touched the side of his head, where a long, white scar disappeared into the hair; its course was marked by the vivid whiteness of the hair that had grown in over an old wound.

"It was a matter of a fraction of an inch. I should of been dead. But the bullet glanced a mite off my thick skull. And, after that, I went out and lived with nothing but guns for three months. At the end of that

43

time, I could take care of myself with most. I don't mean that I was a wizard, but I was able to hold my head up in most crowds."

"I should have to learn," said Anthony sadly. "And that would take a great deal of time?"

"Three months, for me. For you—I dunno. Maybe three weeks. Maybe a little less. Because you look as if you could learn, eh?"

"When I find her," said Anthony, "then I shall see if it is necessary—"

"And if you're a dead man before you ever lay eyes on her?"

"She is somewhere in Dodge City!" said Anthony desperately. "And I am sitting here, wasting time!"

He started to his feet.

"Wait!" said Parker. "You can't go without a gun. And if you'll give me ten minutes, I'll show you the parts of a Colt, and tell you how it works. Believe me, Castracane, you'll never learn anything in your life that'll be more useful to you than facts such as I can show you!"

Even that brief time was grudged by Anthony. He poised the question back and forth in his mind and then he nodded with a sigh.

"I'll take that time," said he.

And he followed his companion out behind the saloon into a long, vacant yard.

"This," said Parker, "is the way that you shoot, west of the Mississippi. I mean, there are other ways. But the other ways are simply ways of dying. And this is a way of living."

44

He stood facing Anthony.

"You are a gent that has it in for me," explained Parker. "I come around a corner quick and I meet up with you. What do I do? This!"

He made two motions so swift that none but a practiced eye such as Anthony's could have followed the gesture. His left hand jerked open the face of his coat. His right hand darted up to his left armpit and swung down again bearing into view a long and polished revolver. It snapped out and exploded so suddenly that Anthony gave a start and a gasp.

"There's the dead man!" said Mr. Parker.

And Anthony, turning about, saw a neat round hole drilled into a post ten yards behind him.

"But you didn't take aim!" said Anthony.

"No."

"And you didn't cock the revolver?"

"No."

"Then, what in the world happened?"

"This!" said Parker. "When I bought this gun, I did what every other sensible gent on this side of the river does. I took it apart and I filed away the part of the mechanism that connected with the trigger. That's a dead trigger, lad. Dead as can be! Then I lightened up the pull of the hammer, so that it flicks back dead easy. And, after that, I learned how to work that hammer back and let it fall with the movement of my thumbs. Just catching the hammer on the second joint of the thumb, and letting it fall when it's high enough. And I practiced until I was able to do it fast, and shoot straight. And now mind you, Castracane—I'm no champion. There are hundreds of men out here that can get out a gun faster than me, and hundreds that can shoot quicker and straighter. But still I'm fast enough and sure enough to always be dangerous. And you can bet, old son, that even the wildest and the wooliest of them, if he knows about me, is not going to tackle me unless he absolutely has to. That's all I want. Not scalps, but just safety. And that's why I say to you: Take this here gun, young man, and treat it like it was a part of your own flesh and blood. Because you can never get too good at it!"

If Abdullah Khan, of Brooklyn, could have looked into the back yard of that saloon a little later, he would have found his talented pupil confronted, at last, with the perfect task—a thing which could never be done perfectly!

For Anthony, with a borrowed holster under his arm, suspended by a strap from over his shoulder, was learning how to whip out the heavy Colt and swing it toward the target and fire—

"Not using your eyes, but just using your ability to guess. You *guess* a bullet at a target, when you're fanning a gun. You *wish* it into the right line. You *think* it on its way."

And Anthony practiced devotedly, patiently, steadily. All his life he had been a student with many teachers. He knew how to concentrate with heart and soul upon one task. He had the mental and the nervous stamina. He had hand and eye and arm made perfect for such schooling as this, and the strides of his progress were amazing.

Time, I am sorry to say, ceased to exist for Anthony. The face of Muriel Lester was smoothed away from his mind. Soul and brain became an utter blank upon which could be inscribed the new teachings of this new master.

Time ceased to exist for Parker, also. He could remember his own first clumsy fumblings with weapons, and he could not understand the swift surety with which this youth progressed from step to step. Until, suddenly, the shadow of the high board fence fell across his feet and he looked up with a gasp.

He touched his ammunition belt.

There were only three cartridges left in it!

And he said: "Son, I've got to leave you for today. But I want to tell you this: You've learned the alphabet, and you know the first words. All you need is practice, until you can speak the language. What you got to do is to take every second you can get for that same practice. And in the meantime, for a week or two, you pray to God that you don't run into any gun fight."

"I want to pay you for the gun, and that knife—" began Anthony, looking guiltily at the sinking sun, while the thought of Muriel rushed back upon his heart.

"Forget that!" said Parker. "This here has been a pleasure for me. The chances are that you're gonna fill an early grave out here. But if you don't, then one of these here days I'm gonna be able to say: 'Sure, I gave him his start!' So long, Castracane! I got one best hope for you—which is that you don't find her!"

CHAPTER VII

IF ANTHONY HAD BEEN A REALLY CLEVER DETECTIVE, he probably would have had no luck whatever in finding the quarry he had come so far to hunt. Just as he would never have won the kindly friendship of Parker if he had possessed even a part of the hard shell of a man of the world. But now, as he walked aimlessly down the street, very conscious of the weight of his new revolver which hung under the pit of his left arm, he came straight upon Muriel Lester walking out of a shop with a bundle under her arm and advancing toward a surrey in the front seat of which was a tall, darkly handsome fellow, reining two high-headed horses, and in the back seat a brown-faced woman, wonderfully overdressed. She looked to Anthony very much like Queenie, the trapeze artist, ready for an outing; like Queenie, too, mounting aloft on her aerial trapeze, ready to shed the outer layer of her apparel and appear in slim tights and the fluffy skirts of a ballet dancer.

But these two were seen by Anthony only from the corner of his eye. It was Muriel Lester who mattered, and he went straight to her and stood before her, white with excitement.

"Thank God," said Anthony, "that I've had the luck to find you!"

As for Muriel, she turned even whiter than her cavalier. And as she looked up at him out of wide eyes, he could see that she was trembling from head to foot. It was as though she were seeing a ghost, not a reality.

"Anthony Castracane!" breathed she. "It *can't* be that you're here!"

"I have come to take you back," said Anthony, happily.

"To take me back?" she echoed.

"Because I know that you must have been forced away. You would never have gone if you had not been forced—"

She tried to press past him.

"I can't stay," said Muriel, whiter than ever. "If only I had guessed—I am sorry—I didn't know—"

She was stammering pitifully when a voice rang behind Anthony: "Stand aside, youngster, and let the lady pass!"

Anthony looked vaguely behind him and saw that the tall, dark man on the front seat of the surrey was apparently in a high passion. But what was that to him? Here was his lady before him. And he restrained her with the merest touch upon her arm.

"Is it this fellow in the carriage that forced you to come, Muriel?" he asked. "I don't want you to explain everything, but only—"

A hand gripped his shoulder and jerked him around.

"Confound you!" exclaimed the man who had just

leaped down from the carriage. "What the devil do you mean by laying hands on Miss Lester. Muriel, get into the surrey!"

"One moment!" said Anthony, and stretched a hand toward the girl.

There was a wrench at his shoulder that was intended to hurl him to the ground, but the lessons of Kilpatrick and Barney and Jumbo made Anthony only a little steadier than a rock upon his feet. He shrugged off that tearing grip and then, with a little gesture, he sent the tall man staggering heavily backward.

Then he stepped forward again to speak to Muriel, but she was transfigured with a sudden fear.

"Run, Anthony!" she cried. "Oh, Jack, don't hurt him! He doesn't know—"

It seemed to Anthony the most bewildering thing in the world that anyone should intercede on his behalf to keep him from being hurt. But, half turning, from the corner of his eye he saw the tall man bring up with a crash against a post, and at the same instant a gun winked into his hand by a motion almost too fast to be followed. There was the tenth part of a second for Anthony to act in, and he leaped far back as the gun roared and a bullet hummed past his face, so close that the hiss of it was like the warning of a striking snake.

Another bullet and another and another followed, almost too fast for counting, but as the Colt exploded for the second time, Anthony was back through the doorway which yawned behind him and stood breathless on the inside, with the scream of

Muriel ringing in his ears.

And he was helpless. Utterly and dreadfully helpless! He knew well enough that only by the grace of swift feet and a good deal of luck had he been able to escape two strokes that had been intended for his death. He had staggered a man who was not accustomed to being thrown off his balance no matter by what hand. But the snaky speed and surety of the stranger's hand seemed to Anthony almost like witchcraft.

What could he do now? If he stepped through that doorway, he would have three or four bullets through head and body before he could fall to the ground. And a dead man would be of no possible help to Muriel Lester.

So he leaned by the wall, head down.

One bitter regret filled him. If only he had struck with a clenched fist instead of brushing the other away with a gesture!

But now he had to stand chained to his place, while he heard stamping hoofs and grinding wheels carry away Muriel Lester's excited, protesting voice.

"You have killed him, Jack, and I'll never forgive you! A poor, silly boy—and he didn't know—and his blood is on my head. Oh, Jack! Oh, Jack! What—"

A rattling noise of approaching horses blotted out her voice, and Anthony raised his head in agony.

He was met by grim smiles, on the faces of half a dozen men who sat in that room. They had not broken up their card game. That diversion continued steadily. But they favored Anthony with these odd, faint smiles.

"Are you trying to get famous, kid?" said one of them. "Or are you tired of living and want Diamond Jack Kirby to pay your funeral expenses?"

"Was that his name?" asked Anthony.

"You didn't know that, I guess?"

"I never saw him before."

"And it ain't likely you'll go out of your way to see him again. No, kid, the wise thing for you to do is to drift. Because, if you didn't know Diamond Jack before, you know him now!"

"I know him now," said Anthony slowly. "I begin to know him now. And I thank you for that advice!"

And he walked straight out into the street.

It cannot be said that all jugglers become as deft with their wits as with their hands, but it is certain that Anthony had picked up the faculty of learning rapidly.

His hands were utterly tied if he stayed in Dodge City. He stood in the most imminent danger of death. And he was as helpless before Diamond Jack Kirby as an infant before thundering Zeus.

So he did, straightway, the very thing that had been advised.

He left Dodge City, but he left it with a brand new Colt, in addition to Parker's loan, and a burro loaded with provisions and scores of pounds of cartridges. He had oil and rags for the cleaning of those guns, and he determined to work slavishly until he had mastered this new craft.

He had worked long hours over other things, before this. When he was a mere youngster, he had had many a dreadful fall while he was mastering the double somersault. But he had so perfected his skill in that difficult feat, at last, that he could spin twice through the air while flying from cantering horse to cantering horse. And upon the knifework of Abdullah Khan's teaching, had he not labored for months and months before he became a proficient?

He found a lonely hollow, fringed with trees. There was no one near. Only, at night, he could see the lights of Dodge City, twinkling like evil stars on the edge of the sky. And, in the day, he could see false clouds rising on the horizon, over the squat roofs of the town, and he knew that new cattle herds were pouring into the place.

He ate, he slept five hours a night—and he worked with those guns!

For eighteen hours a day, he was constantly at it. A third of that time would have killed a lesser man. But Anthony was all the purest steel, supple and mighty. And if he had worked before in the hope of pleasing a crowd, he was working now in the hope of saving his life.

It was not all shooting. If it had been, even the heavy poundage of ammunition which the burro brought out would not have been enough. But there were other things which Anthony worked at. He learned, by hours of steady application, to work the Colt into the holster and out again as fast as thought. He set before himself a mighty ideal—to make that Colt move as rapidly as the trick card in a pack. He knew exactly the speed at which cards may be manipulated, and he strove with all the tremendous agility and strength of wrist and fingers to duplicate that movement with heavy guns. It could not be quite done, of course, but early in his practice he came wonderfully close to it. And in his hours of rest, he would sit or lie, and juggle the guns from hand to hand. Until he could sit with eyes closed and snatch a gun from the holster, fling it spinning into the air, and, still with eyes closed, catch it again as it came down. It had been a difficult trick with Indian clubs. It was ten times harder with a clumsy Colt. But after all, such tricks were putting him more and more intimately in touch with his weapons. They were becoming more feathery light to his touch each moment.

As for the speed of the draw, it seemed to Anthony, after a few days, that even Diamond Jack Kirby could not have produced his weapon with any more lightning dexterity.

Hitting a target once the gun was out was a different matter. If Anthony had not been blessed with all the gifts of a natural shot, he would never have learned. But he had those gifts, and consequently he was learning with a prodigious speed.

He had half a dozen stumps arranged in a loose circle around the central spot from which he did his shooting. At the end of three days, he could sink bullets consistently into a trunk as thick as a man and five yards away. At the end of a week, he could do the same with trees ten paces off. At the end of ten days, he could drive two bullets out of three into a trunk the same size, fifteen strides off from him.

This does not seem like a great achievement, but as a matter of fact any proficiency whatever was a most remarkable thing, considering that other men worked an hour a day simply to keep their hands in! But when he had reached this point, Anthony felt that the time had come to strike back at the great adventure.

CHAPTER VIII

HE WENT BACK TO THE TOWN AS HAPPY AS ANY miner who has struck gold, the difference being that the ore which Anthony carried was securely locked in his heart only—and his burro went back to town with an empty pack.

"I want to find Diamond Jack Kirby's house," he said to the first man he met.

And he was shown to it as readily as though it had been the church—or the cemetery.

Just on the edge of the spreading town, fenced in behind a rapidly thickening hedge of fir, was Diamond Jack's house.

In front of it Anthony paused a moment and made sure that each gun was loose in its holster. He had a very grave belief that he was about to die, but that would not hold him back. For Anthony had never yet learned to change his mind.

Then he opened the gate and walked boldly down

the path, which was laid with red bricks. Other little, narrow red-brick walks wandered here and there through the garden. Everything looked so comfortable and so civilized that Anthony could hardly believe Dodge City was roaring not far beyond those surrounding walls of greenery.

He was at the door, now. And he had to take a deep breath before he was able to knock.

Then he waited, but suddenly he heard lightly running feet down the hall, and the screen was opened, and Muriel Lester broke out with a little cry of happiness and stood before him.

What he heard, as she came flashing through the doorway, was a joyously bubbling "Jack!"

But now, looking up to wider, heavier shoulders than Diamond Jack had ever worn, she shrank back a little from him.

"It's you again!" she breathed, and she clutched at the doorknob as though she feared that he might offer to do her a harm.

It bewildered Anthony. And he said gloomily: "I've come back to ask you once more—the same question you didn't have a chance to answer before Diamond Jack began shooting at me."

She pressed a shaking hand against her mouth, and stared wildly up to him.

Then he went on, growing a trifle grim: "You were to see me that day at noon. And when I went for you, your house was empty. I saw you at the train, though you didn't see me. I thought for a moment that you had been making a fool of me. But I *couldn't* believe that, after all. I had told you that I loved you, Muriel. You couldn't have made a joke out of that!"

"You see—" she stammered. And then she stopped, afraid to speak the truth. "I meant no harm to you."

A red fury leaped across the eyes of Anthony.

"Tell me this: When you said that you'd wait for me, did you mean it?"

"I only meant—" she began.

And then all her courage melted from her. She snatched the screen open and fled into the house. A hand reached after her. She slammed the heavy door and shot the bolt.

Back to the living room she fled, with a ghost pursuing her. It was partly her own conscience, and it was partly sheer dread of that big angry man in front of the house.

There she found that same passive brown-faced woman whom Anthony had seen in the carriage with Muriel and Jack Kirby ten days before.

"Now, my dear," said she, "what has happened?"

"That same man—he's back!" gasped Muriel.

"The same big fellow who tried to speak to you two weeks ago?" said Mrs. Kirby. "I thought he had his lesson that day. Now leave him to me!"

"He mustn't be harmed," breathed the girl. "Only, I'm frightened to death. He's terribly angry. And you mustn't leave me!"

"Stuff!" said Mrs. Kirby, whose nerves were of steel, like those of her son. "Leave this to me for half a minute, and then I'll be back."

In the kitchen she found the Negro cook at his stove and a little woolly-headed Negro boy peeling vegetables in a corner.

"George," she said to the boy, "go to your master and tell him that the same man is bothering Miss Lester. He'll know what I mean, and he'll know what to do. Run at once!"

So George left his pan of potatoes and scampered gladly from the back door and like a dark arrow through the town until he came to a rambling, low-built wooden structure which carried a boldly painted legend above the door:

EVERY GUN DRAWN IN THIS PLACE IS AIMED AT
ME AND I SHALL ACT ACCORDINGLY.
JOHN KIRBY

Little George had seen that legend before, but it never failed to send a shudder through him. A chill was trickling down his young spine as he presented himself at the entrance where a hawk-faced man well garnished with revolvers kept the door.

"What's up, George?" said he. "You look like you've been running."

"The boss's mother sent me. I got to see him quick."

"His *mother* sent you? Then it must be important. You come along with me!"

He led the way through long, low rooms, cooled three times a day with sprinklings of wet sawdust—

rooms for roulette, for faro, and for half a dozen other regular institutions of the place—and every room opened invitingly upon a long bar which ran the entire length of the building, for John Kirby knew well enough that there is nothing which excites a thirst faster than winning at cards, unless it be losing at them. And he knew, furthermore, that a brain-befuddled gambler is a sure loser in the long run. So he had planned the rough outline of his establishment with all appropriate care.

It was the late afternoon, and the real rush of business would not begin until the evening fell and shadows had idealized Dodge City and all that was in it, including the Goddess of Chance. For the harsh sunlight shows us the truth of many things whose real faces we cannot see by the flicker of dim oil lamps. However, in a little private room at the very rear of the gaming house Diamond Jack, at this moment, sat at a quiet game with three others. They were all, like himself, professionals. They had come, as the saying goes, "loaded for bear," and the particular bear meat which they wanted on this day was that of Diamond Jack. So far, they had made very fair progress. Diamond Jack was several thousand down when there came a tentative rap at the door, twice repeated, and Diamond Jack stood up.

"You ain't leaving us, Jack?"

"You ain't disheartened, Diamond?"

He turned and smiled on them. He was a beautiful man, was Diamond Jack, and nothing became him so well as his smile. He knew it, because there was nothing about himself that Diamond Jack Kirby did not know. So he studied to use it often, and in good fortune and bad, and in pleasant company and dangerous, the same brilliant smile was often on his face.

He said, merely: "Gentlemen, there's nothing but a fire in the house that would drag me away from this table—as long as you'll do me the honor of caring to play at it, or until I've lost my bankroll, my house, my land, and the studs in this shirt that I'm now wearing! Whatever it is, I shall only be gone a moment."

So he opened the door and stood before the two.

"Now, George?" said he. "Who sent you?"

The doorkeeper had discreetly fallen back.

"Your mother, Master Diamond, she says that the same man is bothering Miss Lester. She says that you'll know what to do!"

Not so much as a shadow crossed the face of Diamond Jack.

"Run back home," said he, "and tell her that everything is all right."

George vanished. He would as soon have disobeyed a bright angel or a black devil as this same Master Diamond.

Diamond Jack passed softly on to an adjoining room where three or four men were lounging. Day or night, there were always two or more in that chamber. And there were some in Dodge City who called it the death cell. When Diamond Jack entered that apartment, he was in the custom of speaking his real mind a little more frankly than in other places. And he said now:

"Boys, there is a big hulk of a tenderfoot in this town. He bothered me ten days ago, and I thought that I shot close enough to keep him away for good. But he only waited to get up a bit of fresh courage. Now I want him turned out of Dodge City, and turned out in such a style that I can be sure he'll never come back. Do you understand? I don't mean killing, if it can be avoided. On the other hand, you can't manhandle him unless you take him by surprise. He's a bull in strength. If it will help to make you a bit keener for this work, I can tell you that he is bothering Miss Lester, and I think you all know that I intend to make her my wife in a very few days. You may use your own discretion. Chick, you had better go. And Tommy, I think."

He left them, and went back to the gaming room he had just left.

"I have been gone a minute and twenty seconds, my friends," said he, and he took his chair. "Larson, I think you deal. . . ."

And the game went on.

Chick and Tommy needed no further instructions. They simply looked to the condition of their guns, and then they started on the trail. But there was a grim set to their jaws which told plainly that they considered this no simple task.

For they knew exactly whom their master meant.

They had heard of the way big Diamond Jack had scattered lead in this man's direction. And when Diamond Jack shot four bullets without striking his target, something was decidedly wrong!

They knew, furthermore, every detail of the manner in which this same bulky stranger had flicked a knife through the arm of Cherokee Dan. And had done it to save the life of a man he had never seen before!

To attack such a person was no light matter, and since the affair was left to their discretion, they intended to take no chances whatever. Guns were to be their reliance, first and last and all the time. And they hoped to leave a dead man on the street before they went back to report. As for the law—why, what law was there in Dodge City stronger than Diamond Jack's?

No law, indeed, except that which rules in every man's conscience, and conscience was a burden which rested heavily on very few in that age of smoke and iron.

CHAPTER IX

THE SUN HAD FALLEN LOWER IN THE WEST. ALL THE city was flooded with golden and rosy light which filled the deep mouths of the streets and turned the blowing dust clouds into softly moving halos. And as the pair moved on toward the outskirts where Diamond Jack's house stood, they perceived Anthony in the distance, a great figure of a man, moving slowly down the center of the street, with his head fallen, and a burro trudging honestly and patiently behind him.

Something in the mere dimensions of that man gave them pause, for a moment.

They would have liked this business much better if they had been in the heart of the town with a crowd around them, because in any crowd there were sure to be at least a certain number of friendly eyes prepared to swear that the thing was done in "self-defense." It was so easy to build up a case. Any movement that a man made toward his hip was, presumably, a reaching for a gun. And after that all was in self-defense, as a matter of course.

But out here on the edge of the place, with no one in the empty street to see—why, it was strangely like naked murder. Chick looked to Tommy, and swore softly. And Tommy grinned mirthlessly behind his beard.

"We'll give him one warning," said Tommy.

"And then for God's sake shoot straight."

"He's only a tenderfoot."

"If he was so easy, would the chief of sent two of us?"

It was a convincing argument, because Diamond Jack was notably sparing in the number of agents he dispatched upon these necessary businesses. He was proud of their individual prowess. It was his boast that one of his men was equal to half a dozen of the ordinary brand of gun fighters. And he selected them by hand, so to speak, out of the precious garden of ruffians which perennially sprang into bloom in Dodge City.

So the pair came on until they were within fifty yards.

"Now?" said Chick beneath his breath.

"Two more steps, to make sure," said Tommy.

Forty yards.

"Say when, Tommy!"

"Now."

"Hey," yelled Chick. "Fill your hand, you damned—"

He did not have sufficient time to complete his speech. That honored formula by which another gentleman was invited in the West to draw his Colt meant nothing to Anthony, but the double flash of guns which accompanied it was eloquent enough.

He was so startled that he leaped a little to the side automatically. Lightness of foot had saved his life when he first stood before Diamond Jack Kirby. And the same instinctive sense of the boxer saved him again. For two bullets tore through the air where he had stood the instant before.

Those bullets were hardly gone before the Colts were out in Anthony's hands. Ten days is not long to most men. But ten days to Red Anthony, trained as he had been, were enough to make half the matter an affair of a new, extra sense. Thirty yards was twice the distance at which he had been practicing, but still, these targets were slightly larger than the ones he had been accustomed to firing at. Beyond that, there was the most decisive element of all. The vast majority of us are only 50 per cent effective when the crisis comes. But there are a few, one in a hundred thousand or so, who respond better when the climax is more terrible. They are your "money fighters" or your "money horses"; they are your tactical geniuses, who never think really well except on the battlefield. And Anthony was one of these.

But, even so, I have never been able to understand why he escaped death in this second gunfight of his life. I knew both Tommy and Chick, and they were cool hands. They were very cool and practiced rascals, indeed, with records so long and so black that even Dodge City shivered a little as they passed.

I think that what upset them most of all was the sudden flashing of a pair of Colts into Anthony's hands.

"Tenderfoot, hell!" groaned Tommy. "He's a two-gun devil!"

And a double stream of lead issued from Anthony's guns.

He tore the dust at the feet of the pair. But as their own bullets nipped past him, his aim grew better and steadier. In a trice he dropped Tommy on his back. Chick spun around with a yell, clutching at his shoulder. And then, seeing himself alone, he dropped his gun and fled.

The whole affair had not filled six seconds.

But why had not Anthony gone down before the guns of these experts? It was partly surprise at the sudden and terrible fire which a tenderfoot had opened upon them; and, perhaps more than that, it was a feeling that they stood before a strange and mighty man. I myself have seen Anthony in the middle of a battle. And the transformation in him was like that which flame makes in a dry bush.

Twice Anthony covered the fleeing man, and twice he knew that he could not shoot at any man's back.

He looked yonder to the fellow in the dust, and then—he calmly broke open his guns, one at a time, and loaded them!

That was Anthony! That was the Red Anthony that the West was to come to know!

He counted the bullets he had fired. Four from the right hand, and three from the left.

"I must speed up that left thumb," said Anthony gravely.

And he finished loading his guns and stepped forward to the fallen man.

He thought at first that the fellow had been shot through the head, because blood covered his face. But then he saw that it was merely a glancing bullet, such as that which had wounded Parker on another day.

So he picked up Tommy by the back of the neck and carried him to the side of the road. In transit, Tommy recovered his senses, and he bethought himself of the knife in his girdle, and reached for it. But he changed his mind. There seemed too much iron strength in this man who carried him thus lightly with one hand! No single knife thrust, surely, could dispose of him. And therefore Tommy let his knife remain untouched.

He was deposited against a tree stump.

A dozen people, in the meantime, had appeared in the street to see what had caused Chick's yell, rather than to examine into the cause of the fusillade. Because screeches were less frequent than volleys of shots in Dodge City.

But when they saw that no one was dead, they turned back into their houses, rather disappointed.

Anthony sat down on his heels before his captive.

He said: "Did I ever see you before?"

"You never did," said Tommy, wiping the blood from his beard.

"Did I ever wrong you?" said Anthony.

"I dunno that you ever did. But hell, man, what are you tryin' to do? Do you want to make me crawl? Because I ain't that kind! You got a gun, you got the drop on me. Chick, the hound, sneaked off. Well, I've give others their medicine, and now I'll take mine, but I ain't gonna yap about it first!"

And he glared fiercely at Anthony.

He was a sprightly fellow, that Tommy, not big, but looking bigger than he was because he had a very small head. The smallness of his head was a perpetual agony to him, and he had tried to increase its apparent dimensions by letting his hair grow long and by cultivating a flaring beard and widely forked mustaches. But these growths of hair only served to make the face itself seem more ridiculously diminutive.

I think it was a savage intentness on establishing his essential manliness that had made Tommy into a desperado. I think, indeed, that he would have been one of the mildest fellows in the world if it had not been that people were apt to take advantage of him on account of that childish head of his. And, therefore, he had made himself into all that was not natural to him.

Anthony looked at him calmly.

"I don't wish to shame you," he said. "There's no advantage to me in doing that. That's a bad cut on the side of your face, which is punishment enough. And all that I ask of you is: Who sent you out to shoot me?"

Tommy heard, but he did not believe.

And, for that matter, he had good reason to doubt. The code in Dodge City was simple, but it was distressingly to the point. If you tried to kill another man and he got the advantage over you, he killed you. If he shot you down and saw you helpless, streaming with blood, with none to assist you, he calmly stood over you and drove a bullet through your brain, and nobody blamed him. It was part of the code; it discouraged assassination!

No one knew this better than Tommy. He had prepared himself to die. He expected death with an absolute certainty. And so he put on his boldest front and sneered deliberately in Red Anthony's face.

"You're gonna soft-soap the news out of me, eh?" said Tommy. "No, kid, that game don't work with me, either. Only—I wish to God that I had knowed you was *not* a tenderfoot. Because then I would of come prepared to shoot a mite straighter. Who taught you that footwork, big boy?"

Said Anthony:

"I'm not a tenderfoot any longer. I've been practicing with the guns for ten days. And now I want to
beg you once more to tell me who sent you after me?"

The first part of this speech fascinated Tommy.

"Ten days?" he snorted. "Ten hells! *I* know how
long it takes to sling two guns at once! As for the rest
of it, now I've said my say. Don't think that I'll loosen
up. You got the guns, and you got the drop. So finish
off the job!"

Anthony regarded Tommy for a long moment. He
was sadly tempted to wring the information out of this
man by sheer physical torment. But he had been raised
all his life to understand that the worst sin of all is for
a big man to use his superior power over a smaller
fellow.

One of Tommy's guns lay in the deep dust of the
center of the road. The second one Anthony caught up
and tossed over the fence so that it would be out of the
way of temptation. He drew the knife, also, and threw
it after the Colt. Then he stood up and strode on down
the street, leading his burro behind him.

CHAPTER X

IN ORDER TO UNDERSTAND WHAT PASSED IN POOR
Tommy's mind at that moment, you have to understand that all his life he had been kicked from pillar to
post until he learned to demand his rights at the point

of a gun, and after that he had received just as much as his guns warranted and no more—hatred and threats from some, and hatred and fear from others.

But now he found himself lying with blood still slowly trickling down his face and his head reeling, not from the shock of the bullet which had so nearly taken his life, but from the destruction of all his preconceptions of the world and the people in it. For, according to Tommy, he should have been dispatched into another life before this big stranger strode away. And that he found himself in possession of his mortal body in this same Dodge City was a miracle to him.

It thawed through the beliefs of half a lifetime. It melted all the iron in the heart of Tommy. And suddenly he jumped up and ran after the tall man, forgetful of his wound.

Anthony turned in haste.

"Well?" said he sternly.

"Stranger," said Tommy, "I can't let you go like this! I should be in hell, by this time. And here I am, still, to ask you what can I do, maybe, to make up for the skunk that I've been to you!"

"You can tell me," said Anthony crisply, "who sent you to attack me."

"It was Diamond Jack Kirby, of course. Everybody knows that he's my boss. But it's the last time that I'll pull a gun for him, even if he was a closer friend of the devil's than he actually is!"

"Kirby sent you," nodded Anthony. "That's likely. And yet I don't understand how Kirby could have learned so soon that I have come back to Dodge City."

"There was a message from Miss Lester," said Tommy. "She said that you was bothering her and that she wanted you out of the way. Though that must of been a lie, because you're not the kind to bother a girl that—"

He had struck Anthony a great deal more cruel blow than if he had used a shotgun—both barrels at close range.

"*She* sent to have me murdered?" asked Anthony. "*She* sent to have it done?"

And he reached for the trunk of a sapling that stood beside the road and leaned heavily against it. And the tree bowed and shuddered under his weight. Tommy, watching him in awe, saw in Anthony's face more agony than he had deemed possible in human nature, and his own soul seemed a small thing indeed, compared with this!

He said gently: "I understand how it shapes up. It's the fine, clean look of her and her big eyes that fooled you. But then, would she of hooked up with one like Diamond Jack unless she was crooked and hard? Or would she even be in Dodge City if she wasn't a bad one?"

He named the very thoughts which were plunging through Anthony's soul like angry comets smashing his old universe to bits.

As you have seen, he had not really known much of the sorry world in which we are all cooped. The circus tent had housed both his body and his thoughts. And the pegs outside the big tent had been the outermost limits of his horizon. He had lived very much like one in a dream. His work absorbed all his faculties. And though he could have seen enough good and evil in the people around him in that circus, if he had cared to open his eyes and look, he had always been too busy to see the facts; for he had never known anything other than this world, and that with which we are most familiar is usually that which we least understand. We must leave the place of our birth and return to it from a strange land before we know that it is actually something made of earth.

If the lion tamer drank and swore—why, that was the lion tamer's ugly way! And if the ringmaster was a pompous prig, why, that was simply the peculiarity of the ringmaster. And if some of the girls painted a bit too much, they were only to be smiled at and pitied, poor things, for trying to improve the natures which God had given them.

For you see that Anthony had always been ready to look for the very best in everyone whom he met. And no doubt it was for that reason that so many people had endowed him with the best of their stock of knowledge. Abdullah Khan was not a communicative fellow, and yet he had poured out all that he knew at Anthony's feet. Kilpatrick was a surly devil, and yet he was like a father to Anthony. Jumbo was a stupid boor, and yet he was a patient and wise teacher for Anthony. So that young Castracane had grown up feeling that this world of ours is crowded from edge to edge with human kindness, goodness, and truth.

I suppose that we may figure to ourselves Mrs. Wagnall as another serpent in the garden of Anthony's Eden. And little Muriel Lester was the Eve.

Now he was wakening to the fact that he had been thrust from one false universe into another of reality.

Indeed, all the knowledge of self and life that youth and manhood usually gains by slow years of experience was now crowded upon Anthony in a single flaming instant. Muriel, he felt, was most unexplainably false and wicked. Therefore, there was no truth and goodness in the world!

So Anthony left one universe of illusion, leaped across reality, and passed into another sphere where all was as false as the first one. He had thought that there was nothing vitally evil; now he thought that there was nothing vitally good. And the rest of this history must attempt to show you the wild and strange ways by which he had to travel before he learned that there is a halfway house that is neither divine nor damned, but merely human. I do believe that our young Castracane was something of an angel unspotted with sin. And, most certainly, he afterward became a devil with very few touches of light. However, of that you may judge for yourself when I have presented all the evidence. If Tommy had known the actual facts, Anthony would never have been flung into these throes. But Tommy was not consciously falsifying. He was simply coming as close to a true repetition of what he had heard as he could.

Now that he saw the big man so stricken, he went on

to supply as much additional comfort as he could, for he shrewdly guessed at a romance beneath this.

"You see," went on Tommy, "a gent like Diamond Jack, he ain't a fool, whatever he is. And would he pick out for a wife some baby face that didn't know nothing? No, old timer, he would pick out something hard-boiled. You bet on that and you win! And— what's up?"

"I don't know your name," said Anthony, breathing hard.

"Mostly, I'm called Tommy. Just that. And you?"

"I'm Anthony Castracane."

"Anthony Castracane, I'm glad to know you. About this here job that I tried to do on you, me and Chick, I'm sorry that I ever—"

"I want you to do a great thing for me," said Anthony. "I have sworn to myself that I'll never see this creature again—this girl—do you understand me?"

"Yes," said Tommy, a little frightened.

"She thinks that she's had me shot and pushed out of the way. God knows why she should have wanted to do it, except that there's a fiend in her! But now I want you to wash the blood from your face and go to her and tell her that I understand everything, how she sent murderers to get at me, and that now I understand her, I despise her. Will you do that?"

"I'll do that," said Tommy, overawed. "It's a hard thing to talk like that to a pretty girl, but I owe you something, old timer, and I'll do it!"

"Thank you," said Anthony, and he turned away down the street.

"And you're bound for where?" called Tommy after him.

"You'll know later," said Anthony, and moved on his way with such long, swift strides that he was soon out of sight around the corner.

With the huge presence of this man removed, Tommy felt a good deal less strong, and he suddenly remembered that by this confession which he had just made he had secured for himself the great John Kirby's irrevocable enmity. In the sudden panic which possessed Tommy, he seemed to see the dreadful, smiling vision of Kirby flashing before him, guns drawn.

Not that Tommy was a coward. But it is possible to fear a man more than the death which he can deal you. At least, so it was with Tommy.

With this feeling of blighted nakedness, he first of all hastened to the center of the road and picked up his first revolver, which had fallen in the dust. There was a little clot of mud over the trigger, and he knew that mere water had not made that coagulation. That gun would need thorough cleaning before he could ever depend upon it again.

Next, he hunted in the field until he had found the gun and the knife which big Anthony had thrown there.

With gun and knife in his possession, he felt much more at ease. If he were cornered, now, he would be able to give an account of himself, and now he turned toward Kirby's house to find Muriel Lester.

It would have been much better if he had taken Anthony's full instructions to heart and washed the blood off his face before he went forward. But Tommy was in such a state of high nervous excitement that he had forgotten the pain of his wound, forgotten the wound itself, forgotten even the state of his precious beard and mustaches for the first time in years. For they had been to him almost in the place of a soul.

He went hurrying forward with his heart full of the greatness of Anthony Castracane. There was still an ache in his neck where the big man's grip had fallen upon him. And Anthony's deep, strong voice still seemed to him to be booming in his ears.

He reached the garden gate and kicked it open. He reached the front of the house and beat against it.

And little George opened the door.

The sun was on the western rim of the sky, and it blinded George so that he saw only a silhouette and heard a familiar voice saying: "I want Miss Lester—quick!"

CHAPTER XI

GEORGE TURNED AND FLED BACK IN HASTE.
He found Muriel still with Mrs. Kirby.

"There's Tommy, one of the boss's men, at the door, asking for you, quick," he repeated faithfully.

So Muriel went, and found Tommy not on the porch with a blinding sun behind him, but now standing in the hall where she could clearly see his bleeding head with the raw, red gash across it, and the blood-entangled beard and mustaches. For the first time in Tommy's life, he looked as terrific as he could have wished. What a pity, then, that there was only a girl for an audience!

He looked like a very specter to Muriel Lester, and she cried out: "What has happened? To you—and to Jack! Has there been—"

He pointed an ominous finger at her. Even in this moment poor Tommy could not help being more actor than real. And as he spoke, he enlarged the volume of his voice and sank its pitch to something near the register in which the great throat of Anthony Castracane spoke.

"What's happened to Jack, I dunno. What *will* happen to him, I can pretty close guess, but the main thing right now, is to tell you of what happened to your murdered man."

"My murdered man!" echoed the girl.

"You dunno what I mean, I s'pose?" said Tommy with terrible irony.

"My murdered man!" she repeated, still stunned.

"Your murdered man! I said it before and I say it again. Are you gonna play innocent right to my face, when I know everything? Don't I know that you sent to Kirby to have it done? Didn't I hear him say so? Didn't I go myself with Chick, and get this slug across the head, and Chick another through the middle of him trying to get the big gent out of the way?"

Through the house a scream rang and knifed suddenly through even the cold heart of Mrs. Kirby. She started up and ran to the rescue.

"You have killed Anthony!" cried the girl.

"You're gonna weep, now. You're gonna yell and bawl and say that you had nothing to do with it!" snarled Tommy, wild with excitement. "You're gonna play baby some more, but it don't go down. Not in Dodge City! We know a crook here, when we see one, woman or man! It was you, through Kirby, that sent the pair of us to do that murder. And it was nothing but fast guns in the hands of Castracane that kept us from downing him."

"Do you mean that he's still alive?" she broke in on the torrent of his words. "I thank God for that! And if Jack dared to try such a thing in my name—"

The raised forefinger shook in her face. Mrs. Kirby had reached the hall, by this time, and encircled the girl with one arm, but Muriel pushed her away with a sudden strength.

"What does this mean, Tommy?" demanded Mrs. Kirby. "And how do you dare to—"

"You're in it, too," said Tommy savagely. "I might of guessed that if Kirby was in any hellishness, you'd be behind it! I'm here to tell the both of you that I'm through with you and I'm through with Diamond Jack, too. I've found a better man than him. And now I'm here to speak for Anthony Castracane, that says that he sees through you, y'understand? And he despises you, and he's done with you. And there ain't nothing in the world so sneaking, or so crooked, or so low as you. D'you hear? That's the word that I'm leaving here from Anthony Castracane."

And he turned on his heel and strode out from the house, making his steps as long and heavy and swift as he could—like the stride of young Castracane. It would have been illuminating to him if he had remained to hear what followed in that house.

For Muriel Lester had turned on her mother-in-law-to-be and said fiercely: "I understand. You sent word to Jack to have Anthony murdered, and if he were anything less than a hero, he *would* have been murdered!"

Even Mrs. Kirby was a little shaken, but she kept her voice under control with a vast effort. She had never approved of her son's intended marriage. For Mrs. Kirby was a firm believer that birds of a feather must flock together if there is to be peace and strength in wedlock. But she dared not show her thoughts, for she knew that Diamond Jack was desperately in love with this soft, pretty face.

"My dear," said she, "do you think that Jack is the sort of a man who needs to do such things? If he has an enemy, does he send out hired ruffians to fight for him? Muriel, are you so foolish as to doubt what Jack can do, when he's already thrashed this lumbering hulk of an Anthony under your very eyes?"

"Thrashed him?" said the girl, more savagely than ever. "I am not blind, and I saw him draw guns on

Anthony when Anthony's hands were empty—do you call that a thrashing? I haven't dared to ask myself what sort of a man Jack can really be, when he would do such a thing. But I *shall* ask myself, now, and I shall ask him, too!"

"Muriel, my dear," said the older woman, "I am not going to ask you to believe what I have to tell you. I only want you to be quiet and yourself, once more—"

"I was never more calm in my life!" said Muriel, trembling from head to foot. "If there is anything to say, I would like to hear it now!"

"There is this, for one thing—this Castracane is a professional fighter who—"

"What utter nonsense!" cried Muriel. "He's as gentle as a lamb!"

Mrs. Kirby's smile was colder than ice.

"And you have just heard how your 'lamb' has beaten two admitted gun fighters?"

"Admitted gun fighters!" exclaimed Muriel, clasping her hands together. "Admitted gun fighters, and hired by who? Who has employed them? And at whose orders would they attack—"

"Muriel!" said the older woman, stung with anger that whitened her face. "You are talking like a child—and like a wicked child!"

"I want the truth, and the whole truth, and I shall have it!" said the girl. "And oh, if the things which I dream are true . . ."

"And then?" said Mrs. Kirby, trying to smile, but only making a dreadful grimace.

"I shall leave this house instantly. And—I wish to heaven now that I had never come! I wish . . ."

She bit her lips to keep back the tears, but the vision of the bloodstained man rose suddenly before her, and the thought of the giant Castracane, and how one day he had worked with the strength of a hero and the happiness of a child to tame a horse in her father's pasture.

So the tears came suddenly flooding, and she bowed her head into her hands. But when Mrs. Kirby would have comforted her, she turned and fled to her room.

It left Mrs. Kirby with her hand on the knob of the girl's door. But after she had turned it and found that the door was securely locked, she stood back with a little shudder.

"Jack," she said aloud, "will rage like a demon when he hears that this has happened."

And she went to her own corner of the living room and sat down in her own chair and closed her eyes.

Perhaps it was better that the climax should come now. This baby face was no person to turn her out of the heart of her son! And besides, if Muriel ruled Diamond Jack, it would soon mean the undoing of the wild, free life, the end of everything, the bringing of Jack himself to some stupid, plodding existence, his shoulders in a harness, pulling the heavy burden of a family up the hill of life!

Such were Mrs. Kirby's thoughts.

She was a very wise woman, in her own way. And yet, as she recalled how the girl had faced her, such a rage filled her that her sun-browned face grew a swarthy red and she yearned most of all for some means of humbling this young impertinent.

Another thought came to her, and it made her start and wince with guiltiness to think that she had not reached the same conclusion many vital moments before.

Here was the big man, Castracane, victorious in an open battle with a pair of her son's most dependable warriors. And what would Castracane do next? It was plain that he had not only beaten Tommy but made a convert of him to a new cause, and therefore would he not have drawn from the latter everything that Tommy knew—and a little more?

Plainly he would, and if there was savage and revengeful blood in him, he would be laying plans at this instant for revenge upon Diamond Jack.

She called sharply, and little George's woolly head appeared at the doorway. His eyes were bright and round with fright, so that it was plain he had heard at least some of the things which had been said with raised voices in that house during the last five minutes.

"George," said Mrs. Kirby, "go straight to your master again, as fast as your legs can fly. And tell him—no, I must write it. Heavens, how much time I have wasted!"

She ran to a desk in the corner of the room, and snatching up pen and paper, she scratched down on it:

JACK,

Castracane has beaten Chick and Tommy. And Tommy, like a weak fool, has gone over to Castracane and probably told him everything about who sent the two of them on that errand. It seems that this Castracane is not a tenderfoot, after all, but a madman. A fighting demon! The instant that you read this, be on your watch. He is apt to attempt anything! Jack, guard yourself, and then come straight home.

Something has happened here of the greatest importance.

MOTHER

She sealed it, almost trembling in her haste. And then she pressed it into the hand of George together with a heavy, broad, shining silver dollar.

"George, put on wings and go to your master. Go as fast as if a greyhound were chasing you all the way. Hurry, hurry, hurry! And you'll have another dollar if you get it to him in time!"

"Ma'am," gasped George, as he leaped for the door, "I'm there and back already!"

He tripped over a chair, landed on his head, rolled to his feet, and darted from sight.

CHAPTER XII

THAT SAME CARD GAME WHICH HAD BEEN PRO-gressing so unfavorably for Diamond Jack Kirby when the first message came to him from his house had changed a great deal. For, having dispatched two messengers of mischief, he had gone back to play with a smile as bright as ever, and just a shade more of iron resolution. That shade was enough to make a great difference. And the sense of his greater strength troubled the others. They became a bit more uncertain in their betting, and he more assured. In five minutes he had won his first considerable stake of the game and the very next hand he repeated.

He won back the three thousand which he was short, and he advanced steadily. He took a thousand, and another. He was fairly sweeping the board before him, and the self-satisfaction of the others had turned to a deep chagrin, when there was another hasty tap at the door.

"Go on and see what it is, Diamond," said one of the players. "The last call give you a change of luck, and maybe this one'll turn you back again. But make it a quick play, will you?"

"Not more than a minute and twenty seconds, gentlemen," said Diamond Jack, and he stepped smiling through the door.

A gasping, panting little Negro stood there before

84

him, a sweat-stained envelope in his hand, and the gambler ripped it open and read the message.

He was one who made up his mind very quickly. And he placed a ten or a ten hundred with an equal precision and carelessness. But this message he read twice over before its meaning seemed to dawn clearly on his mind.

For it was not a thing to believe. It was not in the cards, as the saying has it. It was as if a man led a pewter plate instead of a slip of pasteboard.

In the first place, it was an impossibility that one tenderfoot could have beaten two such expert gun fighters as Chick and Tommy. In the second place it was certain that nothing in the world could make Tommy desert the flag of the house of Kirby until he found a greater man. And in the sense of cool nerves and fast hand and ready wit, Diamond Jack was equally assured that his equal did not exist upon the plains. But to desert him for the sake of a lumbering, thick-witted, simple tenderfoot!

However, he had that assurance from one whose word meant more to him than the assurance of any man. He had grown up in the habit of taking his mother into his councils. And if he could forgive the evil that was in her and her wit, it was because the sins which she counseled were always for his advantage, and not for her own. Whatever the means she might sink to, devise, or advocate, the end was always the pure and clear one of the welfare of John Kirby and his march upward and onward in the world.

"But first, we must have a little more money, Jack. Then we leave the gambling business and forget that we ever had anything to do with it. There are ways of getting a grip in politics, and your father used to tell me about some of them. Well, Jack, when the time comes, we shall put on another name as smoothly as a new suit of clothes. You will grow a pair of mustaches, and in the twinkling of an eye you will become a grave, serious, smart young politician—with a good presence, Jack, and perfect control of yourself when you stand in front of a crowd—"

"With a gun, mother!"

"Or just your tongue. Tush, Jack, Dodge City is only an accident for you. You are meant for greater things!"

It does not seem the proper place to introduce such material as this. But we pause for this instant, just as Jack Kirby paused over that letter, and look into his mind.

His first thought being that there must be a vast mistake somewhere, his second one was that she would never have sent such a message unless she had been assured that she was right in every detail she reported.

Then if Tommy had confessed as to who employed him that day, and if there was sufficient strength in this Castracane to enable him to beat two such tried gun fighters as Chick and his companion, surely Mrs. Kirby was right and, before long, danger might invade even the house of Diamond Jack himself!

Yet he felt it was only a long chance. He had spent some most active years in building up for himself a great reputation, and he did not know of the man who would lightly face him, man to man. Far less could he imagine any human being so lionlike as to invade his gambling house.

"Go back and tell my mother that everything will be all right, and that I am coming to her within half an hour," he told George.

And as the Negro boy scampered away, he went again to the death cell.

There were three of his trusties in that little chamber, now.

"Boys," he said curtly, "Castracane has beaten Tommy and Chick. Tommy has turned yellow, or crazy, or both, and told who sent him. And there is one chance in ten that big Castracane may come here to make trouble. In that case, you'll be looking for him."

He turned on his heel and went back to his game. And as he entered he said quietly:

"I have twenty minutes to continue this game. Or else we'll stop now, as you please."

"Stop now?" growled one of them. "A good time to stop, when you're winning, Jack."

"If you want revenge, you can double the stakes. As far as that is concerned, the sky's the limit!"

And he pointed upward with his flashing smile. But they had no heart to double stakes on Diamond Jack. Others had tried that system before, and the result had made Jack rich. So the game went on while Kirby's watchdogs left the death cell and distributed themselves here and there through the building.

Business was waking up, now. The sun was down. The shadows were deepening with breathless speed through the streets, and men began to look about them for amusement, and remembered Diamond Jack's. Some came to find a quiet corner for a secure talk, since the Diamond's house was known as the one place in the town where guns were never drawn. Others came frankly and freely to play. But even those who came to talk usually remained to play, so the tables began to have their clusters around them. The noise of voices momently deepened. The lights were kindled, every one. And the usual tide of money began to flow toward Kirby's coffers.

Just how much he made, no one could accurately say except Diamond Jack himself, but it was freely guessed that he must put away profits of at least a thousand a day, or perhaps ten thousand a week.

As the increasing current of gamesters moved into the gaming house, one of the guards took his place beside the door with the hawk-faced man.

"Big Castracane is amuck," he said.

"Who's he?"

"The gent that nipped Cherokee Dan, you know, a couple of weeks back. The boss sent Chick and Tommy to get him this afternoon. And the word is that Chick and Tommy got theirs, instead. Keep a lookout."

"I never seen this one."

"A mile high and broad, with a wildish sort of a face and long red hair. Young, but not too young, if what

88

they say is right. And if you'll—"

"Hello, what's this?"

"Where?"

"That gent heading across the street toward us?"

"By God, I think it's him! It *is* him! Shake your gun loose and get ready. This may mean a big time, old man!"

Before the doors there was ever a little crowd pooled, made up of the restless and the uncertain. There were some who wished to go in but feared on account of stories they had heard. There were some who wished, but who feared because they had already dropped many a month of earnings within the humming gulf of this house. But ever and anon a few detached themselves from the group and drifted slowly, almost shamefacedly, toward the doors.

Because you never can tell. The next turn of the wheel, the next roll of the dice, or the next chance of the draw may make you rich.

And no matter how much you have lost before, at the doors of the gaming house there is always tempting prattle:

"It's a straight game, anyway."

"There was Filmore, last week. He kept his money on black and doubled five times, and then he quit a clean winner. He took down forty-three thousand dollars, they say! Diamond Jack come out and shook hands with him and advised him to put that money in the bank. And he *took* the advice, too. The lucky hound!"

"Luck or nerve! But he'll never have to work again—that's certain!"

"No, he'll never have to work again. He packed up his prospecting kit and sold it for five dollars. Lefty from Louisville bought it. And if you want to know who done better than Filmore, there was old man Kennedy that . . ."

Now, through such talk as this, stepped the tall, commanding form of Anthony Castracane, as big and as light-footed and as long-striding as ever.

But there was a great change in Anthony, and though I was not there to see him enter the door, I know what it was, from others who *did* watch.

He had always possessed the presence to make himself one in ten thousand. It was only the matter of lighting the fire in him and blowing it to a flame, and now the fire was lighted with a vengeance.

Half an hour or so before, Anthony was as quiet and mild a fellow as you could have wished to see, looking not a whit more than his twenty-two or three years. But since that time, he had stood through the baptism of fire, and he had returned fire with fire, and struck down two.

He had tried his guns and not found them wanting, and you may be sure that whatever he was when he faced Chick and Tommy, he was twice as much now. For to all that he had been there were two great qualities added. One was confidence, such as a proved man feels in himself and his tools; the other was a deep and abiding rage, such as will carry a man through a long battle.

No wonder that the crowd gave way a bit for him and opened before him a straight channel to the doors.

CHAPTER XIII

ANTHONY'S CALM AND STEADY APPROACH SAVED him from being shot at a distance. The guards at that door were used to seeing troublemakers. But the troublemakers in Dodge City usually came with a roar and a whoop, a gun or two gleaming in their hands. So Anthony was allowed to come straight up to the entrance before a voice barked at him:

"You ain't wanted in here, Castracane! Back up!"

And the hawk-faced guard reached for his gun. He was a fast man, like all of those employed by Diamond Jack. But a hand without a gun is faster than a hand loaded with a heavy Colt. Heavy as the walking beam of a great engine and fast as a high-speed piston, Anthony's arm shot forth with no warning word, and a fist of iron struck home. Mad Anthony was silent. But there was such a fury in him that he miscalculated his aim by a whole handbreadth. Instead of landing on the head of the other, his knuckles lodged on the man's neck and the base of his jaw. And that, certainly, was all that saved his life.

Consciousness was knocked out of him. He fell with a lurch that staggered the second guard, Plummer. And that stagger spoiled the aim of Plummer's bullet, which was honestly intended for Anthony's heart, but

91

which merely grazed his head, instead.

And before Plummer's active thumb could release another slug of lead from his gun, the Colt was torn away from him and he dangled at the end of Castracane's mighty arm.

"I want to see Diamond Jack Kirby," said Anthony. "Will you bring me to him, or will you stay here with the other murderer?"

And he jerked his unoccupied hand at the man on the floor. Plummer followed that gesture with his eyes, and he saw his companion lying as limp and crushed as though he had just been broken under the foot of an elephant. Blood poured from mouth and nose and ears, and he lay partially on his back, his eyes half opened but as sightless as death itself.

That one glance was enough for Plummer. His courage and his good nerve were twitched away from him like a cloak from a swimmer, and he stood shivering in the cold fear of death.

"I'll show you," he stammered to Anthony.

And straight down the room he marched, with Anthony behind him.

There was a gun in each of Anthony's hands now. And eyes which could follow the spinning flight of fifteen balls high in the air, circling down toward his waiting hands, could flick like lightning across the room and see the dangers which he was passing on either side of him.

Every gamester in the place had come with a rush to watch. Yonder were two extra guards who should have attacked at once to free their brother in arms, Plummer, as he went by. But they had seen this Castracane, with his bare hands win an entrance to the hall. And that sight was, somehow, enough for them.

It was a magnificent procession, though there were only two in it.

At the door of the little rearmost gaming room, Plummer gave the signal with his hand. And that door was opened immediately by Diamond Jack himself. In one shining instant of glory, he had just showed a hand that won nearly fifteen hundred dollars for him. The smile on his lips was a little more sinister than usual as he looked out.

"Well, Plummer?" he asked. "What do you—"

Doom descended upon Diamond Jack. Or rather it shot straight out toward him in the form of Castracane's reaching hand. That grip fell on Kirby's shoulder, but it instantly rendered his whole right arm almost nerveless. His left arm was still free, and that hand twitched up, serpent quick, to tilt the gun from its holster.

Once more the fist was swifter than the gun.

It was only a short, bobbing blow, but it landed along the Diamond's clean-cut jaw and his knees turned to water under his weight.

Anthony trussed that helpless body under his arm, and he turned back to the crowded rooms.

They had been excited before. But they were breathless now. For here a man had taken Diamond Jack's gaming house without firing a shot. It was a sort of magic that even Abdullah Khan could never have rivaled.

Not a soul stirred as Anthony carried his burden into the big main room except one hopeless drunkard who was wobbling to and fro, trying to strike a crack on the floor with the lash of his blacksnake whip.

Past him went Anthony and caught the blacksnake from the numbed hands. The drunkard gaped after him, but no more thought of trying to recapture his whip than he would have thought of attempting to redeem it from a whirlwind.

Straight to the big central pillar of wood that held up the wide ceiling went Anthony. And with a thong he tied Diamond Jack's hands to the post.

Consciousness was beginning to struggle back to Diamond Jack's brain, but it had not completely returned. He stood wobbling, very uncertain, and the crowd watched him in amazement. They were accustomed to seeing this man rage like wildfire on the prairie. And now he was not even as bright as a candle flame.

They saw Mad Anthony rip away the clothes of his victim. The stout cloth gave under his grip like rotten rags, and Kirby stood naked to the waist. That rough treatment had brought his senses to him almost entirely. He looked desperately around, but no one moved to interfere.

If a cat seizes a mouse, the other mice may stir and squeak in their holes, but they do not come out to the rescue.

Anthony Castracane turned back and faced the crowd.

"I've heard that there's no justice in Dodge City, gentlemen," said Anthony, "and so I've come to take a little justice for myself. This man Kirby sent two hired men to kill me. I had their own confession and I came here to ask Kirby if he could deny it. Kirby, do you hear me? Can you deny it?"

"It's a lie!" said Kirby. And then he called: "Joe! McGregor! You've still guns! Are you standing by and letting this damned disgrace happen to me when—"

The blacksnake hissed wickedly through the air and the lash seamed Kirby's back with crimson.

"*I* am talking to you, Kirby," said Anthony, "and if you have anything to say, speak to me!"

He swung the blacksnake at a balance and kept a Colt poised in his left hand.

"Do you hear me?" called Anthony, flashing his eyes over the faces in the crowd, and seeing that not a hand was raised to help the fallen master of the place. "I asked you if you sent two hired men to murder me, Diamond Jack. What do you say?"

"I'll see you burning in hell," groaned Diamond Jack through his teeth, "before I'll open my lips to speak another word!"

"They fired eleven shots at me," said Anthony, "between them. And you, yourself, Kirby, have shot four bullets in my direction. Besides that, your man at the door tonight evidently had his orders. He tried to kill me as I came in. Which makes sixteen shots, I believe. And for every shot I am paying you with leather instead of lead, Kirby. A stroke of the lash for every time that I've been shot at. I've heard the sing of the bullets. You can taste the lash of the whip. It has a sour taste, Kirby, eh?"

These words seem very mild, as I put them down, but I was standing there in a corner of that room, and as they were voiced in thunder by Anthony, I took my first full look at him and I quaked to the very bottom of my soul. I had never seen such a man before. I had never dreamed that such a man was possible.

If I could close my eyes to what he was, then it would seem impossible that he could have turned his back on that crowd, with so many of Kirby's own bought men among them, while he flogged that master criminal and gambler. But as a matter of fact, at the time I remembered hoping that no one would be so utterly lost in folly as to attempt to lay a hand on the giant. For he seemed a giant as he swung the whip, and the long red hair flew out across his shoulders, and he made his count:

"One for the first bullet, Kirby, and two for one I dodged as I jumped through the doorway—and three for . . ."

With every count, the long whip snaked back and darted forward. A red weal appeared on Kirby's back, and presently his skin was a crimson plaid—with the dye blurred and running from mark to mark!

At first, Kirby gave one shrill cry of agony and rage.

But after that he mastered himself with wonderful power of mind. I really think—for I could see his bowed, blackened, convulsed face—that in the extremity of his shame he did not actually feel more than the first stroke or two.

And so this miracle took place, in Dodge City, in the gaming house of Kirby himself—that a tenderfoot walked into the house and blacksnaked Diamond Jack himself before the eyes of the world!

It would have been different if it had been almost anyone else. There were a thousand better men in the town. But there was none so strong as the Diamond.

The sixteenth lash was driven home. Blood now flowed in a steady, broad current down Kirby's back, but he stood like a pillar, unwincing, as Anthony Castracane threw down the whip and whirled about on us. And as he spoke, he strode slowly around the post, so that all of us could see his face.

"Look at me, gentlemen," said Anthony. "I want you to mark down my face and keep it in red in your memories. I came to your city for no harm to any man in the world. I came here thinking that no man could be a hound with more teeth than heart in him. But I've learned otherwise, and now by the eternal God you shall pay for it. I'm going to start treating you for what you are—dogs! And I'll make you lick the hand that beats you—now get out of my way!"

And Anthony walked through us toward the door.

"He's mad!" whispered someone beside me.

I thought so, too. But I also thought that he was

damned. And I suppose that both of us were right.

But more than anything else, I knew I had seen something that deserved to rank among the miracles.

Someone cut down Diamond Jack. But even the fall of the Diamond was nothing compared to the heaving of this new star over the horizon. The one topic of conversation in Dodge City, the rest of that night, was how many men would be killed by Castracane before he himself went down.

CHAPTER XIV

WHILE DIAMOND JACK WAS TAKING THAT FLOGGING at the hands of Anthony Castracane, the cleverest wits in Dodge City, instead of worrying about the situation of her son, were busy with the problem of Muriel Lester. Because, after all, Mrs. Kirby knew that her boy had always proved greater than the opposition which rose against him, and she felt reasonably sure that there was far too much power in him to go down before any clumsy outlander like Castracane. So she sat by the window with all of her mind concentrated on Muriel.

Her problem was clear and simple in the statement. When Diamond Jack came home he would want to know why he had been called upon to put Castracane out of the way. And that would involve explanations and more explanations. And, finally, Jack would go in and sit at Muriel's side and they would explain everything to their mutual satisfaction, as was the custom with young lovers. So that the great blunderer, the great opponent, would be Mrs. Kirby.

It was a serious crisis. And she determined to drive Muriel Lester from the house. The instant that she had reached the decision, she also knew the way of handling it.

She went to Muriel's room, and when the girl opened the door, Mrs. Kirby looked at her with a good deal of satisfaction. For there were traces of tears on Muriel's face, and one who has been weeping is not apt to be calm in the face of another crisis.

Said Mrs. Kirby, in a voice colder than ice:

"You have had enough time to think over your conduct, my child. And I trust that you have something to say to me."

"You think that I should apologize, of course," said the girl.

"I don't suggest," said Mrs. Kirby. "I have only come to ask a question, not to make a suggestion."

"I wish a thousand times that I *should* ask your pardon," said Muriel Lester. "But not until I have found out something more about what has happened."

"And what do you wish to know?" said the mother of the Diamond. "For perhaps I can tell you."

"It is something that you *cannot* tell because it concerns Jack only."

"My son and I are very deep in one another's confidence," said Mrs. Kirby.

"Then tell me if you can—*did* Jack—could he *possibly*—have sent two hired murderers to meet Anthony Castracane?"

"Are you still harping on the stupid Italian?" asked Mrs. Kirby, with a certain smile which was one of her chosen weapons.

"He is as American as you or I!" said the girl, wincing under that smile.

"Dear Muriel, my dear, silly girl," said Mrs. Kirby, still with that same contemptuous expression, "you should know before you marry Jack that he is not an ordinary man and therefore he does not follow ordinary standards in his conduct."

"I am not speaking of standards," said Muriel, "I am speaking of murder."

"In Dodge City," said Mrs. Kirby, "the two words become confused. And since you are to live in Dodge City for a time, you had better grow accustomed to the new way of thinking."

"Frankly," said Muriel, "I won't believe until I hear it from Jack himself."

Mrs. Kirby yawned a little, to cover her growing nervous excitement. She felt that she had entered on this battle so far that now she must do or die.

"Child, child," said she, "do you think that you are marrying a white lamb with newly washed fleece? Don't you know that Jack is a man among men? Or do you think that a professional gambler can run his business without having to use his guns now and then—in Dodge City? Or, if you are in any doubt, ask

100

others what they know of Jack's record. He is known as a man, I thank heaven!"

She said it with a pride which was not altogether assumed, because nothing warmed her heart more than the thought of her son's courage and fighting hardihood.

"He is giving up that life," said Muriel, more tremulous than ever.

"He is giving up what, my dear?" asked Mrs. Kirby.

"The gambling house."

"Muriel, my dear!" smiled Mrs. Kirby.

"He has promised me—a hundred times—and you know it!"

"Have you lost your sense of humor?" said Mrs. Kirby. "Do you think that a man gives up a thousand dollars a day?"

"Do you mean that he will continue with it?"

"And why not, child? If you can marry him in spite of his business, he will find a way to keep you after the marriage, in spite of the same business!"

"You are speaking your own opinion and not his," suggested the girl, growing stronger with anger. "I shall talk with Jack when he comes home!"

"You will," nodded Mrs. Kirby, letting her own passion flare up her eyes, unrestrained. "I shall see to it that you remain here until he comes!"

And stepping back through the door, she took out the key, closed it swiftly, and turned the lock.

After that, she went back to wait. Muriel's blank, terrified face, as she saw herself locked into the room, gave her some assurance that the girl would be frightened enough to wish to escape at once. And if she wished to, the locking of the door was an idle gesture because there was the window on the opposite side of the room, so close to the ground that even a child could not have feared to climb down from it.

So Mrs. Kirby sat down and waited through the grimmest moments of her entire exciting life. She told herself over and over again that she had showed Muriel so much of the truth about her fiancé that if the girl had a spark of spirit in her, she would leave at once. But still she doubted. She had not very much faith in the courage of this soft-voiced child, and if Muriel were still in the house when Jack returned, then in five minutes Mrs. Kirby's hold upon her son would be broken and gone forever. She would become a detested stranger in his life.

All of these things were as certain as fixed stars to Mrs. Kirby, and so, through the side window, she ceaselessly scanned the rear yard of the house, for it was that way that Muriel must pass if pass she dared.

And then the garden gate clashed, and a long, rapid stride approached the house. It was Jack's step. Many and many a time the heart of the mother had leaped when she heard that step, but now she turned cold. She felt the wreck and ruin of her life falling about her— and the strong step of Jack sounded on the porch—the front door creaked open—

And at that moment, Mrs. Kirby saw Muriel Lester hurrying across the yard, and through the side gate into

102

the field beyond, swiftly lost behind some tall shrubs!

So, after all, the wits of the mother had won! She felt the blood rush to her head. For an instant she could not move. She could hardly breathe, so vast was the relief and the thrill of triumph.

And then Jack entered the room and stood before her.

He was a vision that could make even his mother's Spartan heart quake.

For, straight through the town from his gambling room, disdaining any disguise, too proud to conceal his shame from a city that already knew it, Diamond Jack had marched with the blackened blood congealing on his back and now he stood half naked in his home before Mrs. Kirby.

He said tersely:

"Don't ask questions. I've been knocked senseless by Castracane's fist. He dragged me to the central post in the big room and tied me to it by the hands. And he flogged me with a blacksnake before the entire crowd. They didn't raise a hand to help me. That's the story. I'm not a man but a dog until I find Castracane and kill him. Get some water and wash my back!"

She was a proper mother for a hero—or a gunfighter! She hurried to the kitchen, and returned almost instantly with cloth, lint, salve, and hot water. And he sat smoking, with a face made of smiling iron, while she washed and dressed his back. And not a syllable did she speak, though sometimes fury, and agony of shame and sympathy for him, half blinded her eyes.

"Where's Muriel?" he asked suddenly.

And, at that, she burst out suddenly: "Don't name her to me! Not now, Jack! She has been raging against you—accusing you of trying to murder Castracane."

"That's Tommy's work," said Diamond Jack.

"I tried to talk to her. I begged her to listen to reason. I even cried in front of her, Jack."

"Mother, you should never have done that!"

"She slammed her door in my face and locked herself in! That was enough answer for me!"

He started to his feet, quivering with passion, but his voice was as steady as ever, as he said: "I'll see to that!"

She threw herself in his way.

"Not now, Jack!" she begged him. "Not while you're in a rage. You might say some violent word—and she's so sensitive—it only needs a touch to make her throw you over—"

"Does it?" he said through his teeth. "But I'm as cool as stone. I'll know what I'm saying."

He pushed her aside. And she leaned against the wall, trembling, drawing her breath in gasps, while she heard him stride to the door of the girl's room, and knock at it.

"Muriel!" A pause. "Muriel, do you hear? It is Jack!"

And then: "Muriel, if you won't turn the lock, I'll have to force this door. You're acting like a sullen child. I wait for a few seconds, that's all."

Those seconds were beaten out by the mother's pounding heart.

Then she heard a crash and rendering of wood. The floor shook as Diamond Jack, bursting into the room, checked his lunge with a heavy foot.

Instantly he returned, quiet as ever, but with a thousand devils in his face.

"She's gone through the window!" he said.

"She never would have dared!" breathed Mrs. Kirby.

"Of course she would never have dared. It's Castracane again. He must have come straight here from my place, and he's taken her away with him. But I'm almost glad of it. It makes the thing perfect. Why shouldn't I have a thousand reasons for killing him, instead of ten?"

CHAPTER XV

WHEN MAD ANTHONY LEFT THE TOWN, HE WAS striding away at full speed, like a man escaping from a plague city, and as he walked along, he only struggled to increase his pace. He broke into a run, and pushed a swift mile behind him before he would pause to look back to the sinking lights of Dodge City. He felt that he could breathe a cleaner air now. Back yonder was Muriel Lester, and more of the black-hearted, wicked race of women. Back in Dodge City remained Diamond Jack, and others of the under-handed, serpent-wise race of men.

Ay, and some one of them was following on

Anthony's trail. For a shadowy form of a horseman loomed between him and the lights.

"Who's there?" called Anthony.

"It's only Tommy!" sang out a cheerful voice.

"What will you have with me?"

"I'm only guarding your back, chief."

And Tommy loomed before him and above him, the white streak of a bandage gleaming clearly where it had been bound around his head.

"Have you left Diamond Jack because his teeth are broken?" snarled Mad Anthony.

"That's pretty hard, chief," said Tommy. "But you're feeling a little heated up, just now. I'll wait back here until you've cooled down a bit!"

"I want none of you," said Anthony. "I want to be alone. Do you hear me?"

"I hear you," said Tommy, and he reined back his horse.

But he had not the slightest intention of taking the back trail. He merely followed at just such a distance that he was always able to see Mad Anthony's looming head and shoulders moving before him through the night.

A red star showed in the distance to Anthony, the gleam of a campfire somewhere on the plains, and he aimed for it, not because he wished to reach it, but because it was the only guiding mark in sight.

Now and again that star went out. And sometimes its beams were fractured into a thousand thin rays that flared into a rosy haze as the light shone through a small slit. He came still closer, and now he could see that the fire was surrounded by tall, clustering rocks. Shadows of men and horses moved inside or outside the standing pillars of stone.

So he veered off a little to the side, for the last of his desires was to see more of the black-hearted race of man that day.

By chance, as he came to the point of his course which was closest to the fire, someone threw a great armful of dried brush into the flames, and immediately a great crackling irregular dragon of fire leaped into the air, and for an instant the prairie showed far off, as bright as though under a setting, red sun. And, by that light, Anthony had his first sight of the Salton Bay.

For a startled moment, as he came to a halt, he thought that he had seen by a trick of fancy a creature made out of the crimson flame itself, so brightly did that polished red body shine!

Then, as the bright column of fire died down, the sight of the great stallion was lost to him.

But Anthony could not stay away, now, no more than a child can keep from some miraculously desired toy, because here was the very thing made to his desire—a horse strong enough to bear his weight and swift enough to take him rapidly across the darkness of the plains, he did not care where, so long as it were far!

So he turned in and walked straight upon the camp. Behind him came Tommy.

What Anthony saw was a group of a dozen men, dressed more like Indians than whites, some within the circle of the rocks and some outside the circle. Their mustangs were scattered here and there, hobbled for grazing during the night. But within the rocks, in a favored place, was the Salton Bay. For, of course, they would sooner have trusted diamonds out of their hands than that horse.

Two or three of them had watchful eyes, and guns turned toward Anthony as his big form came looming through the night.

He looked again at the horse, and the blinding beauty of the stallion burned more fiery than ever into his very heart. Even to any lump of an ordinary man the first sight of the Salton Bay was a startler. But Anthony knew horses and had an instinct for them. It would have been strange if he had not, having lived all his life among them.

He glanced back from the great horse and found the central figure of the group of men. It was a short, wide-shouldered man, with a face sun-blackened and shaded even darker by a growth of untrimmed beard. That was Jay Madison, of whom you have heard—the man who was stolen away in his childhood by the Sioux and raised by them, until his white blood asserted itself—or his bloodthirsty temper, as some say—and he was forced to leave them. They had his scalp, too, in the end, so that I suppose they felt their work in raising him had not been wasted.

He was not a very imposing fellow, but by his

place by the fire and something in his eye Anthony had no trouble in recognizing him as the chief of the party.

"I want to buy this horse," said Anthony, and pointed to the stallion. "What's his price?"

There was a general gaping, all around the fire. They looked upon Anthony as though they had already heard Dodge City give him his nickname of "Mad." But Jay Madison was composed enough.

"Well," said he, "I suppose that he's for sale."

The others turned and gaped at Madison, still more stricken with wonder.

"He's for sale," said Madison. "I suppose about fifty thousand dollars would be right for him."

"Fifty thousand?" repeated Anthony angrily.

"Ay," said Madison, and let a faint smile show on his dark face.

At that moment, Tommy drifted up beside the rocks and a cry broke from him instantly: "My God," said he, "am I seein' things, or is that the Salton Bay?"

"It's the Salton Bay, son," said Madison quietly.

"It ain't possible," said Tommy. "Madison, how could you of caught him?"

"With these," said Madison, pointing to the men and horses around him, "and with about a year and half of work. That was all!"

"And you've gentled him, too!" said Tommy, still struck with astonishment, as he watched the great beautiful creature standing quietly by the fire with no hobbles on his feet. "Is he for the races?"

"When I can get a jockey to sit on his back, yes," said Madison.

He turned to Anthony, who stood gritting his teeth with impatience and desire.

"Or," said he, "if you aim to really want that horse, I dunno but that I'd let you have him for a hundred dollars—if you could ride him, partner."

Five twenty-dollars bills were instantly counted into his surprised hand.

"There's your money," said Anthony, "and now I'll take the horse."

"By riding him, son," said Madison, grinning in an evil manner. "Only by riding him. Charlie, will you saddle the Bay?"

"He's bad medicine, then?" asked Tommy.

"You'll see, if your friend has the nerve to get onto him," said Madison.

Charlie, in the meantime, had brought the saddle, and the big horse stood quietly enough while it was strapped on his back, but his ears had flattened and his nostrils flared.

He was led forth into the starlight beyond the fire.

And Madison put the hundred dollars which he had just received under a stone.

"Are you risking the Bay?" groaned one of his men.

"Hell, no," answered Madison under his breath. "But I want to see him make a fool out of this big gent. I ain't taken the money, have I?"

And he pointed to it under the stone. It was a neat quibble, perhaps, but Jay Madison might have known, by one glance at Mad Anthony, that he had to do, now, with a man to whom quibbles meant less than nothing.

There was plenty of advice on the tip of Tommy's tongue but he refrained from uttering it, partly because he wanted to see the fun, and partly because he was not altogether unwilling to see his friend the giant have a fall. It would bring him a little nearer to the mere human!

So he saw Anthony mount to the saddle.

It was not the way that most men mount. It was an easy leap that sent him flying into place and jammed both his feet into the stirrups at the same instant. Not a difficult trick to describe, but in order to accomplish it you would practice half a lifetime—as Anthony had done.

And, at the same moment, the Salton Bay turned into a Pegasus. I mean he jumped into the air and stayed there, only coming down now and then in the middle of an aerial figure eight to tap the ground and mount again.

They had done their very best to ride him, Madison and his crew, and while they tried and failed, he had learned about all that a horse can master of the bucking game. In one glorious flare he tried all that he knew against Anthony, and for five minutes he fought as though mad. Forward and backward, and up and down, now whirling like a top, now flinging himself bodily backward to the ground, he strove to get that clinging burden out of the saddle.

And twice he was on the verge of winning, as

Anthony's head grew blurred and dizzy. Once both the stirrups were lost to Anthony, and once again, while the spectators shrieked with a savage glee, it seemed that the stallion was surely pinning the big man beneath him as he toppled backward. But instinct helped Anthony after his clear wits were in a fog. One does not live twenty years on the backs of horses in a circus for nothing.

And suddenly the Salton Bay made a last frantic leap, descended on stiff legs, and then raised his head and sent his long whinny ringing across the plains. It was his signal of surrender.

CHAPTER XVI

HE ANSWERED THE REINS, TOO, THOUGH WITH THE unwilling, stubborn head of a horse which had not yet learned just what it means to be mastered. Now he stood again by the fire, his body burnished and darkened with sweat, and an awed circle of men standing about to admire him and watch the blood-stained froth dropping from his mouth and the red danger light in his eyes. And the dust of the hurricane which he had just raised had not yet finished settling as they stared at him and at the man who had sat out his worst efforts. It had been a very even matter. They could tell that by Anthony's glazed eyes and by the blood which was trickling from his nose. But still, he had won, and victory, like failure, does not have to be easy in order to be real.

"What's this gent?" they had gasped at Tommy in the middle of the struggle.

"Go on to Dodge City, and you'll find out!" he had told them. "All he's done lately is to tie Diamond Jack to a post in his own joint and blacksnake him. The other things don't count! Ye-a-a! Watch that red devil fight!" as the stallion skyrocketed into the air, twisting himself into a knot.

So, on the whole, this little circle of men had learned about all that they needed to know concerning Mad Anthony Castracane. They knew that he had manhandled Diamond Jack, a name to conjure with far and wide across the prairies, and they knew that he had beaten the great stallion in the fairest of fair fights.

And as they stared at him, I am sure that even the dullest heart among them must have been stirred a little, seeing this horse and rider, so perfectly mated, the one to the other.

I have never known the exact dimensions of the Salton Bay. Neither have I ever known Mad Anthony's exact poundage or inches. But I know that both were giants, and each seemed framed for the other.

"All right," said Jay Madison, who was the only quiet eye in the entire circle. "You've had your fun, young feller, and now climb down out of that saddle and let's see if you ain't been shook to pieces."

Anthony's eye had cleared a little, and this chal-

113

lenging speech served to bring all his wits back to him with a leap. He eyed Jay Madison keenly. A day or two before this and he would have dismounted, all unsuspecting, but now he had learned his lesson, that there was no real virtue in the hearts of men.

"I've ridden the horse, and I've paid you the money," said Anthony. "Here's another fifty for the saddle. I suppose that that leaves me free to ride away on the horse, doesn't it?"

"Young feller," said Jay Madison, even his dark color whitening a little with excitement, "maybe you dunno it, but I've chased that hoss for a year and a half. I spent thousands of dollars buying hosses and hiring gents to help me chase him. And I can make all of them thousands back showing the Salton Bay in the towns along the prairie and charging admission to him. And after that if I couldn't ride him, I could sell him into a stud and make enough to retire on. You're offering me a hundred dollars for that?"

"I made a bargain with you," said Anthony slowly. "I don't want to be foolish and I don't want to be crooked. But I made a bargain, and I paid you the money, and I rode the horse."

"Your money, hell!" snarled Jay Madison. And he flashed at his men a glance that made them move their hands back to their guns. "There's your hundred dollars lying under that stone. I never took and kept it. I was just havin' my little joke with you, stranger. And a good thing if you'd just climb down out of that there saddle before me and my boys start another *kind* of a joke on you!"

He had risen to his feet again, his hands on his guns, and every one of his men leaned a little and waited for a signal, like runners on a mark.

It was then that Tommy showed that there was something in him.

He stepped close to the fire, where all eyes could see him. He had only delayed long enough to twirl out his mustaches to their full ridiculous length and to comb his beard into some semblance of order. But Tommy was really never ridiculous to the men of the plains. They knew too much about him to smile at his peculiarities.

Said Tommy now:

"Hey, Madison, and the rest of you gents. This ain't pie that you're asking for, but trouble, and the kind of trouble that comes in two lumps instead of one. Because I tell you that this gent Castracane don't stand here alone. I'm with him, boys, and I dunno but that the pair of us could account for three or four of you."

"Tommy," said Madison, "you're talking damn foolish. You belong to Diamond Jack, anyway. What in hell are you doing here with this Castracane, as you call him?"

"I'm here to show you," said Tommy, thrusting out his weak chin beneath the mustaches. "I'm hating trouble with you, Madison, but I'm with Castracane."

"It's a good play," said Madison, eying the pair dourly. "But the horse stays here, d'y'understand? So get out of the saddle, Castracane!"

Anthony, steadying himself as his sense of balance and clearness of eye returned, had rested his hand on the topmost fragment of one of those steep, narrow rock piles, and now, as anger began to stir in him and his muscles automatically contracted a little, he felt the whole rock pillar stir beneath the pressure.

It was that which gave him the hint upon which he acted, now that he saw action was necessary. He leaned a trifle out in the saddle and planted his feet firmly in the stirrups. His knees took a tremendous grip on the strong barrel of the Salton Bay, and suddenly all his power was thrown with a jerk against the rock. There was such might in that arm of his that it staggered even the Bay. But it sent the great stone toppling forward toward Jay Madison.

There is no doubt that Madison would have had his guns out to shoot, that instant. But though he might bring down Castracane, the great rock would, the next instant, have brought him down. So he leaped backward with a shout, and at the same time the stone fell and, landing squarely across the great bonfire, knocked out ten million sparks which flew like a myriad of stinging wasps into the hands and faces of the whole crew and set their clothes on fire in a hundred places.

Enough of that volley landed on the big stallion, too, to make him whirl about with a snort of terror and leap away into the starlight.

Behind him was a maddened turmoil. Guns were out

and shooting half blindly at the fugitive, but the majority were yelling with pain and astonishment and beating the fire out of their smoking clothes, so that the first to rush away in pursuit on a horse was Tommy himself.

He had hardly started before his heart sank.

He was well mounted. None of Diamond Jack's men was allowed to keep any but a horse distinguished for wind and speed. He knew that his weight in the saddle was scores of pounds less than Anthony's, and yet he was left momently lagging more and more to the rear until it seemed to Tommy that he was riding a rocking horse which pitched back and forth and up and down, but had no forward motion whatever, compared with the flying shadow which drifted away in front of him, growing dimmer and dimmer.

Then the shadow slowed, at the very moment when he thought he was to be hopelessly distanced, and he dashed up to find Anthony sitting in the saddle, impassive, with the Salton Bay tossing his nervous head as though impatient to begin devouring the prairie miles once more.

"They haven't followed," said Anthony as Tommy came up.

"They ain't gonna be in any hurry," replied Tommy. "They've hunted the Bay for a year and a half, and they know that they can't catch him in a night again, not even when there's a man on his back. But they'll come, sure enough. I know Jay Madison!"

"I know him too," said Anthony. "I know him for a

sneaking trickster!"

"That's the most doggone decent name that's been used for Jay Madison in a long time," grinned Tommy. "But no matter what else he is, he's a wolf on a trail, and he never gives it up. Oh, we'll hear from him again, sometime!"

"We?" said Anthony. "That's why I stopped for you, Tommy. I want to know why you're trailing me."

"Why," said Tommy, "I dunno but you could be able to answer that for yourself."

"I think I can," said Mad Anthony. "You're waiting for a chance to worm yourself into my friendship, and then to take advantage of me and pay back the wound I gave you with interest. Is that it?"

"Why," said Tommy, as smoothly as ever, "that's one way of looking at it. But another way is this. When you come up to the fire, and when you was arguing with Madison, I had you against the firelight."

"I didn't think of that," muttered Anthony.

"And that made a good enough show for shooting, even if I had been half blind, which I ain't. So if I had been laying for a chance to put a bullet through you, Castracane, why shouldn't I of pulled the trigger then?"

"It's true," said Anthony. "I don't understand it, but it's true! And more than that, you stood shoulder to shoulder to me when Madison was talking—why, man, what made you do that?"

"I dunno," said Tommy. "Except that I figured that you and me was together. Bad luck and good,

118

together! Like bunkies, d'y'understand?"

Anthony reared his great head and looked gloomily across the darkened plains.

"Besides," went on Tommy, "though you aim to think that most of the folks in the world is skunks—and maybe they are—here and there you'll find a friend, and I thought that maybe a friend would come in useful to you, you having enough enemies already!"

"Enemies?" repeated Anthony vaguely.

"Like Chick, and Cherokee Dan, and this here Jay Madison, who ain't so easy as you made him look tonight—and there's Diamond Jack Kirby, too, that's been beat only once in his life! So, big boy, if you'll have me along with you, shake hands on it, and you'll find that I'm worth my salt!"

"I don't want you," said Anthony. "But if you wish to come, you may. You bought that right by standing with me tonight. But I don't want you, Tommy, and I don't trust you, and all the time that you're with me be careful of the moves you make, because I'm watching you day and night as if you were a snake!"

CHAPTER XVII

EXACTLY LIKE A SNAKE, INDEED, HE FELT TOMMY Plummer to be, and like a snake he treated him that evening on the prairie, talking little or none and keeping at a secure distance so that he could watch the other from the corner of his eye. But Tommy pretended to pay no attention to this disagreeable treatment. However, he felt that time would right these matters. In his heart there was nothing but attachment to the big man, and he felt that he deserved the suspicion which was now being doled out to him.

When time came for the night halt, he made no protest when Mad Anthony made down his bed at a considerable distance. He himself turned in without attempting to come any closer. And he went instantly to sleep, with the security of a good conscience.

But Mad Anthony slept only brokenly.

You must understand that the lessons he had recently been receiving about the wickedness of human nature had been of the harshest kind, and when he thought of Tommy he was baffled, but he was fairly sure that there must be some manner of trickery behind the pretended friendship of this hired gunman of Diamond Jack's.

Dawn had hardly grown to be more than a pencil stroke of light along the eastern horizon when Castracane stood up from his blankets, rolled his pack, and then led the Salton Bay to a safe distance. After he had mounted, he threw one glance behind him to make sure that his companion had not yet taken notice of this desertion. Then he sent the stallion into a soft trot, which he presently increased to a gallop when he was sure that the noise of the hoofbeats would not come to the sleeper's ears.

Somewhere before him on the western horizon was

the goal of his journey. He did not know exactly what he expected, but first of all he wished to plunge into the distance and bathe himself, as it were, in space, until all traces of this unwelcome companion had been lost behind him.

Just what he should do when he *was* alone in the wilderness, Mad Anthony had not the slightest idea. But his mind was in a curious muddle as he journeyed on across the vast prairie. First of all, he felt as though he were remade in entering upon this new and spacious freedom of the spirit. And then again, he felt the weight of a new knowledge of humanity.

He could see that he had been raised in an odd ignorance. For instance, he now knew that all women are wicked and evil spirits. That had been amply demonstrated by the deceits of Muriel Lester. If she, with her lovely face, were bad, then all womankind was bad. So much for the women of the race.

On the other hand, it was apparent that there was little but wickedness among the men, also. Witness such persons as Cherokee Dan, Chick, Diamond Jack, and perhaps above all Tommy Plummer, who had first tried to murder him in an open street fight, and who failing in that was attempting to wheedle his way into the confidence of Anthony Castracane!

Of course, he knew that some of the men in the circus had been rather good fellows. But when he looked back upon them with his cleared vision, he could see that even those nearest and dearest to him had certainly been spoiled by grievous flaws. There was no doubt to him now that Abdullah Khan was a very great rascal and liar and imposter, poor Jumbo a conceited and stupid ox of a man, Barney and Kilpatrick were a pair of ruffians, and as for Mr. Wagnall, his craft and his cunning and his wiles made him appear to Anthony's imagination like a veritable snake.

You will say that a conviction of the wickedness of the entire human race was quite a burden for Anthony Castracane to carry with him. And, indeed, he felt exactly that way. He wanted to be alone, therefore, until he had been able to adjust himself to his new ideas; and when he was sure of himself, he would prepare to hatch out a new plan of living. But, in the meantime, he wanted to be a thousand miles away from all that he had known of life.

He had the Salton Bay in a long-striding gallop while these ideas flowed through his mind, and at the same time the prairie was flowing through his eyes in a swift, great river.

He came to a place where the vast tramplings of a herd of buffalo had recently passed, marring the surface of the soil, casting a dark, wide strip across the verdure, and passing on leaving their trail starred, here and there, with the whitening bones of an occasional straggler which had lagged behind and been picked off instantly by the buffalo wolves. Along that trail passed Mad Anthony, also, for he felt that it would be almost impossible for any human cleverness to follow the trail of his horse through such a maze of sign.

The old trail of the buffalo led him eventually toward a broken country, low hills lifting ragged heads against the sky, while the ground became barren and he found himself passing through a desolation where there was hardly so much as a sun-dried spear of grass upon the ground.

He turned from the trail of the buffalo where the current of their march had bent back toward the more fertile plains. For Mad Anthony liked this desolation in which he found himself. It promised a security of loneliness such as he had not found in any other place.

He passed through a gap in the hills and came in sight of a low, walled valley with a brown streak of muddy creek running down its center and a jumble of vast stones cast about here and there over the floor of the ravine. Once a year that water rose when the snows melted in the western mountains, and then the bottom of the gorge was choked with dashing, maddened currents. They could pick up these boulders and toss some and roll others. But afterward the stream shrank small and could only wander idly and fruitlessly through the battleground of giants.

However, though Anthony Castracane understood this, he did not gaze down at the valley long for its own sake. There was something better to see there than mere river and rocks and steep banks to the canyon. For on the farther side of the valley, and at a comfortable distance up its course, he saw a horseman riding with desperate speed, followed by seven others at a little distance behind him.

Anthony Castracane unshipped his glass and studied them afar off.

They were Indians, every one, and their shaven or close-cropped heads made them look more like warriors from the same nation, or devils from the same hell, so ugly did they appear to Castracane at the first view of them.

It was plain that there was no hope for the fugitive. He had what was apparently a good horse beneath him, but he was a large and heavy man, and it would have needed another monster like the Salton Bay to carry him with ease and speed combined. As it was, he had ridden his pony to the verge of exhaustion, whereas the pursuers were in very good case with their horseflesh. They had a little bank of animals following them, driven on by an eighth member of their war party, and even while Anthony watched, two of the pursuit fell back, made a lightning change of mounts, and on the freshened horses from the rear they were instantly in the thick of the fight again.

Since they could overtake the enemy with such speed and ease, Anthony wondered why it was that they did not dispose of him at once, and why he heard no reports of guns.

But when he studied the procession in more detail, as it wound closer and closer, he made out the reasons. There were no guns fired for the probable reason that the ammunition had been used up. And indeed, Anthony could see only two rifle holsters in the entire band. Every man had a bow, but even the arrows had been terribly depleted by what had evidently been a very long running fight. The fugitive had still a few shafts left to him, and from time to time he turned in the saddle and threatened the followers with an arrow on the string.

That gesture never failed to make the others waver or draw rein a little or split to either side, so that it was apparent that they had an ample respect for his marksmanship. And he, all the while, contented himself with threats and only once did he discharge an arrow, which seemed to whiz perilously close to the throat of one of the copper-skinned pursuers.

Still, the game could not last very much longer. The galloping horse must fail, and when it dropped, the enemy could scatter and surround the big hero from every side. Then his death would be an easy matter to accomplish.

Anthony had hardly made up his mind about this when the pursued tried a desperate remedy for his situation.

The river, as has been said, was narrow, but at the same time it was extremely rapid, and in places its surface was streaked and flecked with patches of foam. In any case, it appeared that it would be difficult to make the crossing. However, to the side of the fugitive, and directly opposite to the place where Castracane was watching, the surface of the creek was broken by a number of stones which rose to the surface, with water flying white around them, and made a sort of natural causeway across the river.

Straight down the bank toward this quasi bridge went the desperate Indian. And with whip and spur he raised his pony to the work. Behind him, with a yell, the pursuit paused, and now they rained a shower of arrows after their man.

Still he went on. The pony, very tired, but still sure of foot and agile, leaped from rock to rock, clinging to each an instant, and then springing on. Twice it seemed about to slip into the water, and twice it rallied itself and clawed its way back to a firm footing like a great cat.

At length it stood on the farther shore, safe, with the despairing screech of the enemy wailing behind it.

The heart of Anthony swelled with joy. It did not matter where the right and the wrong lay; he only knew that numbers lay on the one side and determined courage on the other. Besides, he loved the strength, the courage, and the dexterity of that lithe-limbed little Indian pony bearing his great rider.

CHAPTER XVIII

NOW THAT THE MAN WAS NEARER, ANTHONY COULD vividly understand exactly why the gallant horse had been failing beneath its rider, and why the pursuers had been taking no liberties by closing too abruptly on their foe, for the man was a veritable giant. He was two or three inches, perhaps, loftier than even great Anthony, and he was limbed and thewed in the same heroic proportions. Such a body of a man seemed almost as capable of getting off and carrying the pony as the pony was capable of carrying the man.

He turned, now, and shook his fist in scorn and defiance at the enemy, and that gesture brought another screech of rage from them.

Their own courage was almost as desperate as their foe's, and they seemed to be on the verge of hysteria at the sight of their quarry escaping.

And now Anthony saw a brave with a fluttering cloud of feathers in his hair suddenly spur his horse down the bank and take to the crossing with a yell. The others did not wait for him to cross, but, spurred on by the sight of this generous boldness, each man rode hastily down to follow his chief's example.

It seemed to Anthony, accustomed though he was to circus exhibitions of skill and trickery, that he had never in his life seen such an exhibition, and that he would never be able to see it again!

But what was most miraculous was that every one of them made the crossing in safety until it came to the young brave who was conducting the horseherd. He, too, desired to distinguish himself by making that perilous attempt. But halfway across the stream, his horse slipped. The pony and the man also screamed with a terrible fear, and the next instant both were rolled under the foaming stream and battered to death an instant later among the rocks that reached like great blunt teeth through the foam of the river.

However, he would not die altogether unavenged.

He left seven comrades on the farther shore, and they had before them a ruined quarry, for the pony of the big Indian had been completely exhausted by its heroic effort in making the ford. Now it staggered along, head down, and presently its hindquarters sank to the ground. It made one pitifully vain effort to rise. But it could not move.

The giant rider, bounding to the ground, stood for a moment regarding his horse and the stream of enemies who were coming up the river bank to get at him. It was plain that he could not escape from them now. He gathered up painted shield and long spears, bow and arrows, in one arm. In his other hand, he lifted a long knife and poised to drive it into the pony's heart.

For plainly when he died, he did not wish his war horse to be taken in pride by his conquerors!

The pony, ears pricked and eyes bright, watched the death flash before it, unmoved. But at the last moment this champion's heart weakened. He slipped the knife back into his belt, laid his hand on the head of the pony with a brief gesture of affection, and then leaped away and placed his back against the steep rock which rose fifty or sixty feet above his head, where among the brush on top lingered Anthony Castracane to watch the fray.

He told himself that he had no interest. He had proved to his own satisfaction that all men were wicked and heartless creatures. And yet his very soul was stirred as he looked down at the giant and saw him standing at the face of the rock shouting in stentorian tones that boomed up and down the valley. In one hand he brandished his bow. In the other arm he held his buffalo shield. As for the enemy, they did not hesitate.

They had lost one of their band only an instant before, and Anthony could guess that they had lost others, too, before the finish of that trail. So now that they had their vengeance before them, they did not hesitate to grasp at it. With a shout and a roar they charged the defender.

He shot one arrow as they came at him. That arrow caught straight on the face of one of the enemy shields, a shield of hardened buffalo hide, stouter than steel and lighter than wood. And that arrow flew straight through this formidable defence and grazed along the warrior's head. It turned him straight about and sent him out of the combat at once.

His companions, as they charged, each drove an arrow straight at the giant, but with a wonderful luck or dexterity he caught all those arrows in his shield. Anthony could see the proofs of his superior might with a bow. For his enemies' shafts either were blunted and dropped harmless to the ground or else they merely stuck in the strong leather of the shield face.

So six of the enemy charged with a hurricane of shrieks and loosed their arrows, but they feared to come to close quarters with that tall hero and the reaching spear which he now poised. Only one, and that the brilliant chief who had dared to follow the fugitive first across the stream, now ventured to press home the charge.

Straight at the big man he flew, his face convulsed with battle fury, his body protected by his shield, and his own lance poised above his head to be driven home with all the force of his body, his driving arm, and his savage little pony's charge.

But the giant waited for this attack with perfect calmness. With his long spear, he feinted to hurl straight at the other chief's body. The assailant's shield twitched down ever so little—just enough to expose above its rim the base of his throat.

That was the target at which the big man drove his lance. And the point went home just as the spear of the horseman struck vainly against the shield of his foe. For that shield was as solid, it seemed, as the face of those rocks! Right through the unlucky rider's throat went the giant's lance. He pitched from his saddle and struck violently against the rock wall. Then he lay crumpled on his face on the ground, quite dead.

The victor planted his foot upon his dead enemy's head. Shield and blood-dripping spear he waved at the six baffled warriors before him, and then he broke into a sort of exultant chant whose words, of course, were utterly lost to Anthony Castracane, and yet he did not need any interpreter to explain to him the general meaning of that war song. It was literally an impromptu and very poetic description of what had just taken place in this battle; then the singer passed on in his thundering voice to proclaim what would happen in the *remainder* of the battle.

It threw his foes into paroxysms of fury. They circled this way and that, their arrows prepared on the string. But his own bow was in his hand, now, and though he had only one arrow left, yet it was plain that not one of the enemy cared to be the hero who would draw that fire. So they remained at a little distance while Anthony wondered why they did not think of scaling the cliff and taking their foe from the rear.

In fact, that expedient instantly occurred to them. Two leaped away to the side, to scramble up a winding way to the top of the cliff, and now those who remained on the valley floor broke into a song of triumph in their turn.

As for the giant, he gave one look behind and above him to the top edge of the rock, and then he drew himself up in silence to receive his death.

That silence did not last long. Feeling the end of his life was coming upon him, he broke into a chant again, but in a different key. He walked up and down beneath the rock with a gravely measured step, and now and again he struck his breast and sometimes pointed to the sky, or shouted to the senseless earth, or, lifting his face, called to the blue heaven.

And Anthony Castracane knew that the hero was singing his death song. He would have given much to know of what deeds in his past the hero was boasting, but at least the story which he was telling in this solemn fashion—a story which had to do with his deeds on earth, his scorn of hell, his service of heaven—kept the four braves in front of him as motionless and as attentive as statues. Perhaps they were entirely rapt in the recital of events. But it seemed to Anthony more than probable that each young brave was taking this lesson to heart and learning from a great and flawless model how an Indian should die with dignity in the face of great odds.

Yonder pair scaling the cliff face, however, had no such interest in the singing.

When they had worked their way to the top of the rock, they came running and dodging through the bushes to gain the proper vantage point, and so they ran straight into Anthony Castracane.

He stood there with empty hands.

Yes, though you may hardly believe it, he had not drawn gun or knife, because up to this point, as you must remember, Anthony had never slain a human being. And it would have been well for many a man if he had not begun on this occasion!

Indeed, I do not think that he would have raised a hand against them, but as the leader of the pair came bounding through the bush and saw Anthony's mighty form suddenly before him, he did not recoil to save himself, but with the battle hysteria working in him, he leaped straight forward and drove his knife at the white man's throat.

And there was Anthony, his hands empty, and death coming at him on the flash of that knife!

However, you may remember that in the circus days

it was in the pinch of a crisis that Mad Anthony was most himself. That empty hand had not learned jugglery in vain, and now it shot up and picked out of the air the Indian's knife wrist. The forearm bones cracked like pipestems under the terrible pressure of his grip, and as this Indian shrieked with fear and surprise, Mad Anthony dropped him and strode past him with a booming shout and met the second Indian's rush with the full, resistless weight of his fist!

CHAPTER XIX

I HAVE HEARD MEN TELL SUCH TALES OF THE WEIGHT OF Anthony's fist that when I think of him striking with his bared hand it is to me as though another man were to strike heavily with a club. And the weight of that blow smashed in the Indian's nose and mouth and hurled him backward over the cliff edge. He fell an inert mass, striking head downward at the feet of the brave who stood at bay below him.

But Anthony had no time to take note of this, for the first warrior whom he had flung aside had drawn a knife and leaped savagely in at him, his ruined arm dangling at his side. But the fighting fury was in Anthony now. At his hip, a heavy Colt flashed into his hand and a double report met the charge. Struck in the breast and the head, the warrior bounded into the air like a stricken wolf, and dropped dead in a sage-bush.

And Mad Anthony turned his attention to the battle beneath.

It stood at a pause, now. The bewildered assailants stared at one another, at their dead companion who had just hurtled down the cliff face, and raising their eyes to the rock ledge, they heard the death yell of their second fellow.

And then Castracane's guns were turned upon them. They did not stay to ask questions now. One arrow whizzed perilously close to Anthony's cheek. Then he was looking down on four riders who had whirled their horses away and were rushing for safety. There was no mercy in him, then, any more than he had seen mercy in them to their brave enemy. From either hand a Colt was spouting a stream of fire and lead and the range was still close. At the very first fire, two of them fell, and a moment later the giant warrior's last arrow was driven through the back of a fugitive.

Three riderless horses ran here and there, and then headed back toward the river. The fourth carried his master on for another fifty paces, and then, pierced with three bullets from Anthony's guns, the brave toppled to the ground, rolled over and over, and lay dead, face toward the sky.

What did Anthony do then?

If you think that the slightest compunction disturbed him for this work which he had been doing, you are very wrong. Instead, there was a savage joy in his heart. He had seen a band of matured fighters of the plains, filled with craft and hardihood and the science of their arms, and he had met them in fair fight and struck them down like a five-forked lightning flash.

But he did not stir from his place until he had reloaded his empty weapons and looked to make sure that the Indian who lay in the bush was really dead. Then he went back to where he had left the big bay tethered among the taller brush.

He had to make a long detour down the ravine wall, and by the time he had ridden two miles down, led the stallion by a dangerous route to the bottom, and then returned to the battle site, he discovered that events had taken a new turn which he had not anticipated.

The giant brave who had fought so heroically was now gathering the fruits of the victory. In that brief interval he had climbed the cliff and returned to the plain. When Mad Anthony came up, he found the big man busily stripping the clothes from the dead and picking up their scattered weapons.

And the first thing that Anthony passed was the outermost victim of his guns, with the top of his head a red blur to show where the scalping knife had done its work. Seven bleeding scalps, indeed, were already tied to the warrior's gory spearhead as he stood up and brandished this weapon toward Anthony. Then he thrust the butt of it into the ground and, leaving it standing and quivering, advanced with great strides toward his deliverer.

I suppose that in the whole world there was no one

who had less fear of other men than Anthony Castracane, and yet he could not help shrinking a little inwardly when he saw this bloodstained monster advancing toward him and saw the joy in that hideous face. For the big brave was in an ecstasy.

He rushed up to the white man, and seizing his hand he pumped it frantically up and down.

Then he startled Anthony by saying in perfectly good English:

"Brother, I thought that it was the Great Spirit who loves all good Osage Indians who stood on the cliff above me and struck the Pawnees with his lightnings. But I see it is a white brother, a son of the Spirit, who has come to help me and grow famous!"

"I am not a son of the Great Spirit," answered Mad Anthony simply. "And I have nothing to do with growing famous. But I saw one man fighting like a hero against seven, and so I couldn't help lending you a hand. That is all there is to it."

The Indian listened to this simple speech with shining eyes which had a good deal of foxlike cunning in them. He did not need a long acquaintance with this huge-thewed white man to see that his spirit was very different from others. Anthony's body was a man's body; but his heart was the heart of a child, and the Osage saw it, or guessed it at once.

However, he went on: "They had followed Kohatunka for three days. All their men and their horses rode behind me. But the Big Crow did not fly away at once. There were ten Pawnees on the trail behind me, at first. Two of them I killed but could not count the coup upon. One was eaten by the river—and here are seven scalps for you who came down with running thunder to help me!"

He took his spear and held it forth to Anthony where the latter could see the seven fresh and bleeding scalps, to be sure, and four others of an older day. He regarded the thing with a shudder of horror. And then he shook his head.

"You are called the Big Crow, are you not?" he asked.

"Yes," nodded the Osage.

"Very well," said Anthony, "I must tell you, Big Crow, that I would have no pleasure in keeping such scalps. If I were you, I would take them off my spear and bury them in the ground."

"Ha!" cried the chief. "Do you think that I would send seven Pawnees out of hell and darkness where they are now up to the Happy Hunting Grounds where they may ride with other warriors on the ghosts of fine horses as if they had died honorably?"

He went on with a savage energy: "No, my people grow fewer and fewer on the earth, but their numbers are the greater in the sky. And every time a Pawnee spirit goes up to join the sky-people, the ghosts of the Osage dead frown and are unhappy and look down on earth, and they blame us for letting a single Pawnee die with his scalp on his head!"

"Very well," answered Anthony. "I can't change you, but the scalps are not for me, and if they give you any pleasure, keep them. You fought a great deal longer and harder for them than I did!"

Big Crow's eyes fairly burned with excitement at this announcement.

"Wait here," said he. "There are other things for Running Thunder!"

Mad Anthony looked down with a smile to the revolvers whose rapid action had won him this stirring title, and in the meantime he watched the Indian cross the stream and presently drive back over the dangerous ford, the entire herd of Pawnee horses. There were twenty-two of them altogether. These the Osage drove up, riding on his wise and brave little pony which seemed already nearly recovered from the effects of its long run.

Next, Big Crow collected the plunder which he had stripped from the dead bodies of his enemies. And he showed them to Anthony one by one. These Pawnees were not boys, but nearly all approved warriors in the prime of their fighting life. They had been on many a warpath before this one, they had brought back plunder, and they had many a squaw in their tepees to labor for their wealth and splendor. So Big Crow laid out beadworked moccasins and deerskin suits cunningly and beautifully decorated with stained porcupine quills. He showed all these to Mad Anthony. Then he made them into a neat bundle and tied them behind the saddle of his white friend. From all the plunder he gathered up the shields and the bows, the spears, and the scattered arrows of the enemy, as many as he could find, and he tied these to the saddles of the seven saddled horses. Last of all, he tied these animals in a group with the rawhide ropes which hung about their necks.

For himself he reserved only certain oddments which he found here and there—such, for example, as a pouch of field-mouse skin which he found on the body of one brave, and another of more formidable size made from the skin of a half-grown coyote, and so on; but on each of the dead men, he found one of these sacks, large or small, sealed and containing unknown articles.

"Look!" said Big Crow. "The scalps of the dead dogs are nothing to my white brother. Neither are these little bags. I shall take them. But you shall have the weapons and the horses and the clothes of the Pawnees. You are now rich. You can go among the Osage and buy twenty wives with such property. Tell me, Running Thunder, is this honest and fair?"

Mad Anthony looked at this sudden harvest which he had gathered off the prairies and smiled a little.

"What shall I do with them, Big Crow?" he asked. "I won't wear the clothes of a dead man, I can't use the weapons, and I hope that I'll never need a second horse. Keep it all for yourself, Kohatunka, and very welcome, so far as I am concerned!"

CHAPTER XX

U NDOUBTEDLY BIG CROW WAS A CHIEF WHO WAS well pleased to see himself getting on in the world, but when he heard this disclaimer from Mad Anthony, he looked again at the white man.

For Big Crow had reasons for speaking English so well. He had dealt intimately with the whites for many years; so much so that he had accumulated a certain stain and loss of honor in the eyes of the savage Osage tribe, and it was to wash off that stain that he had embarked upon the desperate effort of this warpath. It was most strange that he should have been rescued in his time of need by a white man!

However, what Big Crow knew of the whites was learned from the traders, who were generally men who regarded an Indian as hardly half a step higher in the animal scale than snakes, and certainly they had no scruple about taking from the red man everything that they could wheedle away from him. To Big Crow the white man had always seemed a creature in the act of seizing something—money, skins, land—no matter what it was, the white man would find a use for it!

And for this reason he stared more closely into Anthony Castracane's eyes because it seemed to him, at the first, that the big man was simply waiting to be urged more strongly to take the spoils, and while an

Indian loves modesty, he hates the false imitation of it more than all things in this world.

However, the closer he looked at Castracane, the more certainly it dawned upon him that the giant was truly a man of his word, and that he had not the slightest real wish to take this pile of loot.

Now Big Crow was rather inclined to be a rascal, and a greedy one. And had he been a white, he would certainly have seized upon this excellent opportunity to take a booty which, at a stroke, would make him one of the richest men in his nation.

But Big Crow was an Indian, and for that reason he heard Anthony's words with profound attention and a good deal of thought. For this attitude on the part of Anthony Castracane moved the Osage almost more than had the terrible roll of Anthony's guns in the battle.

Among the white men, to take, to accumulate, to grow rich, is considered estimable and splendid. But among the red men of the plains the hero and the greatheart was ever the warrior who gave away property faster than it came to him. And though few lived up to the perfect ideal of what they thought a good Indian should be, still contempt of property was developed among them to a point which the white man could not even comprehend.

However, even among the finest and the noblest Indians of his tribe, and those most in repute for the holiness of their lives and the number of scalps which they had taken, Big Crow did not know a single soul who could have refused such a vast mass of wealth as the entire aggregation of the spoils of this Pawnee war party. It staggered huge Kohatunka.

He was half inclined to strengthen his first impression of the simplicity of the white man and make him out a complete fool. But reason forbade him to do that. No man who was an actual fool was ever capable of riding and commanding such a glorious creature as the red stallion which stood under Anthony Castracane's weight. And what fool, also, except a God-inspired one, could make pistols speak with a continuous voice, killing at every syllable that they uttered?

So Big Crow suddenly put aside most of his desire to laugh at the simple white man, and a great cold sense of awe swept through his very soul, so that his eyes widened and his lips parted a little and he gaped at Anthony like a veritable child.

"Is this true?" asked Kohatunka, completely out of countenance. "Will you take nothing?"

"Nothing," said Anthony gravely, "except one pony. One of them might be useful for a pack horse, I suppose, though I doubt even that."

"You shall have it," said Kohatunka with a fiery energy.

He leaped to his own horse. He combed out its mane and its tail to give it a little finer appearance, and then he led it back to his savior.

"Here," said Big Crow, "is a horse which will never fail you. In hot or cold or in wet or dry, you will always find him true to you. His heart is not weak. His legs are strong. His wind will not finish quickly. Take him, brother!"

"Tush!" said Anthony Castracane, much moved. "You are very kind to me, brother. But this is your own horse!"

"Yes," said Big Crow, "he is my own horse. I trapped him running wild. Other ponies could not carry me. Their knees grew sick under my weight. Their backs sagged, and their eyes turned up. They groaned and died. If I killed the buffalo, I had to run on foot. But then I found this horse. He did not fail under me. We have ridden together for buffalo. We have ridden together for scalps. Hey, little one, have we not?"

The pony pricked its ears and turned its head affectionately toward its master.

"For," said Big Crow simply, "would I dare to give my white brother an unworthy gift? The Pawnees were already tasting my death. Their dead men were laughing in hell—their dead men whom I had sent there. They thought that I would come down to them, wearing no scalp. Or if they could have caught me alive, they would have killed me as slowly as a maggot kills a buffalo. But you, Running Thunder, stood on the cliff and they fell like dead prairie grass when the fire strikes across it. I do not give you a horse to reward you, but only to make my brother think of me and remember that I am grateful!"

So said Big Crow, for all thoughts of rascality and all ideas of personal gain were gone from him, and he now merely wished with all his heart to do the right thing for his benefactor.

"All this is kind," said Anthony Castracane, and there was even a bit of swelling in his throat as he listened to the protestations of this red-handed slaughterer. "But I would take the pony if it did not love you! However, as it stands, I cannot take it. When I spoke to it, its ears would flatten. Every time it pricked its ears at the horizon, it would be waiting and hoping for you to come to it from the edge of the sky. I won't have the horse, Kohatunka."

Kohatunka, in despair, stood a moment, running his eyes wildly here and there, vaguely hoping that some magnificent idea might come to him to turn the argument. But he felt that this man's will was perfectly fixed and settled, and that nothing he could do would alter the matter. So he went with a sigh, picked out the finest horse of the lot, which the chieftain of the Pawnees had been riding at the time of his death, and brought that back to Anthony.

"Where does Running Thunder ride?" asked Big Crow, humbly. "Will he take meat and corn with him? If he goes through strange country, will he take a guide with him? Will he perhaps go through the country of the Osage, so that they may tell him they know the Great Spirit sent him to us on this happy day?"

"I ride," said Anthony, with his usual openness,

"simply to get away from white men. I do not wish them to see me. I wish to be away from them, and therefore I am just driving west, as you see. I have no plans. Can you tell me of a good country to ride toward?"

"I understand," said the big Indian gravely. "There were fools among your own people who struck, and the thunder ran among them, and many fell dead, and then they hunted Running Thunder with hundreds of rifles. Is not that true?"

"No," said Anthony. "I never killed a man before today."

There was an incredulous gasp from the chief. But he dared not doubt. Everything that he heard from this white man was more and more prodigious, so that he began to doubt almost his own senses.

"And," said Castracane, "I hope that I shall never have to kill again. I did worse than kill. I shamed a man."

The Indian nodded. He could perfectly understand how even the smallest shame might be worse than death.

"Come back to my people with me," said Big Crow. "There is no other place half so good for you. They do not do like the Sioux and the Pawnees. They do not have traders come among them. They sell few hides of buffalo. They live by themselves. They drink no firewater. And you, brother, will be very welcome among us because the Great Spirit made you big, like an Osage, and true, like an Osage, and made you like us in everything except the color of your skin. And what is color? A little paint could change it!"

Anthony, listening, decided that this might be a rather venturesome expedition, but he did not mind danger. About Indians he knew absolutely nothing whatever except what he had heard, here and there, in the frontier town where he had lived, and a few random tales that had wandered to his ears in the East, mostly very bloody and romantic indeed!

However, what he chiefly wanted was to secure shelter from white men's eyes, and such shelter was ideally promised to him now. Here was a tribe who kept themselves as nearly as possible secluded from all whites. And therefore Anthony said: "Take me with you, Big Crow. I shall be very happy to go with you and to be one of your people for a while. Shall we start now? Every moment I am afraid that someone will come riding on my trail from behind!"

That hint was enough for the Osage. In another moment he had bounded onto the back of his horse. He led the string of captured horses carrying the saddles and the plunder. The rest of the Pawnee mounts followed more or less closely, and so the chief put his mount into a trot and moved rapidly back up the valley.

CHAPTER XXI

THERE WAS A SUFFICIENT DIFFERENCE BETWEEN these two as they rode along. Both were big, both were strong, both were brave, and both rode on excellent horses. But there all points of similarity ended.

Anthony Castracane rode as he had learned to ride in the circus, sitting straight and easily in the saddle, as dignified as any knight of olden days. But the Indian rode after the fashion of his people, in a saddle strapped upon the center of his horse's back rather than toward the withers, with his feet in very short stirrups which brought his knees up to the top of his pony's neck and threw his back into a curve so that his head thrust forward. Altogether he made the most awkward figure that one could imagine. And yet it would have been hard to say which was the most expert horseman. Grace was all wanting in the Osage until the time of need, and then Anthony knew how the redskin would suddenly sit up and lean forward along the neck of the pony and become a graceful living, breathing part of his mount. But now he was utterly relaxed, except that his keen eyes were forever running forward upon the trail before them and scanning the horizon ceaselessly. He seemed to Anthony not like a man but like a wild beast, moving watchfully through a region of perpetual dangers. And

Anthony, watching, admired and wondered at what he saw.

He was amazed, too, by the easy fashion in which the Indian handled his complicated accouterment. There was the big buffalo shield, feather-trimmed at the bottom, and the long, awkward spear, fourteen feet of it, tipped with a point which Anthony had already seen once dipped in human blood, and decorated now with the dangling, drying tokens of the dead. There was the knife in the warrior's belt, the bow and quiver at his back, now fairly well filled by the arrows which he had picked up from the battlefield. In addition, he had a rifle cased beneath his right leg, and three other rifles were among the spoils taken from the foemen. Furthermore, he had a short-handled, heavy hatchet with a blade hooked down like the beak of a bird of prey. The hatchet could be thrown with deadly effect at a distance, or else it could become a terrible weapon in hand-to-hand battle. And yet all of these weapons were so disposed of by the warrior that he seemed rather decorated than encumbered by their multi-plicity.

He could not help asking:

"How would you use all of these weapons, Kohatunka, if an enemy should ride out of that grove—suppose that big white stump were a Pawnee?"

Kohatunka looked at his white friend with a smile, and then with a flash of the war fire in his eyes:

"Look!" said he.

He snatched the rifle from the case and at the same time he swung his pony away at full speed. The next instant he had dropped out of sight along the side of his mount, the long barrel of the rifle appeared beneath the racing pony's neck, and the trigger was snapped toward the stump.

Then the rifle was cased as Big Crow, yelling like a fiend, circled on the farther side of the tree stump. His war bow of well-joined horn came into his hand and one after another, with wonderful rapidity, he launched a flight of five arrows. Two missed, but three sank in the stump and knocked out puffs of dust from the rotten wood.

Round came the Osage, still screeching and wild with excitement at this simulated warfare.

Then, riding to a little distance, he charged straight at the trunk at full speed, digging his heels into the pony's flanks. At a distance, the hatchet left his hand, and whirling with blinding rapidity through the air, its blade struck deep into the soft wood.

On came the warrior, the long lance now thrust forward. Into the stump he thrust it, and changing his hold like lightning, he snatched out the knife from his belt and buried it, also, in the top of the broken old tree.

"He is six times dead, that Pawnee," said Big Crow, coming back grinning and nodding after he had gathered up his arrows. "And that is the manner in which the Osage fights. But you, brother, have the running thunder in your hand. Does it only play when there is battle and the Great Spirit speaks to you and tells you what to do?"

"It speaks," said Anthony Castracane, smiling, "for two hours a day, while I practice. I have nothing to do with the Great Spirit, Kohatunka, and I know nothing about big medicine. I do what I can by hard work, just as you learned by hard work to shoot your arrows so fast and so straight, and if I stopped practice I would be no good at all."

To this speech, the Osage listened in a respectful silence, but it was plain that he made many mental reservations without accepting the statement. And as they jogged on, Mad Anthony praised the weapons and the ways of Osage warfare.

"Except," he said, "that bullets and powder kill at a greater distance."

"Rifles," said Big Crow, "are the white man's medicine. And as for the running thunder—"

He pointed to the revolvers at Anthony's belt and shook his head in awe.

At that moment, two jackrabbits sprang up from behind a rock and darted off, their ears flagging back with their speed.

The Indian snatched out bow and arrow with great speed, exclaiming: "Strike, Running Thunder!"

It was a hard target, and Anthony whipped out his revolvers with many a doubt in his mind of striking such a mark.

His first bullet struck the ground well ahead of them, and the foolish little creatures doubled and ran almost straight back into the mouth of danger. A second bullet dusted the ground beneath them. A third caught them both in line and laid them rolling on the ground with the life blown out of them. And these three bullets had been fired while Big Crow, for all of his skill, was fitting an arrow to the string and drawing it to a head.

He relaxed his grip, now, and jumping down from his horse he ran to the dead victims and kneeled beside them; he seemed at first almost afraid to touch them, but then he lifted each gingerly and looked over their wounds with wide eyes and gaping wonder.

"If they had been two running men," said the chief gravely, "they would both have died before they could throw a knife even! Do only practice and work make this? However, only a fool would throw away the secret of such medicine as this. I, Big Crow, your friend, do not ask!"

And he looked at the white man with awe and envy.

So they journeyed on up the valley, and left it, and turned onto the plains. Late in the afternoon they sighted the distant tepees of an Indian village; a little afterward, a cloud of Indian boys approached on a sweeping drove of ponies.

They poured around the big warrior with yells, and catching sight of the freshly reddened scalps that dangled from his spear, they fell into a frenzy of joy. They looked to Anthony Castracane like so many frantic young devils as they shrieked with their exultation. Counting the number on their fingers and looking over the spoils of war which their chief was bringing home, half of them continued milling around the veteran and half rushed away at full speed toward the town.

Mad Anthony was almost overlooked, for the time being, until Big Crow reined back his horse and rode at the side of the giant white man. That token of respect brought Anthony some share of the boys' curiosity, but now they were coming close to the village, and all the children's thoughts were to be forgotten.

For in the town itself bedlam was awakening.

First, Anthony heard a great horn blowing a deep and roaring note that seemed to come from a great distance and roll up out of the plain all around them—a most dismal sound, more dreary than the booming of a winter wind. Then a shrill, squeaking, flutelike whistle joined, and immediately afterward there was a pounding of drums of a dozen kinds, and a hubbub of rattles. Above all these notes now sounded the heart-stopping war cries of braves, and out from the tepees there surged a mass of demoniacs.

Anthony Castracane had half a mind to check his horse and ride off to a secure distance, it looked so like a hostile charge, but he checked the impulse and steadied himself to meet them and watch what happened, for he felt certain that no frenzy of the mob would be allowed to do him injury as long as he stayed with the chief he had befriended.

These maddened celebrants swept in a jumbled mass around the returning hero. Women bounded into the air and shrieked his name, and savage warriors marched beside him, sending their thrilling whoops maddeningly before them.

The horses were separated. Each was led in a long procession by several boys or women, and so the bedlam poured into the Osage town.

They kept straight on until they came to a tent whose flap was raised and in front of which, on a buffalo robe, sat a man so very old that where his eyes should have been there seemed now only a mass of wrinkles with a glint of misty light hidden among them.

Before this seer Big Crow sprang down and kneeled. Two withered, clawlike hands were placed upon his head in sign of blessing, and then the warrior sprang up and went on with his clan toward the center of the town, where there was an open space with a fire burning in the center. The whole of the circular space was instantly filled with the tribesmen, except for the inner circle around the fire. That was reserved for Big Crow, and he stepped into it alone.

CHAPTER XXII

IMAGINE, THEN HOW ANTHONY CASTRACANE'S EYES watched the smoke from the fire rise, lean to the side in the wind, and then float softly and dimly up to the pale, blue-white heavens, and how he looked back again to the crowd of Osages.

They were a race of giants. Not a man that Anthony looked upon, saving one or two elders, seemed to be under six feet in height, and there were monsters eight and ten inches above that amount. Stripling boys had the bones and sinews of mature men, and the women were giantesses worthy of their menfolk. This whole mob, packed closely together, made a dense circle, with all eyes fixed hungrily upon the central hero.

You might think, perhaps, that Big Crow was a little abashed by all this attention, but he was not. He had found an opportunity to arrange himself a little for this ceremony, and what he had done by way of preparation had been to daub a great streak of purple paint under each eye, a branching of vermilion stain in the center of his forehead, and huge splotches of yellow dye on his cheeks and chin.

He ceased to look like a man and began to appear like a devil from the ninth circle of the Inferno.

He had replaced the bedraggled feathers in his hair with a great feathered headdress which swept down from his crown almost to his heels.

Accoutered in this fashion he seemed to satisfy himself and fill his tribe with pride.

But Anthony felt like rubbing his eyes from time to time to realize that the devil who strode and shouted beside the fire was really the same hunted brave he had seen in the ravine.

To complete the picture Big Crow had brought into that sacred inner circle the beautiful little pony on which he had made his ride. Its belly was a little gaunt from the prodigious labors which it had performed, but its eyes were still bright and its step was quick and it followed its monstrous master up and down like a pet dog.

Upon the pony's back had been bound the total mass of bristling spears and arrows, and bows and axes, and even the great shields. The knives and the rifles were added to the load until it seemed that the little horse was a walking arsenal.

But he was hardly less bristling with spoils and importance than his master.

For Big Crow carried all his weapons just as though he were going into the battle over again. Shield, huge spear, bow, arrows, knife, hatchet, were carried by the big man and managed with such wonderful adroitness that he did not seem encumbered.

Of the spoils of the great battle he had chosen only the medicine bags which he had taken with such care from each of the dead men. They were the visible and the tangible souls of the dead warriors, and every time the brave, in his recital and dance, brandished the medicine bags of the Pawnees, screams of joy rose from the crowd.

In this manner the chief strode up and down, with a sort of gloomy ecstasy gathering in his face, but uttering not a word, and so hushed became the assemblage that even the snarling, pushing, whining crowded dogs that were gathered on the outskirts of the spectators became silent also. Anthony Castracane could hear the crackling of the fire and the faint clashing of the big Indian's weapons. There was no other sound for long moments until Big Crow came to a halt and slowly raised his hand toward the heart of the sky, remaining in that posture a breathing space and then commencing to speak.

It seemed to Anthony, though he did not understand a word, of course, a sort of invocation, or an address to the Great Spirit, promising that all he said should be the truth and nothing but the truth.

After that he broke into a sad chant, standing with his feet motionless but his body swaying a little back and forth, and in his voice the grief of a strong man, so it seemed. By his gestures it seemed that he lamented evil days for himself, or perhaps for his entire people. And it was plain by his movements that many an Osage scalp had been taken by their foes, and there had been weeping and lamenting through the tribe of giants.

He made another pause, stamped violently upon the ground, and thrust up his arm bearing his lance so that it quivered against the sky, and the highlights quivered up and down his naked, muscular arm.

This condition, it seemed, Big Crow had endured as long as he could, and finally he had decided that he would strike in revenge.

So much Anthony thought he could make out from the gestures of the huge warrior.

But after that there was a sudden change, and everything became more vivid. Lacking a clue to what had actually occurred, he might have been completely in the dark as to the meaning of this pantomime. But as it was, he could follow the recital more easily than if it had been spoken in English.

The instant Big Crow reached in his narrative the point where he had started on the warpath with his favorite war horse, he no longer stood still. He began the strange, jerking, labored dance of an Indian, and his voice sharpened and raised in pitch.

The whole circle of the audience responded at once. They began to sway a little back and forth. Not a lip was parted except in the rapid breathing of excitement, but guttural sounds rose in the throats of the Osages, and their eyes began to flash. A storm of emotion was patently brewing in them, and Big Crow was the maker and the master of it. For he was an actor who had proved himself worthy of being heard, and if any doubted, they could glance at the dangling, ragged scalps which were suspended from his lance.

He sketched in detail, now, how he had wandered on the warpath until by his peering ahead, and his preparation of his weapons, and the arrow he strung upon his bow, it was clear that he had sighted the enemy.

Another moment, and the bowstring clanged, the arrow was driven deep into the ground, and Big Crow leaped into the air with a shout which was instantly answered by a wild yell from every onlooker.

So Big Crow had attacked the enemy and sent one Pawnee soul to the Happy Hunting Grounds.

But instantly he was pursued, for it was plain to see, as he rushed to the horse and gathered the reins and looked back, that he was about to flee.

The Pawnees followed fast, and the dance grew fast and furious until the knees of the big man sagged and his head fell—his horse had wearied in the long hunt!

And now the Pawnees in overmastering force were sweeping upon him. A gesture of his hand showed the narrow ravine, the high walls which no horse could climb, and the rapid and dangerous water which hemmed him in.

The Osages listened, moans of soft excitement swelling their throats, and the fear and the exhaustion of horse and rider were reflected in their faces.

Closer pressed the Pawnees. Once more the bow twanged and an arrow hummed in the ground, buried almost to the feathers of the shaft. Once more the chief bounded into the air, and the screech of the delighted warriors and the tingling cries of the women and children long echoed his shout of triumph. Another Pawnee had died!

But still they pressed him; still he danced with sagging weariness and was seen to lash at the failing pony. He grew desperate. He scanned the imaginary river which boiled beside him, and turned his horse, he raised his hands to call the Great Spirit to his aid, then rushed the horse at the water.

And by the bounding of Big Crow, and his staggering, you could see the horse valiantly leaping from rock to rock, slipping, regaining footing, and springing on again until it reached the firm ground.

Another riot of cheers from the spectators. Then deadly silence, for the chief, looking anxiously back, sees the foe cross by the same ford which he had used—all save one!—all save one!

He smites the ground with his heel and bounds again into the air. The third Pawnee is overwhelmed in the stream and carried down its current, horse and man!

Three dead, and the Osage warriors are shuddering with delight and excitement. They can hardly keep quiet now. Again and again, as the narrator proceeds, some young buck, mad with excitement, springs into the air, brandishes spear or knife, and utters a loud war cry.

But the main body of the audience follows with tense attention while Big Crow describes how, at last, the pony sinks beneath him.

Upon one knee sinks Big Crow, with rolling eyes and shaken head. He lashes at the air. No, the horse will not rise. So he stands on the ground, knife in hand to slay the horse before he himself dies.

No, his heart weakens!

And Anthony heard a wild, half-sobbing shout from the women and the girls. Such a moment was made to touch their tenderer hearts. And even the warriors listen with bright eyes that flash from the hero to his horse.

Now Big Crow stands with his back to the cliff. He raises his hands to the Great Spirit. He begs the power from the sky to grant him a worthy death. And then he meets the charge with an arrow from his bow—it turns back one charging fox, and the Osage braves yell again!

Their shouts end. They crouch with excitement. The sweep of the Pawnees has slipped away and recoiled, save for one brave who tries conclusions with the standing hero. And now with brandished spear the chief drives home the lance head through the throat of the brave, who falls toppling to the ground.

And from among his spoils, Big Crow selects a medicine bag and raises it high above his head. And in the tuft of scalps, he points out one—

There followed a moment of utter madness. All that had passed before had been hearsay—mere description. But these were the proofs of victory recited by the victor, and the yelling of the tribe burst up to heaven in a roar.

Yet all is not over!

No, there are still six braves of the Pawnees confronting him, and how shall he be delivered?

A groan of anxiety broke from the listeners' lips. They waited, lips parted, to hear the mystery solved.

And now it is plain by the gestures of Big Crow that two of the enemy are clambering up the rock behind him. There is no blow he can strike against such distant foes. He gives up his scalp and his soul for lost. In spite of all his glories that day, down to the Indian hell he must descend before the noonday!

He plants himself—he throws up his arms—he breaks into his death song!

Another groan of immense excitement and grief rose from the throats of these savage fighters as they listened.

But here is doom standing on the edge of the cliff at the back of Big Crow. What saves him? What miracle?

Man and woman and child trembled with dread at such a thought, and suddenly Big Crow crossed the circle with a bound, seized Anthony's hand, and dragged him forth into the innermost circle.

Here, then, was the man sent by the sky-people to be the salvation of the Osage!

CHAPTER XXIII

TOTALLY UNPREPARED FOR SUCH AN EVENT, MAD Anthony looked vaguely about him and shook back his dark-red hair and blushed, you may be sure, like any girl, and then looked down to the ground. For every hand was flourishing in the air, and the young braves were leaping like deer.

Big Crow, arrived at the crisis of his tale, was in a frenzy. His smashing hands, striking the air, showed how both the foe were smitten down. And then, prostrate himself, he showed the Pawnee leaping, knife in hand. He moved as though to snatch the revolver at Anthony's belt and with two imaginary bullets sent both those braves to their long account!

Ah, what madness now! How did they leap! What terrible war cries stabbed the air! What weapons flashed in the sun!

Even those old chiefs, long practiced in all the exertions of the warpath, men with a dozen scalps to their proud credit, now started out of their dignified apathy and added their shouts. And Anthony, glancing up in vast embarrassment, saw strong-armed women lifting their little children so that they could see above the heads of the warriors and mark this fair-faced hero!

Ah, but that is not all.

The four Pawnees on the plain see the danger. They look up. They see the red-haired giant on the verge of the rock, a gun in either hand—and one word rolls repeatedly from the lips of the Osage—Running Thunder! Running Thunder! Anthony knows that is the term which is driving these warriors to madness of joy.

The Pawnees turn and flee!

But here Big Crow stopped in the midst of his yelling, his whooping, his gesticulating and bounding into the air. He pointed to the sky, as though demanding, What man or men can avoid the strokes of fate?

The guns blaze from the hands of the white man. Three Indians lurch from their saddles, and the fourth is pierced by the terrible arrow of Big Crow himself.

Too much glory, if there can be such a thing!

These scores and scores of braves cannot contain themselves any longer. They break from the circle. They whirl leaping and screeching before Anthony. They seem to strike their own breasts with their knives, as though to show that they will die for him as he had offered to die for them. They gash the air with their weapons to show how they will fight for him.

Oh, Anthony, banish vanity, for now your head may indeed be turned for all the days of your life.

Big Crow was not satisfied that his tale should be interrupted before it was well ended. With an angry shout he drove the others back.

And now he proceeded to indicate how he had taken the scalps and the medicine bags from all the fallen, how the white man had come, and how he had offered to him all the spoils: the horses, the saddles, the weapons of the fallen, and the clothes in which they had been dressed. Look! The tribesmen would see how great the prize was with their own eyes, if they cared to look. But what said Running Thunder to these offers?

The voice of Big Crow shook with emotion. He made a gesture with both hands, as though Anthony in that manner had put away the proffered spoils of battle. He pointed, then, to the mighty red-bay stallion. He pointed to Anthony himself, as though to explain that this hero needed nothing more than was already his!

We admire great men for great deeds, but we do not love them for the same reasons. Heroes are apt to be a bit cruel and conquerors are calloused across the knuckles and the heart. But when, now and then, we meet gentleness with valor, and modesty with might, and above all, perhaps, when we find honesty in the place of sheer ambition, we are unnerved, and kindliness flows in upon all the secret places of the soul and a sort of worship issues from us.

Now the Osages had before their eyes the two types of warrior. They had seen Big Crow vaunting his prowess and striding up and down before their eyes and deafening their ears with the tale of his exploits. And now they saw a greater warrior and a braver and more terrible man crimson with shame because his exploits were known; they heard that he had refused with a single gesture what was in their eyes vast wealth and vaster honor, and all the shouting died instantly away. They surged quietly forward and stood about Anthony with shining eyes and happy faces, women and men together. And a little naked urchin, red as burnished copper, fearlessly grasped the big white man's belt and then caught one of those hands which had dealt such havoc among the Pawnees. Anthony scooped him up from the danger of pressing bodies and trampling feet and placed him on a broad shoulder where the youngster shrieked with joy and, with one arm thrown around the hero's red head and the other clenched fist brandished in the air, began to shout something which Anthony, of course, could not understand, but which he gathered was declaration of the number of Pawnee scalps which the youngster hoped to take in the days of his maturity. And now all was laughter and mirth around them.

Big Crow, breaking the way before his white friend, led the way to the largest and tallest of the tepees, and here he placed Anthony on a buffalo robe, and here a middle-aged warrior wrapped in a resplendent painted buffalo robe came forward to meet him.

He was Munnepuskee, the great war chief of the Osages, who had led them in many a famous battle and ruled the tribe with an absolute authority. He made a little speech appropriate to the occasion. Big Crow translated fluently.

Munnepuskee saw that it was impossible to give any reward to the white man. All that the Osages could do was to declare him a brother and a warrior of their tribe, so that hereafter he should have full privileges of voting for the war chiefs, calling upon the nation for aid in troubles, and looking upon them always as a refuge and an ally. As for his home in the tribe, the tepee of Munnepuskee was of ample width, and if Anthony would stay, the chief would be happy to have Running Thunder under the same tent with the rest of his family.

That night there would be a great feast to celebrate the accession of such a warrior to the tribe, and all the Osage Indians would pledge their faith to him, and he his to them, and he would be given their pass signs and their master words, such as introduce Indians on distant trails.

Such were the proposals of Munnepuskee. And Anthony could do nothing but accept.

For that matter, he was glad to see more of these people. He had known nothing of Indians, in the past, except a little by hearsay. And though he saw in them now a childish mob of savages, he felt that there were certain virtues to be found among them, also, and an honesty and faith such as he had not known among whites.

And though Anthony was a very modest man, he would have been a good deal more than human if the admiration with which he was surrounded, here, had not pleased him. He felt as though he had reached a comfortable resting place upon a long trail which had been leading him in what direction he knew not, so long as it was continually away from other white men.

He told Big Crow that he wished to be alone and think over these offers. So he went with the Salton Bay to the prairie beyond the village, close to the bank of the nearby stream.

There he could see the Indian boys, who had already returned to their sport, diving and swimming in the water and filling the air with shrill, piping cries that whistled down the wind to Anthony.

A cool wind fanned the tall grasses of the plain. Up in the sky above him a hawk sailed on effortless wings. A deep, sweet sense of peace passed into Anthony Castracane's heart. He felt that if he could only stay long enough in this quiet realm of wide horizons, he would forget all about the evils which had been behind him, and he would be able to heal, at last, even the wounds which had been left in his heart by Muriel Lester.

Out of his reverie he looked up to see Big Crow passing across the plain with a troop of burdened horses behind him. Big Crow was bound for the first white trading station to blow in the fruits of his great victory!

CHAPTER XXIV

WHEN DIAMOND JACK KIRBY HAD BEEN AROUSED to anger, it was like the fury of an octopus. That is to say, he flung about him many reaching arms which were his agents searching here and there for Muriel Lester and for Anthony Castracane.

He himself had gone rushing along a trail which led to no end. He returned, and when he reached his house in his failure, he sat himself down in the room with his mother.

He had always gone there for consolation, for comfort, and for the wise advice which she could give. And he found her, as always, with imperturbable face and with bright knitting needles. He looked upon those needles with a portion of the childish awe with which he had beheld them many years before, and the manner in which they performed intricacies of fancy stitches and knots while the mind of Mrs. Kirby was far away, launching distant schemes, solving abstruse problems of her home. So she was now—calm, cheerful, level-eyed—and though he knew that she was dangerous to the rest of the world, he loved her all the more because he knew that she made the one exception in his favor. He was the complete horizon which rounded her existence. Her ambitions, her hopes, her despairs, were greater even than his own; but they were totally bound up in his person.

He watched her for a time. He listened to her speaking gaily of how the hedge of sweet peas which was growing in a forest of dead shrubbery in the back yard would soon be blossoming for the second time because she had picked off all the dead blossoms, clipped all the forming pods—

"Mother!" exclaimed Diamond Jack.

She looked up from her knitting, but still the needles flashed and maintained their rhythm.

"Yes?" she asked.

"I've come back to you to talk life and death, not to hear about sweet peas!"

"You mustn't be desperate, Jack," said she. "Desperation will never win!"

He stared at her.

Then he nodded, for he could realize what she meant. In his gaming houses the desperate gamblers who knew that luck must change were always the ones who placed the greatest number of thousands in his coffers.

"That's sense," he agreed. "But how can you be so cool?"

"Because I want to think, Jack. I want to think— think hard!"

He nodded again. And a vast wave of confidence in her and her lucubrations passed out from his heart.

"What have you arrived at?" he asked her.

"Tell me, first, what you've found out."

"Nothing but a hint that there's a girl at Fort Hendon who faintly resembles Muriel Lester. I'm going to ride on that trail, before long. But as for the big fellow, I don't hear about him! He seems to have melted into the plains, and I suppose that he was frightened because of what he had done and knew that I'd soon be after him!"

Said Mrs. Kirby: "I think that you're much more apt to be afraid of him than he is to be afraid of you, Jack!"

Her son stared, and then flushed with anger.

"Do you think that I'm a coward, mother?"

"Dear Jack! How silly to suggest that! What I mean, of course, is simply that it requires a rather sensitive nature to know fear. And there is sense and sensitiveness in you, Jack. But this Castracane is obviously a brute. There is no fear in him. Don't they call him, everywhere, Mad Anthony!"

"They call him that!" said Jack Kirby. "They'll call him Dead Anthony one of these days, I hope and pray!"

"Undoubtedly, if you use good sense, Jack!"

"You think that he's not afraid, then?"

"Not the least in the world," said the woman. "He walked straight into your gaming house, where there were scores of your men armed to the teeth. I have never heard of such madness—such absolute inability to be afraid!"

"I want to forget what happened that day," said Diamond Jack, dropping his square chin upon his fist.

"Not at all," said his mother, turning a little pale. "I should never forget it. I should dwell on it, quietly, and upon all the pain and the humiliation. One learns in that way! One learns a very great deal in that way."

"Tell me," said Diamond Jack, half tormented and half curious, "what have you ever faced that was half as black as this moment of mine?"

"I can tell you, my dear, though I never wished to mention it before. Now, however, I think that I may. I thought that I had married a brave, chivalrous, clever, romantic gentleman. I am sorry to say, however, that one day I had the mist brushed from before my eyes. And I saw that I had tied myself for life to a shiftless, pretentious, stupid, uneducated, overmannered, self-conceited boor. That was a black moment, Jack."

"My father!"

"That hurts you, my dear. It hurt me a great deal more! Partly because I had let him be the father of my boy and partly because I had to have him for a husband! But I thank God daily that there is none of him in you except for the looks, and his looks were the best part of him! They were what blinded my girlish eyes. But in the moment when I saw the truth about him, I swore, Jack, that I would do nothing hastily. I would fight the big fight for myself and for you. And I lived up to my vow. I worked in silence. I prepared myself to endure hells of shame and mortification and disgust. And I lived through them. The result is you—and I am proud of what I did!"

Diamond Jack looked at her as at a creature more than human.

"If you had been a man—" he sighed.

"If I had been a man," said she, "I would either have

been president—or the president's murderer!"

She broke off with a little laugh, but there was still a dangerous thought in her eyes.

"I believe you," said her son with another sigh. "But now what have you thought out for me?"

"I have thought out this. I would have talked to you about it before, but you were all madness and fury. And when I saw the manner in which you started for Mad Anthony, I knew that if you met him, he'd kill you with the greatest ease in the world."

"Mother, confound it, don't say that. There's no one in the world who can safely take a chance with me in a gun fight!"

She shook her head.

"There are men, Jack," she said, "who can face ten fine fighters and live to talk of how they beat the other fellows. There are prodigies. This fellow they call Mad Anthony, they sometimes call Anthony the Great, also, I believe!"

"Do you think that he's one of the giants? He's a simple, half-witted fool!"

"Why, Jack, I'm not comparing him with you. I'm not saying that he's as good a man as you are. I'm saying that he's without fear, that he has the strength of three men in his hands, and that he shoots perfectly straight and as fast as lightning. He proved all of that before he left this town, I suppose!"

"I suppose so," growled the son.

"Now, Jack, if you fight a weak man, you use strength; but if you fight a strong man, you use cleverness!"

"What good is cleverness?" asked Diamond Jack.

"The greatest good in the world."

"Will cleverness beat a bull?"

"Cleverness will tie a bull's legs together and chip off the ends of his horns. Cleverness will show you exactly what a fool this Anthony the Great actually is!"

"You don't advise me to leave his trail, then?" sneered Jack.

"If you left his trail," said Mrs. Kirby, "before you laid him dead, I would never call you a son of mine again. I would fade away out of your life and try to forget that I had ever brought such a despicable creature into the world!"

"By the Lord," breathed Jack, "I think that you mean what you say!"

"Never doubt that, Jack! Oh, I mean it with all of my heart and soul!"

He nodded.

"Ah, there's iron in you. But get on with your ideas!"

"Why, then, I say that when you find someone who's too strong for you, what do you do?"

"I don't exactly know."

"I mean, you borrow the strength of another fellow, don't you?"

"Why, I've had men out by the score trying to find that trail."

"And they've failed you, and therefore that shows that they don't possess the sort of strength of which you're in need. Isn't that obvious?"

"Why, perhaps it is obvious!"

"Of course. And there is only one other kind of strength to use."

"I don't follow your hint, there."

"I mean the government, Jack!"

"What!"

"Yes, I mean the law!"

He gasped with amazement.

"Does it make any difference to you, Jack, whether you stab him to the heart or the law strangles him with a rope?"

"You mean that I should make myself a marshal or get myself appointed a deputy marshal?"

"You have influence enough to manage that!"

"Ay, I could do that."

"Whenever there's a fight, there's a right and a wrong side to it, and if you're an officer of the law, on this border, you're sure to be in the right, no matter what you do to a friendless, unknown gun fighter!"

"Yes."

"And, dear Jack, while it's a pleasure to kill him, no matter how, wouldn't it be perfect to kill the great bull of a man with the same powers of the law which should be used to protect him?"

CHAPTER XXV

THERE WAS A CERTAIN AMOUNT OF POINT TO THE remarks of Mrs. Kirby on all subjects, and particularly upon those which had to do with her son. And as Diamond Jack listened to her, he kept nodding gently, with a smile upon his handsome face.

"I begin to see the possibilities," he said to her. "I'm to take the law and use it as a rope to lasso this wild bull!"

"Exactly," said Mrs. Kirby.

"I never thought of that!" sighed Diamond Jack.

"Because, my dear," said his mother, "you've been accustomed to crushing every man with the strength of your own hand. But you must understand, Jack, that Napoleon had to have an army to conquer the world. As for himself, he was only a fat little man with very bad manners. And you, Jack, will never be able to do really great things in your life unless you consider yourself as a general and keep behind the firing line. You've showed everyone that you have courage enough and that you can shoot straight. That's all that's necessary. No one will ever try to bully you. So I think that the thing for you to do is to keep out of the way of harm and let others take the risks for you. If you want a ditch dug, you hire somebody else to do the sweaty labor for you. But I warn you that if you or any other man tries to meet this Mad Anthony and crush him in fair fight, he'll kill you, Jack, as sure as God made little apples."

"Why, Mother," said Jack, "he's not invincible!"

"I've seen him," said Mrs. Kirby, "and I knew men, my dear, before ever you were born!"

He looked from her flashing knitting needles to her calm, cold face, and he knew that she was right.

It did not take long to put his new will into execution. He was sworn in as a deputy in a single hour from that moment. But Marshal Bisbee, as honest and as fierce a man as ever rode a horse, looked him fairly in the eye and asked:

"What's put the new idea into your head, Kirby?"

"You can make your guess, Bisbee."

"Why, then, I don't like to think that you're after someone."

"Not that," said Diamond Jack, wincing from the accusation. "You see, my viewpoint has changed a good deal. I used to be a drifter, Bisbee. But now I have a business house and a business that's worth a good many tens of thousands. So it stands to reason that the law means something to me, and I want to see the crooks held down."

He added with a faint smile: "Not too much law, Bisbee, or it might put the gamblers out of business. But enough to see that we get a square deal."

The marshal was pleased by this touch of candor, for he himself was the frankest of men.

"I'll be very open with you," he explained. "I want men who can ride and shoot and who haven't any fear.

I know that you're that sort of a fellow, Kirby. If you play fair, I'm glad to have you. If you start using the law for your own ends, I have to say that I shall be after you, Kirby, with all my might; but I think that after all you and I are going to get on well together. Only—I want you to pay attention to the oath which you take together with this badge!"

As for the oath, Jack Kirby did not give it a thought. What interested him was the bright face of the nickel badge which was duly pinned *inside* the lapel of his coat—for he wished to be more or less a secret deputy.

But as he rode again on his way with the new authority under his coat, it seemed to Diamond Jack that his mother was by far the wisest person in all of this world, and that he could never have done better than in following her advice. Now he was equipped with a club which would be wielded, if need be, by ten million hands. And the more it was opposed, the more heavily would it fall!

So reasoned Jack Kirby, and in a way he was right.

He rode straight for Fort Hendon. He had left the gaming house doing a tolerable business and in hands which he felt he could trust. In the meantime, he had sent out word for his minions to gather in the good cause.

He could have picked up a hundred hired men who could ride and shoot well. But that was not what he wanted. Mere numbers were useful, but what he desired above all was a group of men subservient to his will and his money, and all stirred by the desire of something more than pay. In a word, what he wanted was a cluster of enthusiasts who hoped more than heaven to inflict a cruel death upon Mad Anthony Castracane.

He appointed Hendon as the meeting place, not because he knew that he would find Anthony near the trading station and fort, but because there had come to him a rumor that Muriel Lester was in that town. He would see her if she was in the place, learn what he could manage with her, and at the same time the town would serve as a rendezvous for his forces.

The men he had chosen were Chick, who had already been downed by Castracane's guns and who had been practicing with his weapons ever since in a feverish desire to make himself worthy of a second meeting; Cherokee Dan, whose grudge against Anthony was of the most poisonous variety; and Jay Madison, that famous hunter and rascal. For all the world now knew that Jay Madison had brought the finest of wild horses out of the western desert and that Anthony Castracane had taken the Salton Bay out of the hands of the hunter. Those three, added to himself, made enough brains and gun power, he felt, to bring down any one man—granted that they could find the trail of their quarry.

He saw Fort Hendon looming on the sky line at last. He saw it grow from a few hazy lines to a low, broad, rambling cluster of buildings covered over with the heat haze which forever shimmered up from the sun-beaten prairie. Every spring Fort Hendon sat in the midst of green fields, cut across with little ravines, plowed by waters fresh from the melting snows of the western mountains. But after six weeks of that weather, the sun withered all away, the grass turned brown, the ravines dried up except for a few standing, green-faced pools, and the dust began to drift and blow as before across the prairie. But still, Fort Hendon did a considerable business with the Indian traders. It was an advanced post. It was a danger line inscribed across the plains. Civilization began on one side of it; the Great Spirit lived on the other.

So Diamond Jack, when he reached the edge of the town, dismounted, removed the dust cloth from his neck, took off his coat and hat and brushed them clean, rubbed up the face of his boots, and prepared to enter the fort in some style. He could see the fort itself at one side of the town, with a couple of small cannon glancing from its parapet. The voices of those cannon had been all that served to keep away two or three Indian hordes which had threatened to sweep the fort out of existence.

And Diamond Jack could not help smiling to himself. For those glimmering guns represented the strong hand of the law; and was he not also a hand of the same power? Could he not call upon the same forces in time of need?

So he entered Fort Hendon, and the very first person that he met there had a familiar swing to his shoulders; he rode up and called: "Tommy!"

Tommy Plummer turned hastily and gaped at his former boss.

"Why, Tommy," said Diamond Jack, "I'm glad to run into you, even if you left your old job without any explanation. I understand that you've been riding on the trail of Castracane, trying to get even with him!"

"I been riding on the trail of Castracane," admitted Tommy gravely.

"Any luck?"

"He wouldn't have me," said Tommy.

"You mean that he ran away from you?"

"Because he didn't think that I was fit to be a friend of his."

"A friend?"

"That's it."

"Hold on, Tommy. That's a joke!"

"I suppose that it would sound that way to you, but it's a fact, nevertheless. I'm done with the old job and the old game, Jack. Castracane looked white to me. I tried to be a pal of his, but he cut and run from me in the middle of the night. He wouldn't trust me."

"Too good for you?"

"Why not?" sighed Tommy. "I tried to croak him. What reason did he have for trusting me?"

And he shook his head, gloomily.

What Diamond Jack noticed most of all was that Tommy's mustaches, usually so brisk, so wide, so fierce, were now all drooping and unkempt. It was a plain token that the spirit of his former employee was failing.

"I could be a bit hard on you, Tommy," said Diamond Jack kindly, "because you remember that you walked off with some advanced pay—"

"I'll pay it back one of these days," said Tommy, his eye wandering somewhat.

"No," said Jack. "Because your old job is still waiting for you!"

"My old job!" exclaimed the other. "I'll tell you what, Diamond, you got me wrong! When I said that I was through, I meant it, entirely. I'm ready to cut loose and keep loose. I'm finished with the old life, Diamond!"

"Meaning me?"

"You can figure that out for yourself!" said Tommy Plummer.

And with that, he rode off down the street, leaving a stunned man behind him. For this was a defection which Diamond Jack could hardly fathom. He had always looked upon Tommy as an imitation rather than as a real man. And yet even Tommy had been so inspired by Castracane that he dared to lift up his head against his betters!

CHAPTER XXVI

IF YOU LET THE CHILDREN THROW STONES AT YOU, YOU are inviting their fathers and their older brothers to ride you on a rail or even burn you alive. Mr. Kirby thought of this, and he decided that he would have to put down Tommy Plummer, if he did nothing else in the immediate future, for Tommy Plummer had dared to think and speak lightly of Diamond Jack and such things must not be!

His first impulse was to rush immediately after Tommy and call him to a reckoning, and then he remembered that there was hardly a need of doing this. For now he could use the law and the agents of the law as his tools.

On this reflection, he could not help smiling a little. But he drifted down the street in search of someone to do his dirty work for him.

He found that Fort Hendon was filled with people. Pawnees and Osages had buried the hatchet, for the time being, and passed each other on the streets of the town with no more than black looks. White traders, contractors, adventurers, refugees from the law of the East, vagrants, soldiers, squatters from the prairies, cattlemen, prospectors, and more than a few tourists who had come out here to the verge of the civilized world to see what wildness remained in the country. And seeing often a great deal more than they bargained for.

Diamond Jack liked that crowd. He felt that there was money in it and, more than that, he was sure that such a thing as a fast little gambling game would be welcomed by all. His very finger tips itched to have out a pack of cards and fall to work.

He controlled that professional emotion and shrugged his shoulders at the thought of the money and the fun which were slipping away from him.

There were a thousand sights to see, but none more amusing than the giant Osage chief whose eye had been caught by some cubed sugar. He followed the man who carried the bag of the glittering little crystals with ceaseless importunity until, at the last, he had persuaded the white to make a trade.

And what a trade! For the sake of the little bag of sugar, he gave up a fine war pony with a saddle on its back.

A Pawnee war pony, by the way, which was enough sign that this Osage was a fellow who knew his business on the warpath.

Diamond Jack saw the Osage secure this prize and, at once, sit down with his little stack of glistening white treasure in the palm of his hand, turning it this way and that so that the light would strike upon it, smelling it, thumbing it—and at last tasting it!

He rolled up his eyes and made sure that the taste was good. Then a smile of ineffable content appeared upon his ugly face. He chewed up the pieces of sugar one after the other, and then rose from his heels and resumed his way down the street.

He seemed perfectly without resentment because he had resigned his horse for the sake of this trifle of sweet. To the Osage, perhaps, it was simply another sign of the tremendous medicine of the whites that they were able to produce these little rocks, white as snow, melting like water, and hard as stone! He was content with his bargain, and it was because he was content with such affairs that so many businessmen risked their lives as traders upon the frontiers.

Diamond Jack paid no more attention to the Osage. He passed on until he found what he wanted. And that was the local constable.

Kirby began by flashing the nickel-faced badge of his office. And then he made his statement clearly and simply. Mr. Tommy Plummer had formerly been in his employ, had received advanced money, and had decamped without performing the work which it should have represented. By so doing, Mr. Plummer had obviously become a thief. Now Mr. Kirby had recently seen Mr. Plummer on the streets of Fort Hendon and had approached him courteously and had asked when he was coming back to work, and he had been answered most tersely that Tommy did not intend to return. Neither did Tommy say anything about returning the money which he had taken.

What remained was perfectly simple.

"I could call him a thief and pull a gun on him," said Diamond Jack, "but it's no pleasure to me to kill Tommy. He's more foolish than bad. But he needs a lesson. I suppose that you could round him up and slip him into the jail here for safekeeping?"

The constable would and could. He had heard the name of Tommy Plummer. That gentleman, as a matter of fact, was just well enough known to cause some comment no matter where he went.

"It's him that was out with big Castracane when

Castracane grabbed the Salton Bay out of the hands of Jay Madison."

"Do you know where Castracane himself is now?" asked Kirby breathlessly.

"Ay," grinned the constable, "I hear that you'd been glad enough to know where he is—and that you got reason for wanting to know all about him. But the fact is, partner, that I dunno nothing about Castracane, and neither does Jay Madison, or you can bet that he wouldn't be waiting here for you or no man. He'd have some hired men with him, and he'd be streaking across the prairies for that horse. Why, man, they say that Madison worked for two whole years before he got the stallion, and then lost him on a fluke—"

"Castracane stole the horse, I suppose?" asked the deputy marshal hopefully.

"That's what some say, and that's what Jay Madison would like to have folks believe, but the way that I've heard it, and I've heard the yarn from two of the gents that was right there with Madison, he offered to sell the horse for a hundred dollars if the big boy could ride it. He thought that the Salton Bay would eat any man in the world alive!

"But he didn't eat Mad Anthony, and off he went, riding away with that big red horse under him. And that's the truth of the thing, as far as I can make it out, though of course Jay Madison swears that's a lie and that he never offered to sell the horse for a hundred dollars, or that he ever took the money that was offered to him for the stallion!"

"I'll believe Madison," said Diamond Jack slowly.

"Why," answered the constable, "of course that's the most comfortable way for you to believe!"

And he chuckled a little, until the Diamond wanted to take him by the throat.

"I'll get Plummer, though," said the constable, and he started off at once to do that good work.

As for Diamond Jack Kirby, he started now on the trail of the next most important piece of information which he had received; that was from Cherokee Dan, who had preceded him to the town, and it concerned little Muriel Lester.

He found Cherokee Dan sitting in at a game of poker with his gold-plated spurs lying on the table before him as part of his bet.

Kirby saw those spurs disappear in the playing of the next hand; then he tapped Cherokee on the shoulder, and a savage ugly face was turned up toward him.

"Here's fifty, Cherokee," said Diamond Jack. "Sit right back in that game and buy in your spurs."

Cherokee flashed one burning glance of admiration and gratitude at his friend and obeyed. And Diamond Jack said to him: "You might introduce me, Cherokee. This is a little farther west than I've ever been before, and I suppose that I'm not known here."

Cherokee was glad of the opportunity.

"Gents," said he, "this is Diamond Jack Kirby."

Sharp eyes flashed up at that famous name and centered steadily on the young gambler.

185

"I'll just stand by and see fair play all around," said Diamond Jack, and he smiled upon the others.

By the sour looks of two of them it was quite apparent that fair play was something less than Cherokee had been receiving. And now there was such a professional eye fixed upon the game that the couple dared not cheat.

In half an hour, Cherokee had won three pots. He left that game with a hundred and fifty dollars in his pocket and the spurs and watch which he had hazarded before the arrival of his master.

"Diamond," said he, "I was needing you terrible bad just then!"

"The fact is, Cherokee," said his employer, "that the best thing you can do is to keep away from any game of cards until you see that the rest all are drunk!"

"Drunk?"

"Because anyone except a drunk can always see your cards reflected in your eyes, Cherokee. You have no poker face and you ought never to play the game!"

This advice made Cherokee wince, because to be told that one cannot play poker is almost as crushing in the West as to be told that one cannot handle a gun or a horse.

"Now, Cherokee, what about this yarn that I had from you, that you thought you had spotted Muriel Lester here?"

"I only seen her once before," said Cherokee Dan, "and I may be wrong. But I think it may be the right girl, and you said you wanted to take all chances."

"I want to take all chances of finding her," agreed Diamond Jack with a sigh. "Now where have you thought that you saw her?"

"Down by the edge of town there's a hash joint—"

"Go ahead."

"Why, that's where she is."

"What?"

"Waitress in there—or a girl that has the same sort of a look to me."

"Slinging hash? Muriel Lester? Cherokee, you're just batty!"

"Ain't you going there?"

"I'll go there, but it's a wild-goose chase before ever I get there!"

CHAPTER XXVII

H E LEFT CHEROKEE DAN WITH DIRECTIONS TO LOOK up Jay Madison and Chick. In the meantime he started to find the restaurant where Cherokee thought that he had seen a girl who answered the description of Muriel Lester. At the first corner he came upon the same big Osage who had traded a pony and full accouterment for a bag of sugar cubes, now in the act of finishing off a flask of whisky for which, as it seemed, he had traded in two big painted buffalo robes. He reeled a little as he polished off the last drops, whooped with pleasure as the fire ate into his very spinal marrow and seared his brain, tilted the bottle in a vain effort to find another bit of the alcohol, and then shied the flask across the street and ran off down it, whooping.

Diamond Jack Kirby, as a deputy marshal, might well have invested some of his time and energy in apprehending this rambunctious redskin before damage was done, but Jack's interest in the law was purely perfunctory and personal. So he watched the Osage pass yelling from view, and rode on his way with a broad smile.

For he liked trouble, did Diamond Jack, and, being a master of men, he had often ruled the storm with an iron hand.

Now, when he had come to the quarter of the town where the restaurant was situated, he tethered his horse at the rack near the door and forthwith strode into the place.

It was between meal hours, and there was no one to be seen in it except a Negro boy who was busily at work with a pail of suds scrubbing down the floor. He was a ragged urchin who walled his eyes up at the tall stranger with a grin of appreciation for his inches and his good looks.

"Are you looking for chuck, general?" he asked.

"Anything will do for me," said Diamond Jack. "Ask the cook for a sandwich; that will be good enough."

"Him?" chuckled the boy. "Ask him? D'you know what he'd do?"

"And what would he do, then?"

"He's got a flatiron, and an old railroad lantern, and the handle of an ax, and two busted frying pans. They is all smashed up, them things, and they was all smashed by being heaved straight at my head!"

The Diamond grinned in appreciation.

"Let me see that cook, will you?" he demanded.

"It ain't hard to see him," said the boy. "You just push open that door and look!"

He broke into a gale of laughter. And Diamond Jack rose and opened the door in question. The odors of a kitchen rolled out to meet him, and then he saw a fat fellow with a round, red face, busy at work rolling out a quantity of dough for biscuits.

"Archie, you damn little—" began the cook as the door opened, and without a second glance he snatched the ax handle, which lay within convenient reach, and hurled it at the door. Diamond Jack Kirby sidestepped and let destruction go whirling on into the dining room.

Then the fat cook saw what he had nearly done and stood paralyzed with fright while Archie's merry screech sounded from the rear.

"Hey—sis—" gasped the fat cook, and he rushed for shelter behind a girl who was cutting bread at a corner table in the big room—a girl who was dressed in the cheapest of faded calico dresses, but who now turned and gave Diamond Jack Kirby a sight of Muriel Lester.

He expected to see her borne down with confusion and astonishment, but she only grew a little pale and

189

looked him quietly in the face while he advanced with his hands out.

"Why, my God, what's up?" gasped the cook.

And he saw his slavey and waitress leading this brilliant young giant out of the kitchen into the pantry.

"You damn near got blowed to Kingdom Come that time, I guess!" suggested Archie through the doorway.

"Kid," said the fat man, still too overcome to reply, "d'you know who that man is?"

"I dunno," said the Negro. "Do you?"

"Diamond Jack Kirby!"

At the sound of that famous name, which during the past few years had gripped the imagination of the West, Archie was clearly terrified.

"How does it come that you're still alive?" he asked.

"He seen Sis—he seen her—and she led him out like he was a calf with a ring through his nose!"

"Why," said Archie, "I always told you that she was something extra, and when she finishes telling him the way that you been treating her—"

The cook grew whiter still, glanced out the window, and then sat down heavily in a chair.

"And no railroad inside of three hundred miles!" was his first exclamation.

But Diamond Jack's thoughts at that moment were a thousand leagues away from the ax handle which had so nearly reached his head.

Muriel Lester, from the shadow of a corner, looked up to him with bright, fearless eyes, and she was saying:

"I wouldn't go back home to tell them that I had made a fool of myself. I wouldn't go back to that town, to be surrounded by a lot of spiteful gossip—heavens knows about what. So I just came farther west."

"How, Muriel? How in God's name did you get across the prairies?"

"I ran into a wagon train. A man named Parker was running it, and he took me along."

"Parker? Parker? Ah, I think Parker knew you belonged to—that you were engaged to me, Muriel?"

"Yes. Why?"

"I simply want to remember that—because it's interesting to me, and it might be interesting to Parker someday! But you came here—and you went to work—here—in this low—"

"It's not low, Jack. I don't mind it. I like it!"

"Working—with that fat fool—waiting on trash—"

"I don't mind. I like it."

"Drunken hounds pawing you about—"

"They can't touch me," said she, with a faint smile. "Do you know, Jack, that if the greatest man in the world came to this town and dared to speak an insulting word to me, or presumed to treat me the least bit carelessly, I would only have to crook my finger and twenty men would take up the trail of that man—with their guns, too, Jack. I tell you, in my mother's home I never was as well defended as I am here—I was never so free—I can walk down the streets at midnight, and I'm as safe as though I were sitting in a rocking chair in my father's parlor."

He frowned at her as he listened, for he felt that there might be a double meaning in what she had to say. Certainly, it could be taken to mean that she could not be coerced even by a person like himself.

"Well, Muriel," he told her, "I'm glad that's the way you've faced it down. I suppose it was natural for you to do it that way. All that I've been shocked by—you understand—was the fashion in which you left the house without so much as saying good-by to me."

She nodded, seriously.

"I understand," she said. "That was wrong. I've often regretted it. If I'd had the strength then that I have now, I should have waited and talked the thing out with you. But I didn't have the strength. I was afraid—"

"Afraid of a man who loves you, Muriel?"

"Afraid of your mother, Jack; terribly afraid of her, then, and a little bit afraid even now, at this distance. But I can tell you the whole story in a nutshell. I left your house, first and last, simply because I felt that you had hired one man to kill another. You know what I mean, of course."

"Of course, Muriel, I don't!"

"I had it from the lips of Tommy Plummer himself—that he was the man who had been hired to kill Anthony Castracane, he and a man named Chick. But he said that he was through with you and that he'd never do your dirty work again—"

She paused, and the moment of waiting lay with a

heavy burden upon Diamond Jack's heart. It was not in the mere accusation that he felt how completely he had lost her. It was rather in the lack of emotion with which she presented the ugly thing to him.

"Tommy Plummer," he said a little weakly, "is a rascal and a cheap liar. Everybody knows that. And, Muriel, you wouldn't damn a man to prison without giving him a chance to speak for himself, would you? This is worse than prison, because I love you—because you promised yourself to me—because I built my whole life around the expectation of having you."

She shook her head.

"Perhaps I'm not just," she said. "I'm not clever enough to explain everything or even to try to find out the whole truth. All I know is that I believed Tommy Plummer. I thought he seemed too simple to dare to make up such a thing. I believe that you *did* try to have Anthony Castracane murdered. And that's why I left—and why I'll never go back."

He had a wild impulse—which lasted only a moment—to seize her and carry her away with him. But he remembered that what she said was true. There was nothing that could be done. She had merely to crook her finger in this town, and there would be a hundred valiant fighting men rallied around her.

His grief turned into a foolish anger. And then the anger melted and left him weak because he knew that in spite of wounded pride he loved her more now than he had ever loved her in the past. So he stood for a moment frowning at the floor. Then he backed through the doorway, bowed formally to her, and was gone.

By this Muriel Lester knew that her real troubles were probably just about to begin!

CHAPTER XXVIII

J ACK KIRBY, IN THIS BLACK HUMOR, LEFT THE RESTAU-rant and took seat on his saddle again. He had accomplished two things. He had discovered exactly how low he stood in the esteem of the girl, and he had determined with all his might to raise himself in her estimation.

The means which he decided to use were low enough, but they were the first ones that suggested themselves to a furious and headstrong nature. In the first place, he would destroy Tommy Plummer, who had betrayed him to the lady of his heart. In the second place, he would reach Anthony Castracane if it cost him his own life to do so!

Coming down the street, therefore, his head filled with his own troubles and schemes, he heard a screech before him, and a huge Osage raced across the street brandishing a knife and pursuing a frightened white man on a horse. They passed from view around the first shed.

"What's up?" asked Diamond Jack of the grinning pedestrians.

"There's going to be a couple of killings in town

before night—that's all," was the answer. "Kohatunka is on the warpath and he won't stop until he's sunk a knife in somebody and got his head blown off."

"Who's Kohatunka?" asked Diamond Jack, a little curious, because he had admired the magnificent proportions of the warrior.

"Kohatunka—that's Big Crow—he's one of the Osage chiefs, and just lately he and some white man cleaned up a whole war party of Pawnees, and Big Crow came to town clogged with loot the other day. He's been cheated out of everything, now, down to the shirt on his back. All he's kept is his knife, and he's mighty anxious to use that. Oh, he'll be a dead Indian before long. If he comes near me, I'll not start with questions—I'll begin with bullets. He says that he doesn't care much what folks try to do to him because if a hand is laid on him, his white pal will come out from the prairies and clean up the whole town."

"Who's the white man? A squaw man?"

"Some two-gun Jerry that packs a couple of Colts and seems to know how to shoot in the newfangled way—"

"Wait a minute!" exclaimed Diamond Jack. "You don't mean fanning?"

"Shooting from the hip, so fast that you can hardly count the explosions—that's the way that the Osage has been describing it. Running Thunder they call him for the way that he handles his gats."

"Running Thunder? Running Thunder? I never

heard of that. And I thought that I knew of every man on the plains that could fan a revolver!"

Diamond Jack lifted his head again, and he frowned. For one capable of fanning a revolver was instantly someone to be closely counted over as a friend or as an enemy.

"What sort of a fellow? What else does the Osage say?"

"Oh, a lot of fool stuff, as usual. Everything dressed up and put in the hands of the Great Spirit, you understand? But it seems that Big Crow got his back against the wall, and that six Pawnees were about to claw him apart, two of them being on the cliff behind him, when along comes the white man, Running Thunder, and without asking no questions he just turns loose, shoots one of the Pawnees on the cliff, throws the other one over the edge of it, and then drops three of the other Pawnees faster than you can count, while Big Crow polishes off the last of 'em. That's the yarn as we got it. But I've lived on the plains for a long time, and I've never yet heard of any gent cleaning up five Pawnees in one bust, have you?"

Diamond Jack shook his head. His eyes were shining, now, as he listened to this chapter from an epic of the border, because he knew that he was listening to the deeds of a true hero and it expands the soul of one brave man to hear of the mighty labors of another.

"I would give a year of life," he said, "to have a chance to meet that Running Thunder. You couldn't get the real name of the white man out of the red-skin?"

"No. Maybe he didn't know. Anyway, it's probably just some damn renegade that's living with the Osages because he *has* to live with 'em!"

"What sort of a looking man?"

"You could hardly make out. Big Crow gets hysterical with joy every time he starts in telling about his white pal. He says that when this Running Thunder walks along his head is brushing along among the stars and the ground shudders under him."

"That's as much as to say that he's pretty tall and heavy."

"Exactly. You got to pare off nine tenths of their lingo to find out what they're talking about. It seems, according to Big Crow, that the Great Spirit, at the same time that he gave this gent guns that couldn't miss, gave him also the fastest horse in the world, which can run away from the wind and give even a lightning bolt a pretty close rub!"

Diamond Jack smiled and nodded.

"And the Great Spirit wouldn't do no halfway job. He matched up the color of the horse with the color of the gent—a red horse for the long red hair of the rider—"

Diamond Jack Kirby started in his saddle, violently.

"What's that?" asked the other. "Are you placing this gent?"

"A red horse, long red hair, using two guns from the hip—by God, there's only one man in the world that

197

could do all of those things!"

"And who's that?"

"Why, man, where have you been the past few weeks? Have you never heard of the Salton Bay, and Anthony Castracane that took the bay away from Jay Madison?"

"Hello! I think that you may have hit it! I told you that it was some damn renegade horse thief that was living with the Osages!"

Diamond Jack did not wait longer. He turned the head of his horse with an oath and a setting of his teeth. But two things had pleased him. One was the remark that the townsman of Fort Hendon had made—Anthony Castracane was a renegade horse thief! The other was that he had in the town an Indian brave who swore that if he were harmed, he would be saved by the intervention of an all-powerful white friend who, it seemed, must be none other than Anthony Castracane himself!

Now, it was not difficult to put the two items together. Here was Fort Hendon—it would serve as a trap, well manned with fighting fellows, with the whole weight of the military to back them up if necessary.

And yonder was the redskin who would serve as the bait to draw Mad Anthony into the trap. And so, when all was set and ready, Mr. Kirby trusted that he would bag his man without any great trouble—and when the man was bagged, would it be held seriously against him if he shot down a notorious horse thief?

All of these schemes drifted swiftly and sweetly through Mr. Kirby's clever mind, and then he set out to find his friend the constable.

That worthy gentleman had just completed the comfortable act of lodging Tommy Plummer in the jail.

"A damn tricky little feller with his guns," said the constable. "He near planted me, but his foot slipped as he turned to snag me, and the bullet went—here!"

He pointed to a double hole clipped neatly in the side of his coat.

"Oh, it's all right," went on the constable, "because then I managed to tap him on the head with my own gat, and he sat down quick and hard, you can believe me! That was the finish of the fight, of course, and so we carried him off to the jail and let him get his senses back in there!"

"You're a cool fellow, constable," said Diamond Jack. "If we had one man like you in each of these little fighting towns, there'd be an end of hoodlumism! But I'll tell you what—there's a bigger job than Plummer waiting for you!"

"You mean the Osage?" said the constable instantly. "My rule is to leave 'em for the military. You take and mix it up with an Indian and what happens? You get persecuted for having massacred one of 'em, if the news of it gets to anybody high up, and a lot of saps put up a moan about the poor redskin being drove desperate by border ruffians—and maybe if you're lucky you ain't sent to prison, but you have to mortgage your soul to pay your lawyer to keep your neck from being stretched. No, Diamond, I leave the red boys to the soldiers. They can clean up on them. I'd rather do without that kind of glory!"

Diamond Jack listened with a nod of appreciation. The constable was simple, but it was plain that he was not altogether a fool.

"You're right," said he. "I didn't mean in the first place that you ought to do the trick yourself. It's your town and it's your territory. But I'd as soon as not take a hand in this game myself. I'm a servant of the government, and it's up to me to help out where I can—"

"Hold on, Diamond, do you mean to say that you're going to tackle Big Crow yourself?"

"Why not, old timer? I'd like to have your moral support, though. Will you just come along and be on hand to bear witness that I didn't shoot him until I had to?"

"You're going to do him up clean, then?"

"I'm going to take him alive and put him in the jail," said Mr. Kirby, "unless the fool grows so rambunctious that I have to kill him. Will you come along?"

"Like I was going to a party," said the constable with a broad grin. "Because if you can take that Indian alive and put him in the jail, you're sure wasted out here on the plains, old timer. They had ought to be using you in the place of the whole Regular Army!"

CHAPTER XXIX

JUST ABOUT THIS TIME A BABEL OF WILD VOICES WAS raised not far away, and toward that noise the constable and the deputy marshal made their way.

Trouble was certainly up and they could guess that the big Osage was having his share of the fun.

When they got to the place they learned that they were right enough. A householder, seeing the half-naked brave wandering whooping down the center of the street, had taken it upon himself to loose a great savage mastiff and sick it at the redskin.

That would have been very well, in nine cases out of ten, because the dog was a fierce brute, specially trained to fight armed men. But when it tackled Big Crow, it was showing its teeth at a man without fear, with the strength of a gorilla, and the savagery of another wild beast. The fight was like that between a town dog and a wolf. For as the huge mastiff charged, the red man bounded to one side, avoided the rush, and then literally heaved the mastiff off the ground by the scruff of its neck and, holding it in that fashion with one prodigious arm, drove home his hunting knife to the dog's heart.

Then he marched ahead straight for the house of the white man who had sent the dog to the attack.

He kicked open the gate, just as the owner of the house opened fire with a double-barreled rifle. But the first shot missed, and before the second one could be discharged, the brave was inside the field of fire and at the front door of the house. He found the door well secured, so he heaved the carcass of the mastiff through the first window and climbed in after it, while the brave white man only stayed to discharge the second barrel of his rifle wildly and then fled out of the rear door and abandoned the field of battle to the victor.

After this, Big Crow began to smash and destroy right and left while he conducted a feverish search for the whisky which his stomach was craving with such a vast lust.

A circle of neighbors gathered, no man being brave enough to enter and stop the destruction, while the owner of the house stood nearby, wringing his hands and moaning with rage and agony, but afraid to attempt a rescue.

The deputy marshal and the constable heard this tale of woe and took in the situation at a glance, and Diamond Jack did the talking.

He said to the householder: "If you were half a man, you would never have sicked a dog at anyone. But after you'd done it, you would have met him man to man in an equal fight, or if you didn't have the courage to try that, you would at least have stood in your doorway and fought it out with guns.

"But since you wouldn't do any of those things, then it seems to me that you don't deserve the house and the good luck which you've had. I hope to God that

Big Crow breaks everything in the house. But in the meantime, it's my job to go in and stop him if I can. Constable, will you back me up?"

There are various sorts of bravery. There is the courage which fights back when attacked. There is the courage which goes hunting for trouble. There is the courage which ventures in the hunt against the charge of wild beasts. But greatest of all is the courage of the man who goes single-handed to find another, and desperate, man, and try to apprehend him.

There was such a feeling of awe through the little crowd that watched the deputy marshal stride through the gate and approach the open door through which such sounds of pandemonium came, that something like a groan went up from it.

And two or three of the boldest started slowly on behind him. They had been shamed into playing the man—and partly they were merely playing follow-the-leader. But still, they did not get on very fast, and before they passed the door they saw the battle begin, reach its climax, and then its end.

For when Big Crow saw the deputy marshal coming, he left his work of tenderly opening a chest of drawers with an ax and flung that weapon at Diamond Jack's head. It missed him with the steel blade, but the spinning long haft clipped him across the eyes and brought him to his knees, half blinded, stung, and altogether surprised.

Big Crow paused only long enough to utter one thrilling, soul-satisfying war whoop, and went in with his knife to slice open the throat of this new victim and add a most beautiful scalp to his collection.

But when he lunged for Diamond Jack's neck, the latter managed to twist to his feet and to one side past the darting blade.

He closed with Big Crow, putting all the desperate force in his body into his good right hand. That blow traveled straight to the point of the chin.

It stopped the big Indian's charge, set him back on his heels, and made the knife drop with a clatter from his unnerved fingers.

He lurched ahead, his huge red arms fumbling and spreading for a hold, but he had against him an enemy almost as large and strong as himself, and with a brain that was not in the slightest degree befogged with cheap whisky. Inside the pawing arms of the Indian smote Diamond Jack. His right hand spatted upon the chief's drum-like chest just above the heart. His left whipped clean and true against the base of his jaw, and the knees of the Osage forgot their duty and began to bend.

It was no sudden fall. You cannot strike down an oak with a single blow. But the control of his muscles had departed from the Osage. His jaw sagged. His legs shook and bent. His brow was shadowed with a heavy frown.

So he went down to the floor, and before he could rise again the constable, running up hastily from behind, had dropped the noose of a rawhide lariat over the chief's head.

That was the end of the battle.

And it made such a furor in the town as though deaths and heroism were not almost everyday features of the life of the place. But this was different.

One does not go to capture rattlesnakes with bare hands. And one does not advance in the same fashion against a knife-bearing Indian with nothing but one's fists to work with.

Mr. Kirby did not pause to explain that he had by no means intended to use his fists only. His fixed intention had been to tag Big Crow with a half-inch chunk of lead, and afterward to gather in what was left of him, trusting that what was left might be alive and wriggling enough to serve as bait for the trap which was to catch Anthony Castracane. But that plan had been spoiled by the ax handle that flicked across his head and dropped him into a thousand fathoms of darkness, from which he had recovered just in time to hear the end of the Indian's war cry and to see the flash of naked steel before his face.

After that he had fought to save his life, and his bare hands were quicker weapons than a gun.

That was the true explanation, but Mr. Kirby did not pause to make it. There was no reason in the world why the town of Fort Hendon should not have a little harmless pleasure in worshiping a hero, and he was even perfectly willing that they should worship him. It might fit in with what was to happen later, according to his plans. The more of a hero he was now, the less chance would there be that people might place a false construction upon what he intended to do to Anthony Castracane.

In the meantime, his knuckles were swollen where they had driven home against Kohatunka's huge ribs or craggy jawbone. He accompanied the captive to the jail and there he looked over the matter with some satisfaction.

Yonder lay Tommy Plummer behind the bars—Tommy Plummer, smiling with speechless fury and the coldness of settled hatred when he saw his persecutor—and in the steel cage next to him was placed the Indian.

Kohatunka, released from the lariat, bounded at the bars of his cage, wrenched at them with a violence that threatened to make his muscles burst through the thin drawn skin over them, and then, discovering that they were fixed and firmest steel, immovable and unbendable in spite of their slenderness, he yawned, stretched himself, looked around upon the curious whites with contemptuous eyes, and straightway curled himself up on the bare cell floor like a dog and went to sleep.

There he would remain in his slumber for many hours, and not until he wakened would Kohatunka have a chance to reflect upon his disgrace and upon his misery.

"Are you comfortable, Tommy?" asked the deputy marshal, at the bars of the second prisoner's cage.

Tommy Plummer lighted his pipe without haste and blew forth a cloud of smoke, through which he answered:

"It ain't going to work, old timer. It ain't going to work. Who's the next one that you'll want in this here jail? It'll be Castracane, won't it? And lemme tell you that when you try to put hands upon him, he'll lick you again, Jack, just as he licked you before. He'll thrash you where the rest of the world that didn't enjoy the first fun can have a good look at the second."

So said Tommy Plummer, and for the moment he certainly had the victory. Mr. Kirby was so immensely annoyed that he could not help but allow a hand to steal toward the butt of a revolver. And Tommy, watching, laughed with a loud and fiendish glee.

So Diamond Jack left the jail with a good deal of haste. He had seen that the cells were fairly strong. He had seen that the constable had the keys and that the constable was an honest man. He had seen that the jail was to be well guarded against a rescue.

So all of his preliminary labors were completed, and it remained for him to sit back and wait for the ripening of his plot and the rising of the fish to the bait.

He had only to clean his guns and wait. And he trusted implicitly that before another week was out he would have the satisfaction of looking down into the dead face of the man who had wrecked his love affair and banished pretty Muriel Lester from his life.

CHAPTER XXX

WHEN THAT FRIGHTENED CROWD WAS GATHERED around the house which Big Crow was wrecking in his search for possible hidden whisky, there was one spectator who did not care to let himself be seen. He was another Osage, who had heard that Kohatunka was about to get into serious trouble, and when he saw that there were far too many whites on hand for him to render any valuable service to his chief, he hid behind a hedge and watched, and saw the tall man, Diamond Jack Kirby, enter the house and come out again, victorious, with Big Crow borne helplessly behind him.

The Osage followed in the distance, and saw his chief committed to the jail. He took note of the position of the building and all that was around it. He closed his eyes, and opening them again made sure that he had checked off everything in his mental image of the place, for he was a young brave with a reputation to make, and not a single scalp to his credit, and therefore he wished to appear as well as possible in the eyes of the war leader of his nation, Munnepuskee.

After that he headed for the place where he had left his pony and in another instant was scouring across the plains toward the Osage tribe.

He had a twenty-four-hour journey before him, and

when he reached the village he headed straight for the tepee of He Who Knows No Fear.

He found before the tent two warriors, lance in hand, who barred his entrance.

"Running Thunder makes medicine in the lodge of the big chief," they told him softly.

And at the same time a soft chorus of wonder rolled from the tent, as if to attest that Running Thunder's medicine was found to be marvelous indeed in the eyes of those privileged to watch inside.

"I bring sad news to Munnepuskee," said the messenger.

The guards looked at the bloody flanks of the pony which had carried the brave to the village and nodded seriously. Then one of them stepped aside and plucked away a naked boy who was peeking under the edge of the tepee at the ceremony within.

"After all, it is white medicine," said one of them. "You may pass in!"

The messenger cautiously lifted the flap and entered the lodge.

He found inside a picture which would have stirred the heart of Abdullah Khan. For there were the oldest and the wisest and the bravest Osage chiefs seated in a circle, their feet crossed beneath them, their eyes feverishly intent upon the tall form of Mad Anthony Castracane, who stood beside the smoky fire.

From his hands there arose what seemed to the eyes of the messenger, unaccustomed at first to the dim light within the tepee, a fountain of sparkling water.

But instantly he was aware that it was flashing steel, and not water at all. For half a dozen knives were whirring upward from the fingers of great Abdullah's pupil, and not the Khan himself could have performed the trick with more subtle ease.

Juggling was a novelty among the Osage tribe. Certainly never had red men gaped more widely and childishly at any marvel than they did at this one.

Presently a seventh item was added to the fountain of gleaming steel, and that item was a little wicker disk which had once formed the bottom of a basket. It floated up and down, gently and rhythmically, until presently it whirled off to the side. There was a gasp of surprise from the Indians. For would the white magician be able to recall the flying disk to his hands, now that it had fallen away at such an angle from the perpendicular?

No, it reached the height of its ascent and began to waver. It tottered in the air and sank toward the ground—

There was another sound of caught breath, and then a shout of astonishment and pleasure. For one of the six knives had flown like a streak of light from the hand of the white man, and piercing the wicker disk it pinned it quivering against one of the tent poles. The Osages bent back and forth and gasped with joy.

Suppose that that disk had been the heart of a Pawnee warrior—their joy could not have been any greater.

Another knife darted from the magician's hand. It pierced the mat, it pierced the pole, and hung humming beside its companion.

Another, another, and another followed. . . .

And behold, around the little piece of wicker there were six knives arranged in a symmetrical circle, and the hands of the white man were empty!

There was first a little breath of silence, and then all eyes turned to the most important man in the circle, so that he might speak first. Munnepuskee arose and lifted his hand and raised his head.

"Behold, comrades," said he, "that the Great Spirit lives in the hand of Running Thunder, and while he is with us we are safe from all our enemies. The Pawnee wolves howl and gnash their teeth, but they dare not come near the village of the Osages because they fear the thunder that lies in the hand of our friend. We have seen what his medicine can do. I say that the Pawnees are not cowards to stay away from us, for if they came it would only prove that they had become fools!"

There was a universal nodding of heads at this pronouncement. Plainly the warriors agreed with all their hearts that it would have been the sheerest folly to encounter the craft and might of Running Thunder in battle.

They stood up, one after the other. They went to Castracane and they thanked him for his kindness in letting them see one of the little secrets of his cunning. They had already prized him, they said, more than their own best braves. But now they knew that the

Great Spirit was never far from the man whom he favored.

In the midst of this talk, the messenger found the way to the war chief and gave him his news briefly, and yet telling all, just as a sensible Indian warrior should do when he reports a national calamity.

And such, indeed, was this report. Kohatunka had always been one of the nation's foremost braves, but since the day when he brought in seven red and fresh Pawnee scalps, he had filled the eye of the people almost as much as the great white man whom he had brought back with him.

And now this great warrior was snatched away from them!

Munnepuskee frowned as black as night.

In that tepee he could not vent his rage or his disappointment, because in that tepee his friend, the white chief, was now receiving the admiration of the best men of the nation, so Munnepuskee left the tepee and rode through the village on his fastest horse and far onto the prairie. When the wind of a galloping horse was in his face, his thoughts were always most clear and active.

What could he do?

Gather his braves together and with them raid the white man's town and force them to liberate Big Crow?

He thought of that with his teeth set and his eyes flashing. But then he sighed. For he and his men had not been far off on the day when the guns of the fort had made thunder. He knew that it was bad medicine to encounter in battle, and the ranks of the Osage warriors had been constantly thinned by battle with many tribes far more numerous than they. He had not the power for such a coup, and he admitted it to himself with bitterness of heart, you may be sure.

Now, when Munnepuskee had ridden the first strength out of his pony, he turned back with his heart and his brain empty of ideas.

He would call upon the oldest and the wisest men in the village to give him their council. But he made that determination without hope.

He had heard councils called before this, but he had never known them to solve such a knotty problem as this one!

He returned to the city. His people already knew all the evil tidings. He passed Big Crow's tepee, and in front of it he saw the hero's old grandfather with his back turned upon the world and his robe gathered over his head; and from the inside of the tepee he could hear the wailing of the three squaws who called Kohatunka master, and the screeching of a frightened child.

It made the darkness in the war chief's soul still deeper, and he went on to his tent.

It was empty now. But here and there at convenient distances he could see the warriors gathered, expecting the council which would be summoned in this crisis. And yonder and yonder were groups of the young braves beginning the war dance, breaking the evening stillness with their wild whoops.

But war whoops would not undo the steel locks behind which the white men had put away Big Crow. Munnepuskee knew this, and he bit his lips. Then he called two boys to him and he sent them away to summon a half dozen of the wisest heads in the nation. Because great numbers do not make great wisdom, as the chief very well knew.

He himself retired to the back of his tepee and straightway smudged his face with black paint, made of grease and soot commingled, so that he would be able to receive the council in the garb of mourning.

Then, one by one, the councilors arrived and took their seats gravely around the fire.

"The word has been spread through the nation," said Munnepuskee. "You know why I have called you. Already you have been thinking of wise schemes. I have called you to tell me what they may be. Let the first man speak who has found a thought that may help Kohatunka to come back to us!"

He waited, and the silence extended dismally through the tepee.

At length, the oldest and the most withered of the chiefs said:

"In this same tepee did we not see the magic of Running Thunder? Let us know what our friend can do for Big Crow. Perhaps he will have a medicine which will undo the ropes that hold Big Crow and bring him back to us!"

CHAPTER XXXI

O F COURSE DROWNING MEN CLUTCH AT STRAWS; and though it was at once pointed out by Munnepuskee that Running Thunder could hardly be asked to act against people of his own color, still there was nothing better to be suggested than to make the request of the white man. So Munnepuskee himself was delegated to go forth and bring the big fellow to the war council.

Munnepuskee did not need to ask many questions to find out where Running Thunder might be at that moment. Wherever the young men of the nation were assembled, there Running Thunder was sure to be. He was like a rising sun, which called all eyes after him among the youth of the Osages. And Munnepuskee found him now on a broad, level strip of green in a depression by the banks of the river. It was a sort of playground for the children of the tribe; but more than children were there, now.

Munnepuskee, riding his war horse over the brow of the hill, looked down on what he thought at first to be an alarming melee. For he saw three young men of the tribe engaged in a violent contest with Running Thunder himself, wrestling with him, hand to hand! And as the knot swayed back and forth, and the crowded spectators shrieked with excitement, Munnepuskee gasped with fear lest this should be an attack on their white friend.

He even cast a frightened glance upward, half expecting that the Great Spirit, flying to the help of his favorite, would be seen as a dark cloud loaded with lightning in the heart of the sky. But the sky was clear, and looking down into the hollow again, Munne-puskee made sure that this was no savage contest but a mere friendly wrestling match.

He hurried his horse on, forgetful for the moment of all the anxiety which had lodged in his mind a moment before, and only anxious to have a close view of the fun.

And what amazed him most of all was that any man, even Running Thunder, could maintain himself for an instant against three stalwarts of this nation of giants. For though the Cheyennes were more active and perhaps more daring warriors, and the Sioux fleeter of foot, and the Comanches far better on horseback, still there had never been a tribe on the prairies which could furnish men capable of struggling hand to hand with the Osage men. Inches taller and pounds heavier than all the rest of the plains race, the Osage loved to train and use their strength, and wrestling was one of their favorite diversions.

But still, as the quartet whirled here and there, the war chief could see that the white man maintained his feet!

These were not famous warriors who were wrestling against him, to be sure. But they were matured youths, as strong as veterans, and far more supple and swift.

Not one of the three but stood fully as tall as Anthony Castracane. Not one of the three but possessed an equal bulk with the big white man. Not one of the lot but had distinguished himself many and many a time on this same greensward, wrestling with his peers and showing a mastering knowledge of all of the science of that strenuous game.

But the war chief, pressing up to the outskirts of the crowded spectators, saw the tangled knot of struggling men suddenly dissolve. One of the Osage contestants had tumbled head over heels, rolling to a distance, and the other two staggered back from Mad Anthony.

He stood, not spent and exhausted by his tremendous effort against odds, but with his stern, ugly head thrown back while he laughed with the joy of the contest and the wind from across the prairies combed out his long red hair above his shoulders.

Like the Osage wrestlers, he was stripped to the waist. And Munnepuskee, a clever enough judge of powerful anatomy, was amazed at what he saw. He had heard before, from the young men who had gone swimming with the white man, that Running Thunder was a giant to behold. But he had not been prepared for this might of arched chest, and for the rippling muscles that leaped and glided along Castracane's extended arms, so that he seemed magnified in size. He seemed to become a giant, and the Osage trio fell back around him, baffled, and eyed him with bewilderment.

To be checked by one man was enough to have maddened them, had it been any other man than this. But Running Thunder was the proved friend of the nation, the proved hero of the warpath, before whose skill great warriors crumpled like dead leaves; therefore they could afford to be surpassed by him in a friendly game. But for one to stand against three—could that be skill and strength? Was it not rather the Wonderful Medicine of the white man?

Now the fallen man had bounded to his feet with a yell, and all three returned to the attack with excited whoops, like three great, hungry, cunning wolves.

They danced about the white man from three sides. And then at a signal, all rushed upon him, all reached for holds.

What would happen now? Munnepuskee fairly sweated with excitement. Three young giants had closed on one. Three pairs of mighty hands were fixing themselves with tremendous grips on Mad Anthony's body.

What happened was miraculous in the eyes of the chief. He saw the white man pluck away the gripping hands of one brave with consummate ease; saw him gather that unfortunate and lift him above his head at the full length of his terrible arms. With a wrench and a whirl, Mad Anthony tore himself away from the hands of the other two and, striding a pace closer to the high bank of the river, cast his victim bodily into the air.

Over and over turned the Osage in the air with a

frightened yell and then crashed into the deep water with a shout stifled midway on his lips.

The other two were already clinging to Mad Anthony once more. But two were far different from three. How it happened, the keen eye of the chief could not exactly make out. But one of the pair was presently stretched helpless upon his back. The last of the trio bounded to his feet and fled, with Anthony in hot pursuit.

But that race did not last long. One man cannot be invincible in all things, and Castracane's feet could not keep up with this prairie racer.

Away went the Osage like a winging bird, and Castracane gave up the pursuit and came panting and laughing back to the green lawn, just as the half-drowned young brave staggered up the bank from the river.

Here was a time when game might well turn to earnest and knives might be drawn—for these young men had not seen the latest magic which Running Thunder had worked in the tepee with knives!

No, there was not the slightest hard feeling. He saw Castracane walk up to his defeated antagonists and take their hands. All was laughter and merriment. Yes, and more than that. For the white man was making no mystery of the thing which he had done. While the worshiping boys and young warriors crowded around him, he was showing new grips to them—grips which Barney and Kilpatrick had taught him so thoroughly and so long before.

The fugitive Osage returned and shyly took his conqueror's hand in his turn.

"You are an eagle, Two Buffalo," said Running Thunder, for he had picked up a good deal of the native tongue by this time. "You were not touching the ground as you ran away from me!"

And Two Buffalo laughed with as much pleasure as though he had taken a new scalp!

No wonder that the heart of He Who Knows No Fear swelled with pleasure as he watched this scene. He pressed through the crowd, and presently he was leading the white man apart.

There was much policy in Munnepuskee.

He began: "Your friend, Big Crow, sends you many greetings, Running Thunder. He bids you take his tepee and all that is in it!"

"His tepee?" said Anthony, still panting from his work. "Why should I have that? Has he taken a new one?"

"He will never use his old one again," said Munnepuskee. "By this time, the flames are withering the body of Kohatunka—"

"Ha!" cried Anthony. "The Pawnees have sneaked down and clipped him off! Munnepuskee, why have you not called out a party to join the trail? I shall be among them!"

"Good, my friend," said the chief. "We know that the heart of Running Thunder is the same as the heart of the Osage, but this is a thing in which even Running Thunder cannot help. It is his own people who have taken Big Crow. Whether they will burn him or hang him with a rope around his neck, so that his soul will go to hell forever and never be able to breathe, we cannot guess."

The white man was stunned.

"Big Crow has gone to Fort Hendon," he said, "and there is trouble for him there?"

"Great trouble," said the war chief. "They have put him into a strong house with iron bars across the windows."

"They have put Big Crow in jail!" translated Anthony. "What had he done?"

"Nothing," said the chief. "They had already robbed him of all that he had won on the warpath from the Pawnees."

"I know what they have done," said Anthony Castracane. "They have robbed him first, and then they have put him in jail because he asked for the plunder which they took away from him. Listen to me, Munnepuskee. I am not a man to make many promises, but I swear to you that I shall go to Fort Hendon and smash in the door of that jail and bring back Big Crow to you as safe and sound as when he left your village!"

CHAPTER XXXII

THERE HAS BEEN SO MUCH WRITTEN AND SAID ABOUT Mad Anthony's historic visit to Fort Hendon that it is very hard to separate the truth from the fiction and discover exactly what Anthony did and what he did not do. But what is most certain is that when he was an hour out from the village of the Osages, he descried a body of Indian horse cutting in behind, between him and the town of the friendly redskins.

He took out his glass and examined them with care. They had the same cropped hair which the Osages wore, but they lacked a good deal of the stature of those mighty warriors; and when he looked more carefully at them, even in the distance he was sure that they must be Pawnees.

There had been a strong rumor passing through Munnepuskee's village that the Pawnees were constantly keeping war parties close to the town, and that they were waiting for half of a fair chance to get at the red-headed marauder who had killed five of their tribesmen, but Anthony Castracane had not paid any attention to this.

Neither would he consent when Munnepuskee had begged him, on leaving the town, to take with him a sufficiently strong bodyguard of Osages to guarantee his safe passage to Fort Hendon. For he was impatient to be away. It seemed to him that Big Crow must have been shamefully treated. What the Osage might have done in the town to draw down wrath on his head did not bother Anthony; he was not a logical fellow, as may have been seen before. He had the simplicity of a child, as even the Indians had been able to see. And he knew that white men had been most cruel and unjust to him, and therefore he took it for granted that they were cruel and unjust to others—to Big Crow, for instance. So he reasoned from a few sketchy premises to a most sweeping conclusion, and he rode on toward the fray hastily, hungrily, anxious to tear Big Crow out to freedom, and feeling in his great hands a might of muscle and of anger commingled which would snap steel bars like rotten laths.

That was the mood of the red-headed avenger as he started out from the town. And when he saw the Pawnees cutting in across the line of his retreat, he merely drew rein a little on the stallion and swept the plain more thoroughly with his glass.

He was not long in seeing exactly the trouble in which he had placed himself. For now that the Pawnees had thrown an arm between him and his retreat, they showed their hands plainly.

Besides the body of riders behind him, there were three other groups scurrying in toward him from different points of the compass, scattering rapidly so as to join the wings of their flying lines and form a closed circle around the white man.

Anthony Castracane's heart increased in speed and might, but there was no tremor in him, and his head went up, and his eye sparkled in a way which the world was to know more familiarly, in a little time, you may be sure.

Then he cast himself well forward, raised his weight in the stirrups, and called on the Salton Bay.

There had grown up between them a feeling of perfect comradeship during the stay among the Osages. After the first grim battle in which the stallion tasted the strength of his new master's hand and knee, he had never had cause to flinch from a single stroke of Mad Anthony's hand or heel.

For Anthony reasoned as a child might have done:

"I myself often learned slowly! Abdullah Khan used to go half mad over my slowness, and Kilpatrick was wild because I couldn't learn the straight left as fast as people should—so why shouldn't the Salton Bay have time, also?"

And he gave the big horse time and patience and kind encouragement, and though the stallion still had in his eye some of the wild fire of freedom, which would never leave it, indeed, so long as there was a spark of life in body and soul, still he had submitted his heart to his master as well as his body.

He called on the Salton Bay, and the stallion turned into a red streak that glanced across the prairie. Then, with rifle unlimbered, Anthony fired at a chosen spot on the Indian line. He missed a man with his first shot, but he struck a horse. He missed a horse with his second, but he struck a man.

And now the order of the Pawnees was quite broken

up. They felt that the white man was certainly aiming at that selected point for which he was firing. They threw all further discretion to the winds and they rode like mad to make for the threatened point in time to avert the danger of pressure.

So Anthony saw them gather, bunching swiftly on their agile ponies. He was very close, now. He could see their faces clearly, and their war yells were ringing in his ears. And he could even see the streaks of blood which were springing out on the bodies of the ponies where the cruel riders lashed them with their whips.

It was very like boxing, he thought. A few blows aimed hard and fast at the head will make the other fellow raise a high guard and quite forget that there is a body to protect, also. Then a well-chosen driving punch for the short ribs goes home, and the fight is ended.

So it was with the Pawnees. They bunched at the threatened spot, but Mad Anthony had whirled the stallion around and was speeding away faster than ever to the left.

I suppose that he had had one chance in five, before. He had one chance in three, now, and he was using it for all that it was worth. Never did a horse run as the great bay strode along now. The prairie flowed like water beneath him, the grass blurred to streaks by his speed.

And the Pawnees, seeing their mistake, screeched with rage at the trick. They brought their horses up standing. They whirled the ponies around on two legs, the forefeet beating at the air in protest, and with digging heels and lashing whips they scampered to get closer to the fugitive.

Had there been adequate firearms in that party, Mad Anthony would have been riddled, before this, with leaden pellets. But there were only a few rusty old muskets that missed sadly as they roared at the white man.

There were arrows in plenty, however—arrows which at close range could be sometimes driven clear through the body of a grown buffalo bull. And those arrows were hissing through the air about him in most ugly fashion.

He met them with a rolling fire from his revolvers.

The shortened reins he gripped between his teeth. There was a Colt extended in either hand, and now he had range which was close enough for pistol fire. He emptied the first two guns. He saw two Pawnees down—one of them surely a dead man—and before that withering blast of fire from Running Thunder, the Pawnee's advance curled up and sank back with yells of dismay.

It was not a wide gap through which big Anthony whirled. It was not more than a forty-yard reach from the Pawnees on the right to the Pawnees on the left, but that was really enough for Anthony, and he went through like a log whipped down a raging flume.

Not untouched. A raking arrow flicked its sharp head along the side of his temple, and blood flowed freely down.

But a little blood would not kill.

He had the empty set of guns back in the holsters and a new pair in his hands, and as the Pawnees closed in on him, now, rushing into his wake, he turned in the saddle and let them have it again.

They were checked for a second—a second is a vast distance to a man under arrow fire. And before they rallied to follow again, the Salton Bay was making clear running across the prairies and with every stride pulling comfortably away from the red men.

Their voices still roared hoarsely in Castracane's ears, but the roaring died down until it was more like the dim shouting of the waves along a far-off coast. The Pawnees turned into black silhouettes, bobbing small and smaller against the sky line—and then the bay was striding on beyond the reach of danger, his head high, his body covered with sweat, to be sure, but his breathing perfectly easy and his strength absolutely untouched. Mad Anthony marveled joyously at such might of limb and heart. Well might Jay Madison be eating his heart out at the thought of what once had been his and had been snatched away!

Yet Anthony knew that all fear was not at an end.

The Pawnees would cling to that trail like bulldogs. They would never leave it, if it carried them a thousand miles. For they had lost five men before, from this same hand, and on this day another of their braves had been killed, to say nothing of dead horses and wounded heroes.

Oh, they would be sure to cling to the trail with all the might of their souls and the speed of their tough ponies.

So Anthony rode straight ahead, keeping the bay at a long, easy, stretching trot, or at a swinging canter, which the wild-trained creature could keep up as frictionlessly as the stride of a running greyhound.

He reached the banks of the Hendon River. He crossed that stream, swimming the bay across the deeper portion, and then he climbed back into the saddle and turned straight down the banks of the river toward the distant fort.

That night he made three short halts, for less than an hour each time. But the bay could graze and rest, and he himself could stretch himself on the soil, his arms thrown out crosswise, and relax.

Jumbo the strong man had taught him how to do this, and had shown him that five minutes of utter relaxation may be more valuable than hours of trouble-tumbled sleep, so called.

And he needed all the strength that was at his command for the wild work that might be before him the next day.

How *much* he was to need it, even Anthony could not guess. And so, just in the rosy light of the late afternoon, he saw the dark, squat outline before him of the town where he was to make history and make it with a vengeance!

CHAPTER XXXIII

Now, when Mad Anthony was drawing toward the fort, I like always to think of how the forces were gathering together against him in that place. Because when a race is to be run, one wishes to know who has entered the horses, and what weights they carry, and how their masters have planned their running, and the capabilities of each jockey. That is necessary, and particularly if one has put up money on one of the contestants, so that with one's glasses one may follow the shining beauties as they move around the track, each too glorious and too noble to be worthy of defeat.

How much more necessary, then, to know just what were the odds against which Mad Anthony was to struggle in Fort Hendon, and write his name in red letters that have not yet faded from the memory of the old timers in the West, and that never will fade until great deeds of hand and heart are considered worthless things by degenerate men.

I suppose that, take them all in all, a more formidable group was never assembled than Diamond Jack Kirby had brought together on this afternoon at the jail.

If you begin with the Diamond himself, you may be apt to underrate him, recalling how he was beaten so shamefully by Mad Anthony, but then you must remember that never before that instant had he found a man who could live for an instant before him. And that his prowess and his cold nerve had not decreased in the interim, there was for witness the fashion in which he had taken Big Crow with his bare hands—a thing which paralyzed Fort Hendon—a thing which made Fort Hendon troop daily to the jail that it might gape at the thews of the Osage giant, and then more properly appreciate the valor and the skill and the might of the white man who had conquered the Indian hero.

They thought of the Osage's many scalps, and then they knew that Diamond Jack was truly one man in a million.

This was Diamond Jack Kirby. And he had to sharpen the keenness of his soul for fighting, the sense of the one crushing and shameful defeat which he had endured, and, besides that, the knowledge that the girl he loved had been wooed away from him by Anthony Castracane.

You must not think, either, that because the Diamond liked money and power first of all, he was not capable of truly loving. And all the love that he had borne to the girl was now transferred by a cunning alchemy into surpassing poisonous hate for Mad Anthony.

With Diamond Jack, as he walked to the door of the jail, went Chick.

He was a soured man, was Chick. His square-jawed face had not smiled for weeks. And there was good reason. For he, a fighting man, whose whole life and joy was in his battles, had been known to turn his back upon danger and run away—not from an over-whelming mob, but from a single man!

It was such a thing as Chick could not think about. It turned him mad with despair and grief. And he had forgotten his swaggering ways and his wild manners. He no longer shouted and cursed. His speech was rev-erent. His manner was sedate. He walked with a sober step. With a soft voice he addressed his requests to strangers.

And every day, from morning to night, until his wrist turned numb and his fingers forgot their cun-ning, Chick was blazing away pounds and pounds of costly ammunition at targets of all kinds.

He would ride past a fence line and shoot in rapid succession at alternate posts. He would toss stones or sticks into the air and try to break them with a bullet. He would ride with his back turned and then at full gallop whirl about and fire at the mark.

He would run on foot, shooting over his shoulder or to the side. He would drop to the ground, snatching out a gun and firing as he fell. And then, when all was ended for the day, he would sit for hours and hours, meditating upon the errors and the mistakes which he had made, and striving to conceive a higher standard for the next session of practice.

And at night, when the darkness had fallen across the steep edges of the sky and the black ball of the world was hurtling through the infinite space of the stars, then Chick sat by himself, sadly, never speaking. But out of his heart there arose a prayer to the Creator begging that he might have a chance to vindicate his honor and that God would give into his hands a chance to kill Anthony Castracane or to die fighting heroically against that great man.

Such was Chick become.

Marshal Bisbee had said: "Chick will either join the ministry or kill ten men within the next year!"

And all others who knew him echoed the same sentiments.

Chick and big Jack Kirby found at the jail numerous other visitors curious to see the prisoners. They also saw there the other two members of their sworn band. The first was Jay Madison, swarthier and darker of eye than ever.

No razor had touched his face since he swore that he would recover the Salton Bay or die in the attempt, and now he bristled like a porcupine. He looked a little ridiculous until one chanced to meet his eye. And then all sense of mirth departed. He was a little more dangerous than a nest of rattlesnakes or a den of wild tigers.

No one had ever loved Jay Madison. It was said that his own mother had denounced him when he was only a boy. And certainly he had gone through his life respected for his courage, but dreaded like the incarnation of the devil. For there was no joy and there was no kindness in his heart, and it was known that he was as treacherous as the fiend!

Even Diamond Jack Kirby feared this man. He was so full of passion, now, that he had grown as silent as Chick. Some day that passion would break forth, but never until he saw Anthony Castracane.

Such was the third of these men who had sworn to give up their lives, for one reason or another, to the destruction of Anthony Castracane.

The fourth was, in some ways, the most dangerous antagonist of all.

Because the instant that one glanced at Madison or Chick or at Kirby's beautiful face and handsome form, one knew that here was a fellow who must be counted upon. Cherokee Dan, however, was of a different cut. If you saw his back, he looked like a weak stripling. And even when you saw his face, he hardly seemed worthy of note. It was only when evil emotion rose in Cherokee Dan that you knew him for what he was.

He had been among the Cherokees, in the days of his youth, it was said, and there he had married a squaw and lived as an Indian. It was related of Cherokee that on the days when he returned to the tribe to join in a festival, or perhaps to take himself another wife from the tribe, for a brief period, he unrolled a paper and brought out eleven scalps, and that five of those scalps were never taken from the head of black or red man! But that was hearsay. What was more definitely known was that though among the Cherokees he had proved himself a terrible warrior and a great hand on the warpath for the devising of cunning and murderous tricks, still even those wild Indians could not endure the hell fire which was continually burning in his breast. And he had to leave them and go back to the whites.

It happened that Anthony Castracane had interrupted him in the exhibition of one of his little acts of cruelty. But that was not the real reason why he had fastened upon the big man with utter malignity. Others had done him greater wrong than Anthony, in past days, but in Mad Anthony perhaps Cherokee sensed an innate decency, a kindness and rightness of heart. And for these qualities he hated the giant.

He was a talkative little man, was Cherokee. He had a way of sitting and smiling and nodding while he was relating an endless stock of anecdotes. You might take him for a sort of village gossip, an ignorant little man who took a rather disgusting pleasure and interest in the calamities which happened to other people. But you would never have picked him out for a man-killer—not unless you touched his vanity, his pride, or his love of playing the bully and giving pain. Then the devil flashed into his face, and men turned pale at the sight of him!

He was at this moment engaged in a little chat with Tommy Plummer. That is to say, he was chatting, and Tommy was combing his big mustaches with patient fingers and listening devotedly.

He was saying: "I've put up a bet with Judge Morgan. You know the Judge?"

"I know the Judge," said Tommy.

"The Judge, he bets me five hundred to three hundred that you won't last seven days after you get out of the jail. But I figger that you will. I don't think that Kirby will be able to catch you that quick. You'll duck down a hole, somewhere, and he'll have to rat you out, and that'll take time. You can't dig in the dirt as fast as a rat digs. That's what I tell the Judge. But still, maybe he hasn't give me odds for nothing! He seems to feel pretty sure of himself. And I was wondering, Tommy, why don't you try to persuade the Judge to have you put in jail for a longer term, until maybe Kirby drifts out of the country? . . ."

Tommy Plummer sighed and rolled another cigarette. But he was worried, though he pretended to be only bored. Day after day he had heard this death-talk from Cherokee Dan, and his nerves were wearing thin.

This Cherokee Dan now rose from the badgering of the man behind the bars and went toward Kirby, but as he went he could not resist the temptation of pausing in front of the cell which held Big Crow. He put a hand around his neck and then pretended, vividly, to be strangling, rolling his eyes, contorting his mouth, and sticking out his tongue hideously.

Big Crow shuddered, and the ruffian went on, grinning with content.

CHAPTER XXXIV

T HEY GATHERED IN THE CORNER OF THE CELL-ROOM. "Look at Big Crow," said Cherokee Dan. "He's watching us all the time. Though he ain't going to show it, not if he dies for it! I got him all persuaded that he's gonna be hung, sure. I got him all ready for it, and he's dying every day, thinking about it."

"He's dying of starvation, and that's a fact," said Jay Madison, with a growl. "And a damned good way, too. Ain't I right, Diamond?"

Jack Kirby nodded.

He was well contented with these allies of his, and as he looked them over, now, he told himself that he might have combed all the length and the breadth of the prairies without finding three more formidable men to assist him. Indeed, he was not even sure that he *needed* assistance, and he was almost willing to take his chances with big Anthony Castracane hand to hand had it not been that his mother's warning rang like a prophecy in his ears. He respected her wisdom and her instinct too much to disregard such advice as she had given.

However, these three made him invincible. It was only doubted, now, whether or not the big fellow would respond to the bait and enter the trap which had been spread for him with such care.

"Let Kohatunka starve," said Jack Kirby, "but not

before there has been a chance for Castracane to take a try at him. If you think that he will take a try. Do you still keep that idea, Chick?"

"I keep to that idea," said the gloomy Chick. "He'll come in and bust the jail open and take out the Indian, right enough."

"You mean, he'll try it," corrected Cherokee Dan, grinning until all his yellow fangs showed.

"He'll try it, and he'll do it," said Chick.

"Hello!" snapped Jay Madison. "What the hell kind of talk is that? Are you buffaloed already?"

"I'll take nothing from you, Madison!" said Chick, turning more grim.

"You'll take the truth, though!" returned Jay Madison, his dark face gathered in a scowl. "And that truth is that you've had enough of Castracane, after him beating you once!"

"You lie!" said Chick calmly, and rested his hand on the butt of his revolver.

"I lie? Me?" echoed Madison huskily, his teeth set.

And in another instant two guns would have been in the air and perhaps both men would have fallen, since it was hardly possible that either could miss at such a distance as this.

"Steady!" called Kirby, stepping instantly into the breach. "You know that there's no yellow in Chick, Jay. You know that! And you know that Jay's nervous, or he would never have talked to you like that."

"Ay," put in Jay Madison, "I was kind of free with my tongue, Chick. Let it drop, will you?"

A most ample apology from such a person as Jay Madison, and Chick accepted it with a nod. That was all. He made no profession that all was well between him and Madison. As a matter of fact, each hated the other. But at the present moment, they had on hand work of such great importance to them both that they could afford to pocket up their other spites.

It was ever this way. Day in and day out Kirby had to be on the watch for fear lest one of his assistants should fall foul of another. And every day he never could tell when one of them would meet some other enemy on the streets of Fort Hendon. So he strove to keep them at his own side as much as possible. For he could exercise a sort of authority over them. For one thing, he was paying wages to two of them, and expenses even for Jay Madison. And in addition they knew that, terrible fighters as they all were, Kirby was a little quicker, a little surer, possessed of a trifle more nerve force than any of the rest. Therefore they accepted his commands—to a certain extent.

They agreed, for instance, that it was better for them to sleep in the building adjoining the jail, and that one, or preferably two, of them should always be present in the jail.

As for Kirby, he was rarely away from that post, and he made it a habit to meet his friends in that gloomy little building, much torn and battered where two lynching mobs had broken in and taken out prisoners that they thirsted to hang.

Hang them they did to the branches of a nearby cottonwood, and they left rather a patchwork mess of the jail behind them. They had smashed in all three of the doors, iron staples and all being torn out of the massive woodwork. Then they had beaten through the actual wooden wall of the jail in two other places, and these had merely been roughly boarded across to make up for the attack.

Big Jack Kirby on the very first day had gone over this series of defects with a microscope, so to speak; and when the constable saw him at work, he suggested that they make the jail manproof in order to contain these prisoners securely. But that was not to Kirby's mind, and, as he pointed out, one man could not break into a guarded jail, even when the walls were weak. That was what he said to the constable, but what he said to his companions was even more to the point.

"The shakier this jail looks, the surer Castracane will be to tackle it and try to tear down the walls or kick his way through them, and when that happens we will be waiting."

The others felt that there was much good sense in this, and therefore there was no encouragement for the worthy constable to repair the jail.

But that constable was not ignorant of the fact that something extraordinary was about to happen.

The sight of Jack Kirby and his three companions more or less constantly at the jail was something to wonder over. They received no pay, and yet the constable said that they had volunteered to stay on until Big Crow had been brought to his trial.

The whole town suddenly woke up to realize that the four remained in the jail not because of a special malice which made them want to see the Osage brought to justice but because they felt that some extraordinary event was about to transpire. And there was liberal guessing and much betting as to what that might be.

But all were far from the mark. For not one of the four was chattering. Each kept his advice to himself at the suggestion of Jack Kirby, and therefore the mystery around them deepened from day to day.

In the morning Kirby saw to it that two of them went off to practice marksmanship and keep themselves fit. And the pair which practiced was alternated from day to day. Neither did this proceeding escape the attention of the people of the town. It convinced them that whatever it might be that was about to happen at Fort Hendon, it would be something in which bullets would be flying thick and fast.

So the hours had drifted along, and every moment the expectation grew greater and the waiting was tenser. But on this afternoon Jack Kirby, when there was silence and better feeling among his three assistants, said to them: "We're bearing down into the home stretch now, friends. If we can pull all together, we'll get through this thing in good style. But if we begin to fight with each other, we might as well give up now. We're not going to have to deal with any soft job, you know! So we'll make this a rule. If you can't find pleasant things to say to each other, say nothing at all! There's one more thing that we have to manage if we can, and that is to try to get the crowd away from the jail. There's a half a dozen fools lingering across the street from us all the time. They know that something is going to happen and they want to be in on it, and while they're there they act as a sort of signpost to warn Castracane that there is something in here that he must beware of."

"They're there by the day," said Cherokee. "And you can depend on it that the big fellow is going to make his try by night. He's not a fool."

"He's been with Indians, the last few weeks," said Kirby, "and he may have picked up some of their trickery. Nothing is certain about what he'll do, and he may rush the jail at noon, for all I know."

"With how many Osages?"

"That's the question. How many of them will come with him? But as it seems to me, we don't have to worry about them. They won't stand up to gunfire— not the sort of fire that we'll turn loose on them. There'll only be one man that will press the charge home—and that one man is Anthony Castracane. You keep that in mind!"

It was the one mistake which they made in their calculations, for they did not think it possible that the Osage tribe would leave such a job to a single man, and that a stranger. They were certain that a dozen braves, at least, would join in the attempt, for how could they know that in the eyes of Munnepuskee and his tribesmen, the medicine of the big white man was so strong that numbers were not needed by him for any work of war?

The afternoon passed. The day turned to dusk, and then the first word of what they had been expecting came into town, borne by a galloping horseman—to the effect that a large number of Pawnees that day had chased across the plains a single horseman, riding a great bay stallion, and that they had lost one dead and several wounded in the attempt to bag him.

"It's Castracane!" said Jack Kirby, "and before morning we'll have him on our hands. He's come in by one way, and the Osages have come in by another. They'll join hands near the town, and then they'll start their dirty work. Boys, have your guns clean tonight!"

CHAPTER XXXV

FROM THE OSAGE MESSENGER MAD ANTHONY HAD learned all the details about the position of the jail, and upon the ground at the Osage village there had been sketched a detailed plan of all the buildings near to the fort. On this information he was prepared to act.

He knew very little about the interiors of jails, except that they were supposed to be strong places where prisoners could be safely lodged by the law. But he trusted that if he were in any way able to break into the jail, he would be strong enough to set Big Crow free, and then together they would be able to break out to liberty.

So he waited on the edge of the town until darkness came, then he set straight forward with the stallion.

It never occurred to Mad Anthony that though he himself was large enough to be easily recognized in any crowd or even by night, his horse was far more likely to be recognized because every man and woman and child upon the prairies had heard the tales about the great bay stallion.

He did not think of such things, or that the shafts of lamplight that stole out from partially opened doors and through the windows might gleam along the silken flanks of the great horse, or that they might sparkle in his own long red hair which had made men call him, among many names, Red Anthony.

All that occupied his mind was how quickly he could get to the jail, and how fiercely and strongly he would fight there in order to free Big Crow.

So he passed rapidly through the winding, narrow streets of the little town, which had grown up without order or pattern, along the winding cow trails which journeyed toward the fort.

Not far from the jail there was a field fringed with a dense growth of trees and shrubbery, and here he had planned to leave the stallion.

So he jumped the great creature over the fence and left it there. And as he stood for a time, patting the neck of the Salton Bay and gathering his own resolution for the work that lay before him, he thought that he heard a whispering of subtle voices among the underbrush, and then a crackling, as of footfalls rapidly retreating.

But it did not come into his mind that these noises might mean spies who were watching him. He left the field, vaulted lightly over the fence and strode off up the street, turned down another alley, and so came to the tall fence of solid boards which hemmed in the jail from behind.

It had been specially built in order to hinder a rapid flight on the part of a prisoner, for it was of a height which no man in the world could jump over. Incidentally, it made a shrewd obstacle in Anthony's path, just now.

He estimated the distance to its top. Then he saw that there was nothing nearby by which he could scale the tall fence.

However, there were some most generous cracks in the wall, and putting his fingers through one of these he used a little of that strength which God had granted to his hands.

They were new nails with which that board had been fastened recently, and therefore they did not screech. And Mad Anthony calmly plucked off two of the boards and laid them gently aside. There was now a passage wide enough for him to squeeze through—big enough for most men to run headlong through!

He paused at the gap to look through on the rear yard of the jail. Not, as men afterward conjectured, to rest after the prodigious labors entailed in the wrenching of those two boards away. And many men swore that he must have used some sort of pry. But there was a watcher in a tree above Mad Anthony's head all this time, and he was the man who swore that he saw the thing done with the giant's naked hands!

At any rate all looked wonderfully peaceful to Mad Anthony. Somewhere in the dim distance a banjo was twanging and a Negro melody was floating through the air. Near at hand there was a stir of voices from a group which idled across the street from the jail. The jail itself was dark except for one window, dimly lighted.

That window he would let alone. Instead he chose to circle to the side of the jail. He saw above him a barred window, and climbing up he tried the strength of the bars with his hands. After all, though the iron was stout, it was bedded in wood only, and not well-seasoned wood at that. And it was perhaps not so very prodigious that the wood gave way. Two of the bars of the Fort Hendon jail he plucked forth by the roots and let drop to the ground. He had laid his hold upon the third when he heard a voice behind him shout suddenly: "Ready, boys!"

And he recognized the voice of Diamond Jack Kirby!

He relaxed his hold at the same instant, and dropped as four guns blazed from the shrubs at the side of the jail. There was a jangle of broken glass at the window, and the chopping, heavy sound of big-caliber bullets sinking deeply into the wall of the fort.

But Anthony took only a little scratch along his ribs,

where a bullet had sliced through his clothes. And the next instant one leap had carried him around the corner of the jail.

Why did not Diamond Jack Kirby give his signal with a bullet instead of his voice? That would be a hard question to answer, if one did not know Diamond Jack and his nature, but as a matter of fact there was no great joy to him in blowing the soul out of the giant's body unless he could let the big man know that it was Jack Kirby's will which was sending the bullets on their way!

And so he and his men had a suddenly moving target to fire at—a dropping target, of all the most difficult—and the next instant that target had darted around the corner of the jail.

The whole town seemed to Mad Anthony to have wakened at the same instant. There were shouts everywhere. He saw a full dozen men running into the yard of the jail. He saw lanterns showing. And he saw the lantern light falling on the polished barrels of shotguns and rifles and pistols and some of the new revolvers.

It was amazingly sudden, and stunning in its unexpectedness. But that was Jack Kirby's cunning, he knew, which must have arranged this affair in all of its details.

He set his teeth at the thought, and his stern eyes flared like the eyes of a badgered lion—and then he darted across the open toward the fence through which he had come.

From the hole through which he had broken two guns spouted fire at him—a bullet grazed his head and knocked Mad Anthony headlong.

"He's dead!" screeched the triumphant voice of Cherokee Dan, and he started running forward, firing as he ran, but firing blindly, so great was the intensity of his joy.

The giant's prostrate length stirred. A bit of steel twitched in his hand, and a bullet split the forehead of Cherokee Dan, driven fairly between his eyes. He died without even a final groan, and Mad Anthony, lurching to his feet, lunged toward the huddle of half a dozen men who had been racing forward at Cherokee's heels.

They split to either side as though they were seeing a rearisen ghost instead of a man.

Not a shot did Anthony fire as he raced through them, and not a shot was sent into his body. He sprang through the gap in the fence just as he had come and, doubling down the alley, made for the field where he had left the stallion.

Behind him, out of the turmoil, he could make out the commanding voice of Jack Kirby shouting like another Stentor: "Scatter, scatter, boys! Scatter and you'll get him—don't wedge all together like sheep and block the way for each other!"

Oh, wise Jack Kirby! He damned the wisdom of his great enemy as he saw the mob behind him spill out to either side. It would go hard with the town of Fort Hendon if they allowed this monster to escape!

He ducked from the alley down the next byway and headed straight for the field where the Salton Bay had been left—and saw before him four shadowy forms of men rising behind the fence with glittering weapons in their hands.

He dodged to the side barely in time. Three guns clanged, and a great load of buckshot spattered noisily against the boards of the house behind him.

They had discovered the place where he had hidden the stallion, then, and they had captured the Salton Bay!

That thought rang like a death knell in Mad Anthony's heart. But still he was not done with his efforts.

There were two things which most people would have done, had they been brave enough at that moment. They would either have rushed madly straight at the enemy to die at once or else, back to wall, they would have made a final stand.

But Anthony did neither. Blazing guns were before him, running feet were speeding up the alley behind him, and his one chance was that of melting his way through the solid side of a house wall.

A hitching stone lay nearby. His foot had struck it as he sprang back from the blare of musketry before him. It was long and narrow, and massive and deeply rooted. That stone he tore from the ground, swayed it high, and ran staggering forward with it.

It crunched through the thin, timbered wall of the house like a projectile from a great cannon. His mighty hands instantly ripped the opening wide enough and he leaped through into a cellar thick with darkness, filled with dripping dankness—no light anywhere to guide him.

He lurched forward. His hand struck the railing of a stair and up that stair he sprang instantly, thrust open the door at the top—and found himself in a family sitting room!

Outside there was a roar of voices sweeping here and there—and in the room two children and a woman and an old man were standing petrified with horror. Gunfire they had all heard before, in that wild town, but only a moment before the whole house had shaken as with an earthquake and there had been a crashing blow as though the foundations of the place were being ripped apart.

Now the door to their cellar was thrown open, and they saw a red-headed giant, without a hat, with long hair blown back across his shoulders, and with blood pouring crimson from his head staining again a rude bandage which had been knotted around his brow. Blood, too, appeared on his side, and yet these wounds seemed as nothing to the big man, merely as spurs to his energy.

They could not have stirred, so frozen were they with terror. But at the same instant that the giant entered, the front door of the house was thrown open and into the threshold leaped the squat, active figure of Jay Madison, already exultant because the Salton Bay had been reclaimed for him, but mad with blood lust, now, and keen as a hunting dog upon the trail.

He saw Mad Anthony, and Mad Anthony saw him, at the same instant. There was a tenth of a second's difference in the time it took them to fire. But that made all the distinction between life and death. Jay Madison sprawled on the floor with a bullet through his heart, and Mad Anthony turned from the room with a leap, passed through the kitchen, and sprang out at the rear door.

He saw before him a small gap. Madison's shooting and the uproar which it had caused had drawn attention toward the front of the house, and in that direction the crowd of hunters was swirling. In that direction a rider was sending his scampering horse at this moment, when Anthony leaped like a great tiger at a deer, struck the victim from the saddle, thrust his feet into the stirrups, and whipped his way toward freedom.

CHAPTER XXXVI

IT WAS A GALLANT LITTLE INDIAN PONY THAT Anthony had under him now, and he could feel the stout horse gathering under him. Out from the alley's mouth they darted and turned sharply aside into the broader street, with a blur of shouts and exploding guns behind them. And they went on with a rush down the next alley, turning abruptly into a vacant lot toward the edge of the town, when three men, rifles in hand, ran around the corner and opened a withering fire.

At the first volley, the pony leaped high into the air and crashed to the ground with a lurch that cast Anthony out of the saddle and rolled him headlong along the ground.

He was on his feet instantly, firing as he rose at the three shadows which were running toward him with blazing rifles. He was stunned by his fall. He made out their dim silhouettes, and that was all, but he did not need to strike his mark, now, in order to make an effect. They had seen what sort of execution Mad Anthony could make with his guns, and when their dead man came to life and surged to his knees with revolvers spouting fire, they split in two directions and raced yelling for shelter.

Down the street came the head of the hot riders of the pursuit, and another body of mounted men was thundering down the street beyond, catching Mad Anthony between two dangers.

He saw that, and he gave himself a moment's refuge by leaping the hedge into the back yard of a building larger and longer than any of the others around him. He glanced through the windows into a big, dimly seen room, for there was only a single light burning in it. And it was cluttered with furniture, chairs and tables arranged in orderly rows—a restaurant.

He could hear voices shouting behind him, and particularly the ringing tones of Jack Kirby leading them on:

"He's near to us, now, and we've got him. Go slow and steady, boys. Take nothing fast. We don't need speed, now, but thoroughness. Don't miss a single inch of the ground. Where's the fellow who shot down his horse? I've got five hundred for that man, and another thousand for the fellow who sinks the first bullet into Castracane's body—by the authority of the law!"

Castracane could hear this ringing speech as he leaned against the wall of the restaurant. And he stole forward to the front of the building to see how the land lay there. Every window was lighted, and every door was open. Fort Hendon was blazing with illumination, and by that light Anthony could see half a dozen armed men scattered up and down in the immediate vicinity of the restaurant front.

They were not sleeping at their posts, either. Two gun fighters had already fallen in this street fight, and every man in the town was alert to kill or be killed when they should sight the fugitive. At any instant, now, there would be searchers in the yard of the restaurant. And for some reason, Anthony preferred to die with the light on his face instead of in the heart of the darkness.

He drew himself up and through the nearest window.

Against the wall inside, he reloaded the two revolvers which he had with him and then skulked across the big room and listened at the first door.

He could not make sure that all was silent beyond it, for there was a growing babel of voices outside. After a moment he opened that door and stepped through into a narrow hall—and straight against a shadowy form—

He grappled it with one lightning hand and laid the muzzle of a revolver against the head:

"Be still—don't make a sound!" said Anthony softly.

And a voice gasped in answer: "Anthony!"

It dissolved half his strength and his ferocity to hear his name pronounced. And he reeled back from the girl who had spoken and supported himself with one hand against the wall.

She followed close to him, without fear of the big revolver which hung in his other hand.

"Anthony, Anthony!" she said. "Thank God you've found me! This way—quickly! There's no one else here to see or hear—they'll never dream of hunting in my room!"

His brain refused to act. It was benumbed to childishness, and he let her lead him down the hall, up steeply winding stairs with his shoulders brushing the wall on either side, and so into a little room above.

She turned the key in the lock behind him. She drew the shade close. She lighted the lamp on a corner table. And he found himself looking into Muriel Lester's face. She cried out in a choked voice at the sight of him, for Anthony was never a pretty man, and now he looked very like a sole survivor of the wreck of the world.

He was covered with dust, his clothes were rent, a

bloody bandage circled his head, and the side of his coat was clotted and caked with blood. Bloody, too, were his hands, for they had been pierced by the jagged edges of the boards as he wrenched a passage through the wall of the house.

"Anthony, you're dying!" she moaned at him. "Lie here!"

"I'm not dying. I'm only scratched, not really hurt, Muriel. There's no need—"

But somehow he could not resist when she pushed him strongly toward the bed, or when she took the gun from his big hand, or when she took water and washed his face, or took off the filthy bandage and cleansed his wounds about the head and bound them again with clean cloth. For all the while he was taken up in a childish intensity of interest, by the softness of her touch and the bright tears which escaped, now and then, and rolled down her face.

He did not understand. He only knew that he was wonderfully happy, and the sounds of the hunt, surging up and down about the building, were as faint and far away as voices in a happy dream to Red Anthony.

But now she sat beside him, holding his hands and yearning over him with a broken voice.

"Do you see, Anthony? I didn't know. I thought you were only a big boy, and I didn't dream that they had sent me to tease a lion. I didn't dream it! If I had, I should have died sooner than flirt with you and lie to you, but I thought that you would forget me in three days, in your circus. I never guessed that you would follow me out to the West, and while they've been telling such strange and terrible things of your doings, I've waited here, trembling and sick, because I knew all the while that I was to blame. I knew that it was my fault. I knew that I had drawn you into this. Oh, Anthony, God will never forgive me, but say that you do!"

He could only mutter: "I don't understand. You belong to Diamond Jack. And you're not with him?"

"Didn't you know? The instant I heard Tommy Plummer tell how he'd been hired to murder you—why, I never had been able to see through Jack before that, but afterward how could I stay a moment in his house?"

"You left him!"

"Of course I left him."

He heaved himself up from the bed and sat on the edge of it with closed eyes.

"Are you sick, Anthony?"

"I'm only trying to think it out."

He opened his eyes and stared at her.

"I've been hating you all these days, Muriel; blaming you, you understand. But now if they kill me before morning, they'll kill a man that loves you—"

"Hush! They daren't touch you. I'll keep them away. I'll protect you, Anthony—ah, God help me!"

For at that moment they could hear the front door of the building thrown open with a crash.

She threw a cherishing arm around Anthony, and she

turned half trembling and half fiercely toward the door as though she would spring at the first man who dared enter her room in the search!

Mad Anthony laughed deep in his throat, but be sure that there was no mirth in the sound, but only a world of sorrow and of wonder and of joy such as overfloods a heart.

"Muriel," he said, "I have an idea that there's something more than regret in you. I almost have an idea that perhaps you could love me, dear—"

"Hush, they're coming! Don't you hear?" she whispered. "Don't you hear?"

"Let them come and be damned. It's you that I'm thinking of. Muriel, will you tell me the truth?"

"That I love you, with all my heart—oh, there's no truth but that—only, how shall God teach me to save you?"

"I need no saving!" cried Anthony, truly mad now with joy and bewilderment. "I'll save myself. I could bend iron like wax, now. You've closed up my wounds and put back the blood in my body. And if—"

A footfall crashed in the hall below; the stairs creaked with an ascending weight. Others followed. Voices came flooding up the passage.

"Try this door."

"It's only the girl's room. No need of going in there."

"Kirby says search every inch. We'd better not leave this without a look."

"You're a fool. But have your way."

A hand turned the knob of the door, and then rattled it.

"It's locked!"

"Sure, the kid is scared to death, and she's locked herself in!"

"Hello! Open the door!"

"Let them come in," said Anthony. "I'll rush a way through them—it'll take them by surprise—"

She wrenched one of the revolvers from his hand and leaped to the door:

"If you dare to force the lock, I'll shoot through the door!" cried Muriel.

CHAPTER XXXVII

HELLO, HELLO!" CALLED THE MAN AT THE DOOR. "A spitfire, ain't she!"

"Look here, youngster," said an authoritative voice, "I don't want that door spoiled, and you can't bluff all of Fort Hendon. I'm here to see that no harm is done to you!"

"I won't unlock the door," said Muriel. "I'll trust myself and nobody else!"

"Wait a minute!" called another. "Here's Kirby. Let him handle it."

And Anthony could hear the explanation being made: "It's the waitress, scared to death in there and won't open the door."

"We'll have it open, though," said Diamond Jack.

"We'll miss not a room in this place, because I've got an idea that somewhere in this dump is Red Anthony Castracane. What's her name?"

"By name of Muriel Lester, she calls herself. Go easy with her, Kirby. Mighty pretty, and plumb decent."

There was rather a long silence.

"Are you gonna pass the room by?" asked a voice presently.

Then Kirby spoke through the door.

"Muriel, it's Jack. Do you hear me?"

She looked vaguely, in an agony of fear, at Anthony. And he said, in a whisper: "You can't keep them out. They'll simply break the door down. Ask him to come in alone!"

She cast at him a glance half curious and half terrified.

"No," he answered. "I won't do that! It's not going to be necessary!"

He added: "Tell him he can come in—alone!"

She drew a quick little breath.

"Jack, will you come in alone?" she asked.

"Certainly. Bear back, boys!"

There was a shuffling of feet in the hall.

"Scatter along and hunt through the other rooms. I'll take care of this one!"

And as the footfalls departed she turned the key, the door opened, and Jack Kirby entered, blinking a little at the brightness of the lamp and closing the door hastily behind him.

"Muriel," he said, "of course I didn't want to search,

258

but only to beg you to—"

He stopped. He had seen from the tail of his eye, now, the shadowy form of a big man standing by the wall, and as he turned his head he saw a great Colt leveled at him by a steady hand.

"I'm a dead man," said Kirby quietly. "You can file a notch on the butt of his gun and say that that's *your* notch, my dear!"

"He won't hurt you," said the girl faintly. "Only— you'll find some way to get him safely from Fort Hendon. Will you do that, Jack? Will you so much as give your word of honor—"

She stopped, unable to speak another word.

He looked from her to Anthony's grim face.

"I ought to tell you to fill your hand and then put a bullet through you," said Anthony, with a fierce gentleness in his voice.

"Do it," said Kirby. "The sound of the shooting would call the rest of the boys in to get you and hang you, my lad!"

"I've still half a chance of breaking through, and with you dead behind me there'd be too much to live for, Kirby. Do you understand? And tell me one thing—you were at the jail, tonight. It was you who laid the trap for me?"

Jack Kirby smiled. Never had his courage been so magnificent as it was now under Anthony's gun.

"I had that satisfaction," he said. "I arranged the net that grazed you, old timer."

And he glanced at Anthony's many wounds.

"I laid the net, and it'll capture you after I'm dead and done for. Get your dirty work over with, Castracane. A man can't live forever, and I'm ready to finish now! Castracane, go on!"

And he sneered at Anthony with an iron resolution.

"Anthony!" gasped the girl.

"I won't harm him—I hope," said Anthony. "Because there's still a way out for both of us!"

A flicker of light appeared in the gambler's eyes.

"I'm used to long chances, Castracane," said he. "Name your game!"

"It's this. Suppose that you leave the room and let the boys know that you've found Muriel Lester here— and no one else! Suppose that they finish hunting in this part of the town for me and go off to another section. Why, then, I'd have the better part of a chance to get clean away from Fort Hendon—"

"One moment," put in Muriel Lester, trembling with excitement. "Do you mean to say that you'd take his word for that, Anthony? Don't you know that the minute he was safe from your gun he'd come rounding back at you with a hundred armed men?"

A bright flush stained the face of the gambler. But he looked from one to the other, and said nothing.

"I don't know," said Anthony. "Perhaps he would. There's two chances in three that he would, perhaps. But on the other hand, he's a brave man, Muriel. And brave men can keep faith when they wish to. Besides—I'm not a murderer. I can't shoot him down—Kirby, do you hear? If you'll give me your word, I'll put my trust in you!"

It would have been a strange sight to those who knew Diamond Jack best if they had been able to look at him at this moment, and see the pallor that spread over his face, wiping the blush away, and how his eyes winked shut and then stared wide at Anthony.

Something in the foundation of his belief in the world had been broken away. For his belief was implicit that all men live by craft and cunning only, and the strength of their good right hands, and that trust and faith are things to be left to children's fairy stories.

"Castracane," said he, "are you serious?"

"I am."

"There's no pledge that I could leave behind me with you. Nothing but my word."

"That's all."

"And is that enough for you?"

"We could shake hands on it, Kirby."

"Man, man," cried Jack Kirby, "do you know that I've hunted you for weeks and hated you like a black devil?"

"I can guess that."

"Then here's my hand."

"I'm glad to take it, Kirby."

Their hands closed.

"I'll go out of the room," repeated Kirby, "and I'll tell the boys that there was nothing here, and I'll lead the search to another part of the town—if I can! But after I've done that, I'll come back and find you if I can. And when I find you, one of us goes down. Is that clear?"

"As clear as crystal."

Their eyes shot fire at one another.

"We'll meet with guns talking the next time, Castracane."

"We will."

"And God help the one that's worth helping. Goodby!"

He backed to the door. And there he lingered for an instant, his fine head turned toward the girl.

"Muriel," he said, "I thought at first that you were a fool. But now I see that you were simply able to look deeper into him than the rest of us. If I didn't hate him like the heart of hell, he's the one man in the world that I'd select for a friend."

He wrenched the door open, stepped back into the hall, and the door closed quickly upon him.

They heard his loud step down the hall. They heard his voice calling briskly:

"There's nothing here, boys! We'll get on with the hunt. The scoundrel has slipped through our fingers, but where the devil can he be?"

"Somewhere in this house—you've said so yourself!"

"I was a fool. Nothing is certain about this Castracane except that he manages things that no other man can handle! Come on, and make it quick!"

CHAPTER XXXVIII

THEY HEARD THE DEPARTING RUSH OF THE CROWD OF searchers, and Mad Anthony listened with the girl held close to him, so close that he could feel the tremor of her heartbeat.

"Anthony, what will you do?"

"Win away from the town. But I can think of that afterward. I only want to think of you, now. If I escape, where shall I find you again?"

"Wherever you wish. There's nowhere that I won't go, so long as it's to you."

"To me? I'll be living among the Indians. The white people will hunt me like a wolf after tonight. Muriel, I've killed two men."

"Jay Madison and Cherokee Dan. The whole world will bless you for doing it. And as for the Indians— I'm not afraid of that. I'll go out to you and live with you in a tepee—"

"What! Like a squaw?"

"Do you think that anything a squaw is brave enough and strong-minded enough to do a white woman can't do, also? I could laugh at work, dear!"

"And the shame of such a thing?"

"There's no shame in it!"

He gloried over her, laughing softly.

"I'm not asking you to come to me. I'm coming back to you, one of these days, and I'm coming back free and with clean hands. Or else I'll find another country where I can take you, where the law has no scores against me. Only—can you wait?"

"Time is nothing. I can wait forever. Now you mustn't stay. Every second counts for you. They've gone—and Jack Kirby has kept his word—God knows how! But they'll be back, and he'll be keener than ever on your trail! You can count on that! If only you can get to the back of the Salton Bay—"

"Where will they keep him?"

"In the corral behind the jail. There's no other corral fence in town high enough to keep him from jumping it. They'll be sure to have him guarded there. But you won't risk breaking in to him? You won't do that?"

"I'll give you one promise—that I won't throw my life away."

"Anthony, kiss me, and go!"

He leaned over her. He read her face and reread it as though it were an endless chapter, but then all chapters, even the most beautiful ones, must have an ending. He did not touch her with his lips, but released her suddenly and ran blindly from the room and down the hall.

When he came to the rear door of the restaurant building, however, the first touch of the night air against his face sobered him. Far and near the sounds of the hunt, and the clatter of hoofs as fresh recruits arrived, showed that Fort Hendon was doing its work manfully. And there was reason enough! If you tap a hornet's nest you must expect trouble, and Fort

Hendon, being surely a very nest of hornets, had been shaken to its foundation; it had been literally stamped upon, and now it raged with a determination to uphold its dignity as the very hardest and manliest of all the towns upon that hardy and manly western frontier.

Enough had been done on this one occasion to raise Mad Anthony high on the roll of the daredevils of the West; enough had surely been done to justify his nicknames of "Red" and "Mad." But if he had paused here, he would not have hewn for himself such an ample niche in the Hall of Fame. He might have been obscured, afterward, by the deeds of other desperadoes of the region. For all that he had done before, you might say, had been forced upon him, so people would feel afterward. He had come to achieve a daring exploit in the liberation of prisoners from the guarded jail in the center of the town, and having been trapped and surprised and hunted, he had fought most desperately, and he had managed to kill two famous gunmen in his fight.

But with the town roused, with the streets boiling with armed men, with every eye and ear alert for him, that he should have gone on to attempt what he next tried was almost beyond the credence of the people of Fort Hendon and of all the others who heard of these spectacular deeds.

However, it seemed to Anthony, at the time, the most logical thing to do. And he went ahead step by step, not with any resolute and terrible plan in his head from the beginning, as men were apt to credit him for in later days and years. They felt that such work must have been deliberately schemed. As a matter of fact, Anthony merely felt his way from act to act the rest of that wild night.

And indeed, when he first stepped out into the night and felt the chilly air against his face, and while the shouts of the hunters rang in his ears, he only wondered how he could possibly skulk away from the town.

Even that seemed quite impossible. For suppose that he should be able to get his hands on a horse, if he strove to ride out by even the most obscure lanes, he would be seen, and when he was seen, he would be followed. And no Indian pony, no matter how stout, could bear up for long under the crushing impost of his weight. His flight would not be like that of Kohatunka, when with the threat of an arrow, now and again, he had been able to hold back the rush of Pawnees. For Anthony's pursuers would not be Indians, but reckless white men, each with a gambler's spirit, eager to take a chance to make himself famous by sending a bullet into such an enemy.

All of these things Anthony had been long enough in the West to understand. And, to give an edge to all his apprehensions, at that moment he heard a sudden crashing of guns on the opposite border of the town. It was only a wretched skulking dog which had been creeping frightened through the brush, but the glimpse of the hiding fugitive had brought a dozen guns into action, and the unlucky creature was blown out of this world and into the next before a single yelp could tell the hunters that they had fired in vain.

Exactly what had happened Anthony could not tell, but he knew that those shots were meant for him, and shooting pains of apprehension went through all his recent wounds as he listened.

But now, just as his heart sank to the lowest depth, another sound came trumpeting to him, like a very battle bugle—the neigh of the Salton Bay ringing through the night, and calling for his master with a breaking heart.

Mad Anthony, listening, set his teeth, and in another moment he was slinking forwards toward the jail.

He found a hole beneath the hedge and crawled through it. Very lucky for Anthony that he had not leaped it rashly again; for as he came through, he found two men walking slowly up and down, rifles in hand.

"Maybe they got him then," said one.

"There ain't any chance of that," said the other. "Because if Castracane was down, there would be hell-popping and roaring and yelling all over the place!"

"That may come later on."

"Who'll be the lucky hound to salt him down?"

"Us, we got a fine chance, left here by Kirby!"

"Well, I dunno that I'm sorry. I'm best pleased to be out of the way of his gats. Madison and Cherokee gone in one night! And one man killed 'em! I dunno that I want to be handy around when a sharpshooter like that is working."

They passed on slowly to the other end of the empty lot, still talking, and Anthony skulked out and reached a bush fifty feet from the hedge before they turned and came slowly back. They passed almost within touching distance of him. And had either thought of glancing at the thin-limbed shrubbery, he would not have failed to see beyond the branches the bulky silhouette of the hunted man.

Very lucky were they that they did *not* look, for two deadly guns were waiting for them and out of the shadow peered eyes as burning and bright as the eyes of a tiger. That moment when they discovered Anthony would have been their last on earth, but they did not dream of looking in underbrush for a man who, in their imagination, was rushing at full speed in another part of the town, ready to deal death and destruction.

They strolled on, and as they turned their backs Anthony was up and away once more; and this time he safely reached the street and turned down it, not running, but walking quietly, for in this emergency he guessed that more haste might be a greater temptation to bring the eyes of the enemy upon him.

He crossed the street a hundred yards higher up, turned through a back gate, and presently he came out near the jail, where he could see the tall fence cutting the stars of the horizon. Inside that fence was the Salton Bay, perhaps. He determined to make sure.

He had not gone clear to the edge of the fence when a snort and whinny inside the enclosure told him that he was right. The Salton Bay was there, indeed, and if once he could place himself on the back of the stallion—

He had to pause a moment in order to allow his heart to recuperate from the flurry of exultation which had quickened its beating.

Then he crept carefully on through a scattering growth of brush.

The next instant he saw how the big horse was held.

That twelve-foot fence which secured the back yard of the jail was exactly copied in height and strength to make an adjoining corral in which not animals but humans had been kept on several occasions when the jail overflowed. Two-inch planks, spiked down with great nails, made the wall of wood, and there was only one gate, a six-foot-high door of the heaviest sort of bars. And outside that one place of ingress or egress there were no fewer than five armed men.

How could he spirit the stallion away from such a place as this?

CHAPTER XXXIX

HE PONDERED THE THING WITH A GLOOMY HEART. To leave the town, even if he could sneak away and escape from the patrols which must be riding round and round it, was difficult enough. To escape from the town once the stallion was under him seemed not at all unfeasible.

And there was the key to the situation—there, so securely locked away!

What he did next was the blindest and most foolish step, so it seemed, in all his adventure. He was overcome with a mastering desire to see the big horse once more, to pat his neck, to see his bright eyes glimmering in the starlight. And so he proceeded to think only of how he could get into the enclosure, and not at all of how he could get out!

Even this foolish task was difficult enough. Every moment someone might see him lingering near the wooden wall, and any loiterer there was sure to draw inquiries. He scouted on, however, until he found a spike whose head projected a bit from the fence, four feet above the ground. That was a sufficient toehold for him. And with a foot on that, and his arms stretched above his head, he gripped the upper edge of the fence.

Over he swung himself with a mighty effort of shoulder muscles and, like a pole vaulter, dropped down into the enclosure.

There he crouched low in the shadow of the wall, taking stock of his surroundings. The instant that he had touched the ground inside the place he deeply regretted the thing that he had done. It was a perfect trap, this, and like an idiot he had entered a trap for the bait of a horse—a horse which he could not possibly take away with him!

So it seemed at that moment, and he set his teeth, to keep back a groan, not only that he was finished in his fight for freedom, but that he should have come to such a disgraceful end as this!

The stallion sighted or smelled him instantly, and trotted to him with a shrill whinny, with the stirrups flapping against his sides. For they had not delayed to strip the saddle from his back.

That whinny was like a searchlight aimed at Anthony, but as the giant horse came to him he stood up, hoping that the body of the stallion would shelter him from any but a close observation from the gate. But with whispered commands, with the touch of his caress, he could hardly keep the monster from acting like a joyful dog which has recovered a lost master.

And then a voice called from the gate:

"The Bay has gone crazy!"

"What's the matter?"

Anthony's blood turned cold.

"Look at him over there by the fence!"

"The old fool is trying to paw his way out!"

"Better scare him back from there."

"Son, no horse in the world'll ever get through that wall!"

And Anthony, staring wistfully at the barrier, could not help agreeing. No horse in the world could ever get through it. However, he had plucked away just such timbers as these once before on this night, and his sore and swollen hands could do it again. . . .

But not without making a telltale noise, and the first

noise would betray him. Besides, he would have to wrench away three of the big boards before the horse would have enough room to press through.

With any sort of a battering weapon he would have made the attempt that instant, but there was no such weapon at his hand. Cold sweat was starting on his forehead as he heard one of the guards saying: "I'll just stroll around the outside of the fence all the same, and make sure. Wouldn't have that critter slip through our hands, you know. Old Kirby would go mad, I guess. I think that he values the stallion as much as he does Castracane!"

And through the brush outside the fence sounded the footfall of the inspecting guard.

Every moment Anthony's danger grew greater. Inside and outside there was peril.

"You're a dummy, Sam," said one of the group at the gate. "The horse is safe as can be. Come back here."

"Leave me be."

"I'll leave you be damned. Do what you like!"

"Hello, what's that?"

Another crash of gunfire sounded, but this time close to the center of the town, and followed by hoarse shouting.

All heads were turned toward the noise, and that instant Anthony made up his mind.

The wall was impossible; that was plain. He could not leap it, and he could not dig through under it. And the gate at the end of the corral looked as lofty as a castle wall to poor Anthony. But by a simple process of *reductio ad absurdum* he knew that the gate must be attempted. It was all that was left, and it was better to die trying than to give up meekly to miserable death.

So he swung onto the back of the big horse; and the instant that he was seated there, who can tell what a thrill of might and confidence passed through Mad Anthony's very heart and blood? The tremors left him; he forgot his aching wounds. He became once more a hero!

Leaning far forward, crouched as close as possible against the back of the stallion, he hoped that he could approach the gate very close before he would be seen.

He put the big bay into a trot.

It was too high to jump, that gate. Surely no horse had ever jumped such a height, at least with a burden like Anthony on its back. . . .

And yet all miracles seemed in compass of this winged creature's powers! He would not doubt; he would not doubt, but put all his trust and his might into the attempt. But perhaps the stallion would refuse, and turning from the gate present the broadside view of his rider to the watcher's guns.

If so, that would be Anthony's last moment on earth!

"Hello! Here's the Bay coming to talk to us. My God, ain't he a big one!"

"Look out!"

That cry came as Anthony, with a whisper, and tightening the reins, put the stallion into a gallop and straightened him out for the gate.

"The big fool is going to try to jump the gate!"

"No, smash it down is more likely. He's gone crazy! Get back, boys!"

"Ah, ain't he a grand sight!"

"He's running amuck. Damn him, he'll break his neck on the bars, but he'll never break through them!"

"What's that on him!"

"Where?"

"On his back!"

"I don't see nothing!"

"My God, it's a man—Castracane!"

The last was a wild screech of excitement and fear, for Anthony, seeing that he was discovered, had now reared upright in the saddle; and with a mighty shout he put the bay at the gate.

Up pitched the forehand of the big stallion. He left the earth with a lurch and sailed into the air, ears flattened, mouth agape, held straight and true, in perfect balance, by the controlling hand of his rider.

Well for Anthony that he had jumped obstacles of all sorts in the circus ring; but never such an obstacle as this, and never with Colts to chatter the applause!

A touch of his heels, a shout, had winged the stallion at the last moment.

He shot high. The bars dropped beneath him. The stars seemed to rush into Anthony's face, and his heart turned giddy. From the height he looked down upon the awestricken faces of the guards—frozen by the daring of this incredible adventurer and the prowess of this still more incredible horse!

The heels of the Salton Bay clattered against the uppermost bar of the gate. Down they pitched, and Anthony, guns in hand, fired blindly to either side.

Those bullets of his were not aimed, and they all flew wide, but the Colts, spouting fire, struck terror through the hearts of the guards.

They fired back, of course, like good men and true. But they hardly could have hit the fence itself, at that awful moment, let alone a flying phantasm of a horse and a ghostly rider.

And in a stride Anthony was screened from their view among the trees that grew all over that section of the field behind the jail.

He was away, then, to a flying start, but he could hear the rush of horses ahead of him and behind him; he heard the guards leap into the saddles of their waiting ponies and rush after him with a wild babble of cursing.

Not an instant was lost. They were off at full speed at once, and as Anthony turned his head to listen to the crashing of the brush beneath the feet of the flying cow ponies, an arm of iron struck him across the breast, shot him clean out of the saddle, and flattened him against the earth.

A spurt of fire ripped across his brain, then an instant of darkness, and he recovered his senses with the soft nose of the stallion sniffing inquiringly at his face as though wondering why this glorious race had ended the very moment it was getting under way.

And as Anthony pushed himself up into a sitting posture, he heard the rush of the pursuit go smashing past among the trees, dimly speeding silhouettes—so dim that it was not strange they did not see him where he lay before the stallion.

They had their vision attuned to a giant on the back of a giant horse. They were not searching for one without the other. And so they boiled away and into the street beyond!

CHAPTER XL

ANTHONY, STAGGERING TO HIS FEET, LISTENED TO the departing rout of the horsemen. He heard the rush into the street, and the shouting and the grand confusion as the guards from the corral met the other hunters.

Then up and down the street rushed the divided squadrons.

He breathed more easily, for it was apparent that they were sure he must have passed through the wood and slipped up or down the street. Though how he could have done that unobserved was a miracle. But on this night men did not wait to become logical.

And perhaps Anthony was the wildest of them all.

He looked up to the branch of the tree which had knocked him from the stallion's back. He had no doubt, now, that this rough accident had saved his scalp, because if he had ridden on through the trees into the street, the guns soon would have struck him down never to rise again.

Then he turned back.

And as he came out to the edge of the woods, he saw the low lines of the jail before him, still with its side starred by a single lighted window. But no guard was in sight. There was not a soul to see, and so it happened that the fiercest and the wildest of Anthony's conceptions came into his brain.

Accident and chance had driven him here and there, on this night of nights. It had seemed to the townsmen, baffled as though by the raging of a lion, that all these achievements were the result of careful planning, but it was not until this point in his career in Fort Hendon that he actually struck out with cold forethought to attempt the impossible.

He brought the Salton Bay as close as possible to the jail, and left the big horse safely shrouded among the shadows of the trees. Then he went boldly forward, turned the end of the building, and hoisted himself up to the window from which he had already started to pluck away the bars when he had been fired upon by Kirby and the others. He pulled off the rest of the bars now, working steadily and quietly, and then he reached up through the window, the glass of which had been completely shattered by the bullets which had been aimed at him, and turned the latch which locked it.

He pushed up the sash gently, making sure that no sound was caused by that movement. And after that he leaned through and examined his surroundings.

He could see the narrow interior of the building clearly enough by the flickering light of the one lamp. Yonder he could see Tommy Plummer walking up and down restlessly behind his bars. And Anthony's heart warmed at that sight. Since he had heard from Muriel Lester that Tommy's confession was what had armed her against Jack Kirby, he had taken a different view of the little man. Now he could not help wishing that, besides Big Crow, he could secure the freedom of the white prisoner, also.

As for Kohatunka, that chief sat hunched in a corner of his cell, but even from the distance the lamplight glistened on his restless eyes.

Next Anthony noted the guards. And he rejoiced when he saw that there were only three.

Only three! Enough surely to have turned back any man who was not desperate, but after the odds which Anthony had faced on this night, the sight of three men only made him warm with confidence.

There were two by the door, and one of those men was Chick, silent and grim, leaning on a rifle. The third fellow was the jailer, walking carelessly up and down the jail with a jangle of keys at his belt.

"You fellers might as well beat it," he told them. "You might as well circulate around outside and take a look for the big boy."

Said one of the pair at the door: "Chick, here, says that Castracane ain't going to give up trying for the jail. He says that he knows him!"

The jailer laughed.

And Anthony slipped through the window and began to work his way softly across the floor. He paused presently. Big Crow had stood up to his full height—and suddenly sat down again, and Anthony knew that the Indian had seen him.

Would any of the others look? No, the jailer was saying confidently: "I got to laugh at that. I got to laugh at the idea of even Castracane getting anything out of this here jail while I got two barrels of this here shotgun loaded down with slugs. Besides, even Castracane ain't mad enough to come back to the jail after being so near peppered here once tonight."

"You watch yourself," growled Chick. "You work things out for yourself, but don't try to work things out for Mad Anthony, because he is mad."

The jailer laughed again. He was thoroughly well contented with himself and his ideas of this matter, and he hummed as he walked down the length of the corridor once more. He turned, and as he was beginning to stride back a stunning blow struck him behind the ear, and he fell without making a cry. Only the keys at his waist crashed loudly against the floor as he went down.

"Hello," called Chick. "Did you slip or—God!"

And he pitched the rifle to his shoulder as he saw the great form crouched over the jailer.

But Chick had not the slightest chance. He was late, taken by surprise, and he was facing a gun which dared not miss. The Colt roared from Anthony's hand,

and Chick leaped sidewise, staggered, struck the ground, and recoiled to the floor with a groan, his rifle exploding as he fell and then clattering uselessly upon the floor far from his hand.

Anthony wrenched the keys from the fallen jailer and ran on toward Chick, for the third guard, seeing his two companions down, did not stay to be a dead hero, but fled with yells to alarm the town.

Leaning over Chick, Anthony laid the muzzle of his revolver against the head of this old enemy. But he saw the wounded man was writhing helplessly with pain. So he merely took from him the two revolvers with which he was still armed.

Then he turned to Big Crow's cell.

The Indian, in an ecstasy of fear and hope, clung to the bars, moaning with excitement and swaying himself back and forth while Anthony feverishly tried key after key.

Outside he could hear the wild voice of the third guard shouting, and he could hear other voices answering. They were gathering a sufficient host to attack him as he strove to leave the building. They might turn this into a trap—

And still he could not find the proper key!

He was in a nervous despair—but then suddenly the lock turned, the door sagged open, and the Indian bounded out with a ringing war cry.

Anthony turned hastily from him and leaped to Plummer's door.

"Save yourself, Anthony!" cried Tommy Plummer.

"I'm not here on any hanging matter, and every second is making it worse for you. Leave me be, Anthony, and take care of yourself!"

Suddenly Anthony grew calm and cool. And he was half laughing as he answered:

"If you hadn't said that, perhaps I might have left you here in this pigpen."

"Running Thunder! Running Thunder!" called the Osage. "We must go—"

The lock of Tommy's door turned. He too stepped out and the guns taken from Chick were placed in his hands. From a dead weight he had become a formidable fighting unit.

"Now," said Anthony, "give me your word about one thing. You won't fire at any man, when we try to get out, unless it's a matter of him killing you or you killing him?"

"I'll promise you anything you want, Anthony!"

"Run to the back window. I'll look out the door, and we'll see where the best chance lies for getting away!"

That order was obeyed instantly. And Tommy's voice came presently back:

"There's five here, and more coming!"

"This wall!" called Anthony, and Tommy was instantly beside him.

The two white men and the Indian stared through the door. All the danger that was before them they could not see, and they dared not wait to make sure. Distant shouts were approaching. The night was filled with ringing cries and the rushing of horses.

"There's two men in that clump of brush," said Anthony. "And yonder are four horses at that rack. We'll go out of the door and charge straight at the brush, shooting at it. I don't think that the pair of them will wait to fight it out. They'll scatter. Then turn and head for the horses, you two. I run on past the brush and into the trees to get the Salton Bay. When I'm in the saddle, I'll turn and ride right past the jail again and down that street. You'll have a flying start. Use it for all you're worth, because the Bay will soon be on your heels! Do you both understand!"

"I do!" they told him.

"Are you ready?"

A hungry snarl formed in the Indian's throat by way of an answer.

"Follow me, then," said Anthony, and he leaped from the door and down the steps, his revolver spouting fire at the clump of brush behind which he had spotted the outlines of the two men.

Behind him came Kohatunka, screeching and bounding into the air and waving a knife, far too deep in ecstasy to descend to gunplay. But perhaps his formidable capering did more than Tommy's and Anthony's guns to break the nerve of the two half-screened men before them. For they leaped out from their shelter at once and sped away, throwing their rifles aside to lighten their flight.

Fort Hendon had had enough of Castracane's shooting on this night; and now Mad Anthony had helpers at his back!

CHAPTER XLI

OFF TO THE SIDE WENT KOHATUNKA, RUNNING LIKE a deer, with short-legged Tommy Plummer sprinting vainly behind him to keep up. Anthony saw this with a glance over his shoulder, and then he rushed ahead toward the covert where he had left the Bay.

He was drunk with joy now. His wounds were as nothing, and he was half laughing with a sort of happy fierceness as he ran.

The great stallion came eagerly toward him with pricking ears. It was as though his own tyrannical, keen spirit rejoiced in such a scene as this, with war and death all around him. Into the saddle bounded his rider and sent him away again with a rush through the shrubbery, leaping out into the open before the jail.

He saw a little knot of horsemen wheeling in confusion before him, some pointing one way and some another; for some wished to keep down the street after the rapidly disappearing pair of riders, and some wished to go in the direction in which the chief quarry had gone.

It would have been easy for Anthony to avoid them, but his blood was up now.

He shouted, and the thunder of his voice sent them scattering to either side as though it had been a thunderbolt. Two or three guns were fired at random as he

283

went through, but they were not aimed shots, and Anthony went on unscathed, a terrific figure with the dust boiling up behind him from the stallion's flying hoofs, and his bandaged head, and his red, flying hair.

He sent a blind bullet behind him to keep them back a moment, and the next instant he was around the corner with the Salton Bay running as he had never run before.

And always with pricking ears, and alert head, as though he were finding this the greatest fun in the world! It would have put heart in the greatest of cowards to see the fine animal at work, and Mad Anthony, with a revolver poised in either hand, and the wind stinging his face, raced on through Fort Hendon as never a man had passed through it before.

Half a dozen times figures appeared at either side of the road. And he fired in anticipation of the blaze of their weapons, not to kill, but to unnerve them, for he wanted no blood upon his head beyond what already rested there. He had killed Madison and Cherokee Dan, and he did not regret it, for death had long been overdue to them. But he wanted to have no decent man upon his list after this affair, if he could win through it with his life.

So six blares of fire sent death at him—and missed. And then the houses grew scattering. A bridge rang loudly, smitten by the stallion's flying hoofs, and now he was away into the open country—with the free, sweet sweep of the stars above his head and the limitless horizon drawn far and faint.

Ahead of him he could already see the ponies of the big Indian and Tommy Plummer, laboring side by side and drawn back to him fast by the stallion's terrific speed.

From the rear rolled the hoofbeats of the many horses.

There was not such a crowd as one might have expected. For two miles out of Fort Hendon, every mounted man in the place followed in a long stream the noise of the pursuit, but after that every man on a weak horse knew that this was no race for him. Besides, there were many, well enough mounted, but so far back before they left the town that they decided the stern chase was too long for them.

They fell out, and now the pursuers were running fairly well bunched, a dozen or a score of them— Anthony in the starlight and in the dust which floated behind down the trail could hardly tell the exact amount.

But those numbers were enough. If he called upon himself to account for three men and each of his companions to account for two, there would still remain enough of their foes to wipe them out of existence.

So they could trust only to speed.

That to him was a simple trust, for he had the Salton Bay beneath him, but it was a different matter for the other two. Tommy Plummer was well enough, though by no means on a racer. But he was a good rider, and his weight in the saddle was light, and it is easier on a horse to run ahead than it is to pursue. But even

Tommy was not secure, and as for Kohatunka, his weight was killing his pony already.

The big chief was wringing the last strength out of his horse, but still it did not suffice, and he turned blazing eyes of rage and despair over his shoulder toward the rear as Mad Anthony came up with him.

"Courage, Kohatunka!" called Anthony.

"I am not afraid," shouted the Indian. "But when a man's last day has come, it is his last day and nothing will save him. However, I shall not go to the other world without company!"

And he snatched from the saddle holster the rifle which he had found there, and shook it savagely at the rout which ran in his rear.

"Big Crow," said Anthony, "your day has not come, for otherwise the Great Spirit would never have sent me to take you from the jail!"

"That is true," said the Indian. "It is true that he sent you to free me, but that was only because he did not wish that Kohatunka should die in a cage like a sick dog. Now he has brought me into my own country, where the sky-people can see me fight and die, and it is well! I shall turn back now, brother, while there is still strength in my horse to charge them. And do not doubt that I shall not die alone!"

So said Kohatunka, and brandished his rifle again, as he gathered the reins to turn, calling: "Running Thunder, my glory as I die is that I have brought you to the Osage tribe, and that I leave you with them after me! Farewell!"

Anthony swung the stallion closer, and he gripped the reins.

"You shall not turn back, Kohatunka," said he. "At a time like this there are three men, but there is only one heart among them. If you die, we die with you; if you turn back, we turn back with you!"

For a long moment the Indian's eyes stared into the face of his white comrade. Then he settled grimly to the impossible task of striving to draw more speed out of the pony on which he was mounted.

But it was a useless effort, and with every moment the head of the pursuit drew nearer. They were opening a scattering fire, and bullets hummed closer and closer to the fugitives. Tommy Plummer reined up beside Anthony.

"There was never an Indian," he growled, "that was worth two whites throwing their lives away for the sake of him. Are you gonna do that, Anthony? Look back! There comes big Diamond Jack at the head of the lot of them!"

Anthony looked accordingly over his shoulder, and he saw the glimmering body of a great black horse which bore Kirby swiftly out before his companions.

"It's his fight and mine," said Anthony. "If he had no one with him, he and I could have it out together. Break off to the side, Big Crow! Tommy, ride to the side. Change your direction. They're after me, but they'll never follow you!"

"Yes," said Tommy Plummer, squinting back in fear.

"They're coming fast. My God, how fast they're riding!"

He turned his head toward Anthony.

"Anthony, I'll find you again—so long!"

"Good-by!" said Anthony, and waved his hand, and Tommy Plummer turned his laboring horse away at a sharp angle to the line on which Castracane was riding.

He departed fast from them, falling gradually behind, jockeying his horse along at full speed now.

"Now you!" said Anthony to Big Crow. "You see that not one of them has turned his horse to follow Plummer. Neither will they try to capture you, Kohatunka. I am the game they're after. And they think that they almost have me!"

"Leave you?" said the Osage savagely. "Not while there is life in the heart of Kohatunka!"

"But I'll be safe," said Anthony. "Once you're away and safe from them, I can leave them behind me like nothing at all. Look at the Salton Bay. He's simply playing across the prairie. He wants to be off and away. In half an hour he would drop them out of sight!"

The Osage suddenly pointed straight ahead and then waved to the side.

"It is too late," said he. "They have sent out other watchers. They cover the plains as if with a net, and we are both caught, brother! Ho, there will be singing and dancing when they kill us! I am glad of this. I shall never die on a greater day. I shall be remembered for what I have done, and because Running Thunder died beside me! Together our souls will journey to the Happy Hunting Grounds! Is that not well, brother?"

Anthony, looking anxiously ahead, could see nothing at first where the Osage with a hawklike vision had seen so much. But presently he saw a long line of riders, small against the dimness of the night, and with a wide-flung order, rushing across the plains in a great arc. To the right, to the left, and straight ahead they came!

And Anthony's heart failed in him.

He looked to his rifle. He loaded his revolvers. And he made ready to fight his last battle and to shoot to kill.

Behind them, he could now turn his head and see Diamond Jack Kirby rushing at the head of the men from the town. Kirby should be his first target, and surely he would not miss! But at the same moment there arose from the on-rushing line of riders ahead of them a series of wild war whoops. And Big Crow straightened in the saddle and threw his arms in exultation above his head.

"We are safe!" he shouted. "That is the war cry of the Osage!"

CHAPTER XLII

THEY CAME ON IN MAGNIFICENT STYLE. ANTHONY could see them whipping their ponies to a mad run now. And behind him the men from Fort Hendon seemed to understand the situation with an equal speed. Instantly they whirled their horses about and started back for Fort Hendon at full speed.

But they had been badly spent in the long sprint after Anthony, Plummer, and Big Crow. And the ponies under this tribe seemed ever as fresh as morning.

A series of screeches and battle yells, and they went past the pair of weary fugitives like avenging ghosts under the stars.

It was a sort of fun from which Big Crow himself could not be absent. The roar of his voice was sufficient to make a young brave that passed them check his horse and surrender it to the chief. And off went Big Crow, freshly mounted and hot to get revenge for the manner in which he had been chased across the prairie.

But Anthony halted the Salton Bay and, resting his hand on the pommel, peered curiously after the departing clouds of dust.

There was not a soul near him. There was only the far-off rushing of many horses' hoofs, and now and again the thrilling war yell of an Osage came wavering back to his ear with a dying force.

He went on a mile or two farther, and then he halted on the top of a low hill and waited to see what more would happen. He had not long to linger there. Silence crept onto the prairie. Somewhere he heard the thin call of a coyote, and afterward came the returning beat of many hoofs. The Osage warriors came gradually back, saw his dark form on the hill, and swept toward him in a new charge.

Anthony was almost alarmed.

He had never seen such a demonstration as this, and though his nerves were of the steadiest, still he had a good deal of reason to shake in his boots; for singly or in clusters the Osage braves put their ponies into full speed and went by him with a rush, firing into the air their guns, their bows, and screeching like so many fiends.

In a wild circle they swept around him, and then Munnepuskee suddenly rode up to the battered "madman of Fort Hendon," as Anthony was called for a time after this episode, took his hand after the white man's fashion, and pumped it vigorously up and down.

"We wonder," said Munnepuskee, "for what great thing Kohatunka is reserved, seeing that the Great Spirit has twice rescued him from death by the hand of Running Thunder. We shall think more of him from this moment. But what shall we say to you? Already you had shown that you were a father to our tribe. But what shall we say now? Alas, Running Thunder, you make us very poor. We cannot tempt you with buffalo robes or with horses or guns. We shall only be able to pray to the Great Spirit and beg him to leave you long among us!"

He moved on. There were all the rest behind him, and each with a speech of which Anthony could make out more or less the meaning. His right hand was weary before the procession was ended, and his ears were crowded with thick gutturals. But even this had an end, and finally, in the midst of a shrub-grown stretch of ground, the fire was lighted, meat was produced, newly killed that day on the march, and while it was roasted on a hundred spits, Anthony heard from Munnepuskee the meaning of this most lucky intervention.

For Munnepuskee, though he could not force his assistance on the white man after he learned that Running Thunder intended to ride to Fort Hendon, had nevertheless determined that he would ride out with most of his available force of warriors and act as a party of observation, for the sake of striking when he could, in case Anthony needed help.

But he dared not come too close to the town.

The soldiers would be called out if such a large body of Indian horse was observed near at hand. So he kept them a few miles back and sent ahead a number of boys as scouts, mounted on the fleetest horses. These youngsters would act for him and his little army as feelers, and when something of importance happened in Fort Hendon, they would carry the tidings back to their master and enable him to act suddenly and with surety.

They had come boiling up to him, finally, with word that Running Thunder was loose in Fort Hendon, and that he was driving the city of the white men mad, like an armed hornet among milling cattle.

With that news ringing in his ears, Munnepuskee fell into a dreadful trouble. He knew not what to do or what to attempt. If he attempted to ride on into the town, he would find that even his numbers would not be very useful against the hordes of better-armed whites, and the Osage braves would be mowed down like grass before the prairie fire!

He pushed a little closer to Fort Hendon, therefore, and waited again until another scout came hurrying in and swore that he had seen three riders leave the town, pursued, and one of them had the bearing of Running Thunder on his great stallion.

Behind them streamed a fierce pursuit.

That was enough for Munnepuskee. He gave the signal, and spreading into a great semicircle the Osage tribesmen delivered their charge in the hope of coming upon their friend between that point and the town.

And lucky for the two fugitives that the chief had acted so promptly. So Anthony told him.

"Like a wise father," said he to He Who Knows No Fear, "you have thought out all the trouble of your people. Long before this Big Crow and Running Thunder would have laid dead on the prairie, and the men from Fort Hendon would have ridden back and forward across our bodies!"

The chief was greatly pleased by this compliment. He was about to make a rejoinder with flashing eyes when a clamor broke out on the edge of the night camp, where some of the younger braves and the boys were breaking up wood and pulling brush for the fire.

The word leaped instantly from the outskirts of the camp to the ear of Munnepuskee. Big Crow and some of the others had just come in—men who had fiercely followed up the retreat of the white men toward the town—and they had been able to pick up one prisoner, whose horse had stepped in a prairie-dog hole and fallen.

That word had hardly arrived before the returning war party rode straight into the presence of the chief. Across the pommel of Big Crow's horse was seen the bound body of a big man, whom the chief now seized by the hair and flung to the ground. The body struck heavily, and lay still.

"Look," said Big Crow, smiting his broad chest with his fist. "Fools will dare to reach up their hands to capture the Big Crow when it flies close to the ground. They do not know that Running Thunder will follow and strike them blind and dead. And sometimes there are still greater fools who would chase the Running Thunder. They do not know that the Big Crow has a beak and talons for striking! This man, brother, was not your friend. This man was the chief hunter. I let the others go. I took this one man. I struck him down. And I have brought him to you. May his scalp dry beside your fire and hang forever in your tepee! May he spend ten days in the dying, inch by inch. For that will warm the heart of Running Thunder!"

There was a good deal of exaggeration in Big Crow's speech, but what he had to say excited Anthony so much that he hardly waited to thank the war chief before he ran forward and peered at the fallen bulk of the big man who now lay stretched on the ground, face to the stars.

And he found himself looking into the eyes of Diamond Jack Kirby!

Yet, helpless though he was in his bonds, and certain of a horrible death, Kirby was as composed and collected as though he stood at that moment in the midst of his gambling hall on a most lucky night.

"You have sent your dogs to worry me down, Castracane," he said quietly. "But they shall never have the pleasure of hearing me squeal when they sink their teeth in me. As for Big Crow, he lies. My horse fell and left me stunned on the ground. Otherwise there are not enough Osages under the sky to take me alive. But do I understand that he has given me to you?"

"He has," said Anthony. "He has most certainly given you to me!"

"Very well," said the gambler. "Are you going to stick me like a pig and watch me bleed to death, or are you going to play the part of a man?"

"And what is the part of a man?" said Anthony gravely.

"Tonight," said the gambler, "I had you in the hollow of my hand. I only had to squeeze my fingers shut, and that would have been the end of you."

"That is true," said Anthony.

"Now, Castracane, give me fair play. Take me far enough from this gang of cutthroats so that I can get away if I win. And then let us fight it out hand to hand!"

"I am very slow," said Anthony. "I might not have thought of that for a long time, and so I thank you, Kirby. Because, before God I am going to kill you!"

He turned to Big Crow.

"Do you give this prisoner to me, brother?" he asked.

Said Kohatunka: "Am I not less than a mangy coyote without teeth if all that I have is not my brother's? And therefore is not this man yours if you will have him?"

"Then," said Anthony, "let me deal with him in my own way, and no man follow me!"

And he leaned, and with a slash of his knife he set Kirby free. The fallen man rose and they walked together from the fire.

CHAPTER XLIII

IT SPOKE MUCH FOR THE SELF-DISCIPLINE OF THE Osage tribe that though every soul there must have been eaten up with curiosity, yet not a man dared to move to follow the two white men and see what happened between them.

They walked straight out toward a riding moon, down the hill, past the brush, and into the flawless quiet of the open prairie. Behind them gleamed the red eye of the Osage campfire. Before them was the broad yellow face of the moon.

"Here," said Anthony, "are two rifles and two revolvers, and two knives. You may make your choice, Kirby. How I kill you is no matter to me!"

He added: "And here is the Salton Bay that has followed me. He is like a tame dog now. If I die, you can step into the stirrups and make sure that all the Indians in the world would never be able to catch you! What's your choice?"

"First," said the gambler, "I have to say that if I did not hate you like a snake, Castracane, I'd love you for this thing you're doing. But as things stand, one of us has to die. I'll make my choice. Give me one of those revolvers."

Instantly one was placed in his hand.

"It's a clean gun, I suppose?"

"There's enough moonlight for you to examine it."

"As clean as a dog's tooth," said the gambler presently. "And now, what distance?"

"Close or far, I don't care."

"You're confident, youngster!"

"I am going to kill you, Kirby. Nothing can keep you from it!"

"Bah!" snarled Diamond Jack. And turning on his heel, he marked off ten paces and whirled about.

"Are you ready?"

"Ready, Kirby. Do we start with bare guns, or with them in the holster?"

"I won't be beaten by any of your damned jugglery!" exclaimed Kirby. "We'll start with the guns out of the leather."

"Any way that you want to have it will suit me."

"And what's the signal for the shooting?"

"There's a coyote yapping yonder in that brush, now and then. When it yells again, it's our signal!"

"That will do for me."

They fronted each other steadily, each filled with a keen rage, each hating the other with a cold intensity, the one because he had been wronged, and the other because he had been once before beaten and shamed.

The gambler began to talk, softly, smoothly, and always with his ear bent with hair-trigger earnestness to catch the first waver of the coyote's next cry.

"I wish only that I had a little audience, Castracane. Such as you had when you manhandled me. Do you remember? But after all, not much of an audience is needed! The deed will be enough. Because tonight you've made yourself famous. I admired you, Anthony. Now that I'm about to settle all scores between us, I can tell you that I admired you as you went smashing and crashing through Fort Hendon, raising the devil on every side of you. I admired you and envied you a good deal. I'm strong enough for most purposes. But I can't tear down walls and steal horses away from the very hands of half a dozen armed guards. What devil was in you? Well, in another moment I'll be sending that devil home!"

"You've talked enough," said Anthony. "There's no woman here to admire your fine face, my friend. And right through the center of that face, I'm going to shoot! Do you hear me? Before—"

The yip of the coyote clipped his words short. The two guns tipped suddenly up, and there was a blended double report.

Anthony found himself standing with the wind in his face and the level moon shining. And in front of him there was stretched the long, dark, shadowy form of a man.

He ran to Jack Kirby.

He kneeled by the gambler and turned him on his back.

"Lift me up a bit higher, Castracane," said Jack Kirby. "I can breathe better, then. My face is all blood. What in the name of God happened? It wasn't only a bullet!"

Anthony looked in amazement. The face of his enemy was blurred by a great bruise. And from a cut on his nose the blood flowed freely.

"My slug hit your revolver as you were throwing it up," explained Anthony at last, "and there was enough force to tear the gun out of your hand and knock it up into your face. Kirby, God saved you. And as long as I live, I'll never try to touch you again. There's been blood enough and hate enough between us!"

Jack Kirby rose to his feet, staggering a little, a handkerchief held to his face, for it was a nasty wound.

"Anthony," said he, "whether there was God or the devil in it I don't know. But I've had enough. Only tell me this. Are you really giving me my life?"

"Yes."

"And I can pay you back nothing?"

"Unless you can help me to make my peace with the law, Kirby."

"I'll manage that, if I have to paint myself as black as a crow doing it."

Jack Kirby on a dancing black steed left Fort Hendon that night. Jack Kirby on an Osage pony returned with a bloody handkerchief tied about his face. He went to his room, and there he sat down to write. The town was like early evening, not midnight. Every lamp was lighted. Voices hummed everywhere, as though there had been an earthquake or some other prodigy. And, in fact, what Anthony had done that night, as all men agreed, was little short of a prodigy. And Jack Kirby wrote:

Dear Bisbee,

I've been on the trail of Mad Anthony. He's been to Fort Hendon, smashed the town wide apart, killed Cherokee Dan and that devil Madison, and shot down Chick. He's ripped through Fort Hendon like a tornado, and the military was nearly called out on account of one man!

I followed him out of town, and he was taking along with him Plummer and Kohatunka, the Osage, whom he'd let out of jail. Instead of bagging Castracane, he bagged me. And when he had me tied hand and foot, he gave me a chance to stand up and fight our fight out hand to hand. I took the chance, and he dropped me—and then gave me my life again.

And that is why I'm sending you this letter and confession. I'm the only man who knows Castracane's story, and I can tell you that there's nothing wrong with him under the surface. He came West to follow a girl. The girl tricked and fooled him and that drove him half wild. He met me and I tried to shoot his head off. He was *forced* into going bad. Your first guess about me was right. I wanted a deputy's badge, not for the sake of upholding the law, but because I wanted a legal authority for murdering Castracane. I've failed.

I'm sending you this confession because I'd rather go to jail myself than see Castracane in prison, or dead.

Bisbee, if you hound him, you may win in the end, but you'll lose twenty men getting him.

If you give him his chance now, he'll go straight. As I'm going to go from now on, or God help me for a fool. I've had my lesson!

JOHN KIRBY

Such was the duty which Diamond Jack performed. And he wrote to a very wise man indeed, when he wrote to Bisbee. There was a scant month before a Washington pardon came west with the President's signature. And that was why, on a certain evening long remembered in Fort Hendon, a young giant on a red bay stallion cantered through the streets and stopped in front of the restaurant and strode through the doorway.

It was the dinner hour, and from the crowded tables there arose a sudden shout:

"It's Mad Anthony!"

And some sat still and stared, and more jumped to their feet, and some in frozen terror raised their arms above their heads, but not one dared to show a gun. Then a voice came rich and ringing from the back of the room, and they saw Muriel Lester running forward with such happiness on her face that never a man in that room could forget it the rest of his days. They saw her swept into the giant's arms and carried through the door into the street, and they sat in a stupor, staring at one another.

"Is that the end of Mad Anthony?" asked the proprietor.

Center Point Publishing
600 Brooks Road • PO Box 1
Thorndike ME 04986-0001 USA

(207) 568-3717

US & Canada:
1 800 929-9108